"*Vicissitudes* is not a trend but a discove honored to be in on the discovery of fair, free, funny, beautiful, heartbreaking and heartfelt love. I say it before bed nightly, 'Vicissitudes.' We all need change in the air."

Carol Lee Lorenzo, author,
Nervous Dancer
Flannery O'Connor Short Fiction Prize

"Oh, the delight that is basking in the words of Kim Green! Kim's ability to write what we all feel, to play with language, to be bold, vulnerable and funny has found the perfect home in this important and hopeful love story. As the title suggests, *Vicissitudes* exposes the uncomfortable, controversial and electrifying changes ever-present in human life. It bravely takes a stand for following ones' heart into the unknown."

Jen Sincero, author,
*You Are A Badass: How To Stop Doubting Your
Greatness and Start Living An Awesome life*

"*Vicissitudes* is an impeccably written story with an exciting mixture of suspense, controversy and enlightenment. I found myself shackled to the story with all of its twists and turns. This story left me to question my own level of consciousness. In a time when people cling to the term, 'woke,' this novel creates a tug-of-war with religious principles, cultural acceptance and spirituality. I'm so glad to have read my way into a deeper level of understanding. I look forward to meeting these characters again."

Lakendra Ford, author,
Amaze In Ways

"Kim Green has captured the elation and agony felt by many trans men in their journeys of transformation. I rejoiced in Jahn's adventures through life as a teacher and lover while wrestling with the dynamics of call-out culture and an ever-changing LGBT community's understanding of gender identity and the risks of personal exposure. May his story provide a beacon for other trans men in their quest to find true love and acceptance."

Zander Keig, LCSW,
editor, *Manning Up: Transsexual Men on Finding Brotherhood, Family and Themselves*

"This is a novel for our times…an important Black love story that interrogates a multitude of assumptions of what Black love looks like, how it unfolds in communities and complicates the mainstream definition of gender."

Matt Richardson, Professor of Feminist Studies
University of California, Santa Barbara

"I just finished *Vicissitudes*…I really enjoyed it. It's so timely, real and deeply heartfelt. I was totally engrossed."

Leslie Cohen, Author, *The Audacity of a Kiss: Love, Art and Liberation* (forthcoming)

"Sadly, I just finished *Vicissitudes*. I'm in awe! The writing is provocative, alluring and I feel all the characters' struggles. Bravo! I am so looking forward to the sequel. I want to go help the Transgender Community now. No more suicides…just because a person wants to be their authentic self. You transformed my intellect and thought process on this subject greatly."

Sandra Egnaczyk

"*Vicissitudes* is an excellent novel! A truly sensitive subject which Kim Green handles so beautifully."

Joann Malkin

VICISSITUDES

VICISSITUDES

Love Transforms

Kim Green

TRANSGRESS·PRESS

Typeset by Medlar Publishing Solutions Pvt Ltd., India

DEDICATION

This book is dedicated to my son, Micah London Foster.
Let this story inspire you to see that every day matters,
everyone's story matters, everything matters
and that you, so *matter.*

PART ONE

PROLOGUE

A *perfect day for a wedding. Perfect because it's not mine. That's what my brothers would say and then we'd laugh, do a finger snap and take another swig of our craft beer. Ha ha. Such sarcastic bastards we are.*

Last night I laid my clothes out with my favorite gold chain. I want to look right in the uniform: ironed black pants, polished dress shoes, crisp white shirt and that stupid bow tie. Bethany said don't be late, so I'll be early.

Carving the perfect goatee takes time. You have to pay attention to the angles. The hot water runs and the steam fogs the mirror. Everything I'll need is here: electric shaver, trimmer and a clean white towel. The heat from the cloth warms my thickened skin. The shaving cream hisses and snakes into my palm, filling the room with the foamy fragrance of man. I get hard just feeling the soft scrape of the blade gliding over my moist skin.

Damn! The sting of blood, just below the nose. I rip off a single toilet paper square.

Cover.

Wait.

Disaster averted. Just a shred is all it takes to stop the bleeding.

———— ∼ ————

Walking the grounds of the hotel, I survey the crowd, all done up. There are some prospects, but I'm just here to work. I feel good… as good as a hired hand can feel at a wedding that's not his own. This is as good as it gets when you're being there for a friend, but mostly for her money.

JAHN

The Doctor says you have to find the root of your rage.

On the first day of the blood, Momba jeered, "You ain't no boy! You'se almost a woman. Dat 'dere blood proves it. You'se a guh! I tole you."

I trample through life shaking off nightmares. Momba refused to see what was in plain sight, me. In my dreams, she still hangs over me, toothless grin, her lips forming an oval, laughing at me. She found me soaking in a puddle of womanly blood that never should have been. The more the crimson stream dripped onto the cold white tile, the louder she laughed.

I can still feel the scrunch of my torso against my knees, my arms tightly around them in a desperate embrace. Only the cool of the porcelain commode could soothe my burning cheeks. Hot with protest, I told myself, just stay tightly crouched and try, try, try to dissolve.

Momba's voice doesn't leave. She's always so close, leering, lurking and jumping in and out like a phantom, hounding me with all that I wish to forget. The cringe is constant, the cold wet flecks of tobacco that spill from her mouth still stick to my skin.

She'd wake me every morning with, "Get up! The train is leavin' the station!" "Get yur ass up! Don't be a joker, like *he* was," she'd say, referring to her only son, the one who fathered me. Momba couldn't even say his full name. She had cut him down to a single initial. J was her abbreviation for *Jazzir*.

Momba called my mother, "Dat Guh." And when she pronounced it, she used her deep, guttural belly voice, the voice that flattens out vowels and gives new depth to consonants. Whenever she was in a pleasant mood, my grandmother would call her, "Goldy," which I thought was her name. Turns out, it was just the color of her hair.

When I was in the first grade, "Dat Guh" dropped me off at the bus stop, just like every other day. The final day, she just didn't plan to return. Her last kisses, all sticky and moist, still cling to my flesh like third degree burns.

At night when Momba thought I slept, she'd growl and roar into the phone, heating up her old country friends with stories of our family's unspeakable truths. Always proud of her prophecies, she'd brag, "I *knew* it was gonna be trouble when J. brought that white guh in my house. Can you believe Dat Guh abandoned her own flesh! Thanks the Good Lord I was able."

Like a toxic mist, Momba's words wafted underneath my bedroom door, stealing away my innocence.

CHAPTER

AUGUST
Cielo Spa Resort
Los Angeles, California

*L*ove is all there is. I whisper into her ear.

"Shhhhhh! Mom, I can't hear!" My daughter, Rain, shoos my voice. It's hard to hear over the waves.

The voice of the wedding officiant slices through the air. "Welcome to this sacred space of love. I have come today to join together Rene Harden and Bethany Ricci," says Priestess Marcel, the only person Rene trusts on the rare occasions that spiritual affirmation is needed. My best friend, Rene, has been running from religion for the last twenty years. A lifetime of bitter wars with her mother, Bertha, about her soul's salvation have been relentless.

Being a motherless bride is another thing, besides Lupus, that Rene and I share. Needless to say, Rene's mother, Mrs. Bertha Mae Harden, is absent today. The difference between us is that I lost my mother to an untimely death, suddenly brought on by the overindulgence of vodka and cigarettes and Rene lost hers to the fear of burning in hell, which Bertha was convinced is a real possibility.

The grey dreadlocks that sit in a coil on the top of Marcel's head form a modern yet ancient headdress. Majestically, she turns to the audience and says, "Today, I stand before you to birth a new family. This union will exemplify the power of commitment." She turns to the brides and says warmly, "I've had the privilege of knowing you both and standing under the warmth of your love."

Bethany cannot hold her tears. Rene puts her arm around her.

7

Once again Marcel turns to the audience with her arms raised, "To you, who have loved them, I proudly use the sacred salutation of our ancestors, *Ashe*!"

Rain pulls my shoulder down and whispers, "What does 'commitment' mean?"

"I'll tell you later," I reply, knowing that I need more time to figure it out.

Oh, my sweet daughter, Rain, who has already experienced so many of life's travails... In nine short years, she has already been lulled to sleep by the cacophony of divorce and the fluctuation of love. My little girl has silently watched my body grow weak, playing host to cells that have lost their way, not knowing the difference between good and bad, attacking every cell in sight without discretion. It saddens me to think that with all of the things she's seen, the simple idea of commitment has eluded her.

What *does* commitment mean, anyway? I always thought I knew until I experienced the cold winds of infidelity that rattled my nerves and ravaged my limbs. Rain's father's famous line: "I didn't sign up for this," still rings like a siren.

My attention is lost to the waves that rage behind the altar and the sound of the harpist who begins to play the wedding processional. My eyes close as I imagine myself being sucked into the beautiful horizon. Rain tugs my arm, pulling my attention back to the wedding just in time to see Rene walking slowly down the aisle. My best friend and I have both been through so much since our bodies were stricken with disease. At least, one of us is embarking on a new life.

Although both of our doctors say we are in "remission" as they call it, my once failing body has healed much faster than my heart. I remain slow to emerge, fearing the torrent that intimate love requires. I guess the only thing that I can tell Rain about commitment is that it is just how people *try* to love.

Effortlessly, I spot Rene's meager number of attendees. For the most part, her peers are all members of L.A.'s Black elite who have only accepted her because she is on her way to making partner at the firm. Only a few of those elites, who consider themselves progressive, could bring themselves to be seen at the wedding. Rain and I remain Rene's only family.

The crowd belongs mostly to Bethany. The family is large and lively. The parents, brothers and cousins all wear the same swarthy Italian skin tone with pronounced angular Roman noses and heads full of shiny dark curls. Bethany's film colleagues are all well-known hairdressers, makeup artists and a few budding actors who are all tattooed and pierced, here to pay homage to one of Hollywood's emerging costume designers.

The Ricci family beams with pride, as they watch their only daughter process down the aisle alone, as she wanted. Trailing behind her is Nicholas, her five year old nephew, clumsily carrying an oversized velvet pillow holding two diamond bands. Nervousness makes his little legs sway and the rings bounce off, just high enough to cause alarm. Flying to catch them, Nicholas loses his balance. But just in time, before Nicholas hits the ground, a pair of hairy arms encircle him, standing him upright.

The audience gasps and swoons, "Awwwww."

When Nicholas finally reaches the altar, Rene looks at Bethany adoringly and plants a gentle kiss on her cheek. Marcel gently takes the brides' hands in hers and studies the crowd. Tears come to my eyes as Marcel describes The African ritual of the Four Elements. Handing each of them a tiny bowl from which to drink, she explains that the Four Elements represent all of the stages of a marriage. She explains, "Here is cayenne pepper to represent the spice in your relationship. Here is lemon to signify the sour moments that will come and go. Now, vinegar to show that sometimes there will be bitterness. And, finally, honey to represent the sweetness in your life."

Rene and Bethany listen intently, both of them shaking slightly as the cups come to them. Rene passes on the cayenne and Bethany takes too much of the honey, leaving a small spot on her face. Rene tries to wipe it away but it smears. They both burst into laughter.

Lastly, the brides exchange their own vows. I hide my face from Rain, not wanting her to see the unexpected tears now flowing out of my eyes.

"Ladies, you may now honor your beloved with a kiss."

My arm suddenly flinches with pain from Rain's deep squeeze. Her eyes are scrunched up in agony. She does not whisper but says loudly, "*Eeewwww.* Grownups are *always* kissing! *So gross!*"

Playfully, I pull her head full of thick copper curls into my chest. "You're right, Rain. It *is* gross. Please continue to think like that for the next ten years!"

Once the wedding party has come back down the aisle, Rain blurts out, "Mom, I've got to go to the bathroom." Without waiting for permission, her copper curls are all I see in the distance as she melts into the crowd.

I remain seated, glad that she has the courage to disobey me, once in a while. The poor girl has been smothered by paranoia ever since my diagnosis. Due to my disease, public bathrooms are anathema to me, only representing things that could make me sick. Not only does it take Rain so long to find bathrooms, she spends an inordinate amount of time on her ablutions, wiping, washing and flushing. It takes her forever. I'm so scared of germs that I don't even wash my hands in public places, relying only on an endless supply of hand sanitizers that fill my purse.

It was not too long ago that Rain ended my madness outside the bathroom at Chili's restaurant. She had tears in her eyes. "How will I ever grow up if you are always doing everything *with* me?"

So, I stay in my seat, distracting myself with watching the brides revel in the well wishes of their guests. From the sidelines, joy mixed with regret washes over me. It feels like a lifetime since I was the one all-aglow from the light of everyone else's hopes. The heft of their optimism weighed me down.

As I wait, my blood sugar sinks to a dangerous low. The jitters are taking over my body. Beads of sweat seep through my full-coverage powder as I wait for Rain. Never letting on when I am wilting, slightly dying, it is my custom to suffer beneath fashionable disguises. I am too proud to reveal my imperfection.

Looking for Rain or any sign that dinner is being served, I strain to see over the socializing crowd. The buffet seems miles away, but I decide to go for it. Rain will find me. I'm always dressed in funeral black, no matter the occasion. (Once a New Yorker, always a New Yorker.) I take a deep breath, hoping not to stumble when my high heels meet the uneven but decorative river rock path.

Making my way over a bamboo bridge, I feel a jolt as a cart filled with china and silverware whacks my backside. With a grimace, I turn around to see a waiter who looks like the guy who saved Nicholas. I recognize his hairy arms.

"Excuse *me!*" I bark before getting a good look.

"Man! I'm so sorry," he says with a twinge of embarrassment. Under his breath, he says, "I told them these carts are too heavy. Hope I didn't do much damage." His smile widens as he takes inventory of my body.

His skin is an exotic racial blend; brown with reddish undertones. His dark eyes peer at me from a head covered by a thin layer of dark peach fuzz that protects his head like a cap. The lack of hair only highlights his bountiful lips.

I am taken aback. My frown loosens, "No problem. I'm fine. I'll just forward my doctor bills, if there are any." My eyes stay glued to his details. "Nice tragus pierce," I admire aloud.

"Bravo! Impressive that you know the proper name for it. So, are you a friend of Rene's or Bethany?"

"An old friend of Rene's. You?"

"Bethany is my best friend from high school." After a pause, he adds, "I hope it's not too forward of me… but what's your name?"

He must not see the bulging creases around my eyes and my middle-aged belly that defies exercise. He's too young and vital to have eyes for me.

I take a deep breath before I respond. "My name is Morgan and asking a simple question is never too forward."

"I should get back to work, Morgan."

I notice his pristine waiter's uniform. "Work? I thought you said you were Bethany's best friend?"

"I am, but we're sort of helpin' each other out."

From the quizzical look on my face, he explains. "You see, Bethany knows that I'm saving up for something. So, she 'hired' me…" He makes little quotation marks in the air "… to help with the wedding, which saves her the cost of additional wait staff and puts a little tax-free cash in my stash."

"That makes sense. Well… good luck saving for your… something."

"Don't really need luck, just dough. But thanks, anyway." He starts to walk away and then turns around. "Uhhh, care to make a small donation?"

"Next time! I never carry cash." I say, using the reliable New York City excuse.

Saving for what? Probably, an engagement ring. Oh, if I had only met him back-in-the-day, when I was young. The fact that he had a girlfriend wouldn't have even mattered. He would have been strictly good fun.

Rain finally ambles towards me and I quickly return to my motherself. "Rain, you spend way too much time in public bathrooms. What took you so long? I keep telling you, take it from me, don't catch something that you can't get rid of!"

"At least I washed my hands," she says. "I'm hungry, can we get something to eat?"

"Let's go. I'm starving, too."

My mouth waters seeing all of my favorite foods, lavishly displayed. The centerpiece is a huge smoked salmon surrounded by lemon wedges and grilled asparagus tips. Veggies are prepared in every style possible: sautéed, roasted, stewed, deep-fried, curried and tempura-ed. They each sit in asymmetrically shaped pewter bowls. The brightly colored bowls hold the whole grain and fruit salads.

Rain has the audacity to scowl at the five-star spread. "Mommy, there's nothing here for a kid to eat!"

Trying to be helpful instead of annoyed, I say, "Look, Rain there's a meat carving station over there. Maybe you can get some roast beef or turkey." I start to fill my plate and she just stands there, pitifully holding a fine china plate, with just a few lonely spinach leaves and a handful of grapes.

"You mean the guy with the big tall hat? I'll try…" she says skeptically.

Settling into a seat in the shade, each succulent bite brings the waiter back into my mind. It's probably for the better that I didn't ask his name. Don't need to know it, not looking for anything or anyone.

Rain interrupts my thoughts with a plate of meat. "Hey, who's that guy you were talking to when I went to the bathroom?"

"How do you know I was talking to a guy?"

"You're still a man magnet," she teases me, reminding me of stories her father used to tell.

"He is a waiter who was apologizing for hitting me with his cart. *And*, you should mind your own business."

"What's his name?" she asks with a hopeful grin.

"Don't know. Didn't ask," I say with a full mouth.

"Wasn't it you who said it's impolite to engage in conversation with someone and not know their name?"

"Yes, it was me and I'll ask his name after I finish eating. Will that be OK with you?"

"Suit yourself," she giggles.

After the last drop of curry tickles my tongue, Rain looks at me, waiting for me to move. Losing my nerve, I hear my own hard breaths, just thinking about it.

"OK. I'll be back in a minute."

She has already lost interest.

The excitement of talking to an attractive man makes me tingle. I stand up straighter, despite my achy knee, longing for my untarnished self. Walking towards him, I change my mind. Taking three steps backwards, I yank Rain up out of her seat. "Come with me," I say, and she relents. All around we see guests in full throttle party mode, dancing with their glasses held high in the air.

———————～———————

His back is to us, rinsing champagne flutes, preparing for the toast.

He turns, smiling. "You're back! What can I get you two ladies?" he says looking at Rain.

I stammer. "Hi. I forgot to ask your name."

"Thought you'd never ask. It's Jahn, *Morgan*. See, I remembered yours."

"Hello, John, nice to formally meet you."

"It's pronounced John, but it's actually spelled J-a-h-n," he says handing me a sparkling crystal flute. He looks down at Rain. "And, who are *you*? How'd you like the wedding?"

"My name is Rain," she says as if expecting a prize.

"*Jahn.* That's quite an interesting spelling of the world's most common name," I say before Rain speaks again.

"Maybe, it's because I'm uncommon," he smiles.

"Or, your mother is very creative…"

"Well, it's a…"

"—long story?" Rain completes the man's thought.

"How'd you know that?" Jahn laughs.

Wanting his attention, I interject, "Everything is a long story with Rain."

"How did *you* like the wedding, Jahn?" Rain asks, so comfortable with adults.

"It was really meaningful," he says looking right at me.

Nervous breathiness punctuates as I jump in, "I'd have to agree."

"What'd you like about it, Rain?" Jahn probes.

With dreamy eyes Rain's voice goes all-babyish, "I liked how happy they both looked. And, I *love* Auntie Bethany's dress. She looks like a princess. The only part I didn't like was the kissing! Kissing's so gross!"

I jump in, "Rain doesn't like to see *anyone* kissing."

She rolls her eyes.

He says, "The kid's actually right. Kissing can get tricky."

I wonder whom he's been kissing.

He continues, "Rain is wise beyond her years. Surely, Morgan you know what trouble a single good kiss can cause."

I blush. "Might it be an engagement ring that you're saving up for?"

Then Jahn looks down. "The thing that I'm saving for is definitely *not* an engagement ring! No." He adds, "*Not at all.*"

"I'm sure you have to get back to work," I say, knowing I have said too much.

"There's always extra time for nice people like you and Rain," he says.

I glance at my watch and pick up a glass of champagne, "It's almost time for the toasts."

"Come back and see me," he says.

"I will if I get thirsty." But, he is already serving someone else.

———————— ∼ ————————

"What's a toast?" Rain asks as we walk back into the crowd.

"It's—"

A photographer intercepts us, videographer in tow. He wants a photo. Rain cheeses with her biggest smile and I grumpily show my teeth, absolutely hating pictures of my unrecognizable, older self.

With a thick accent, the photographer tilts his head. "You can do mush better than that! Give me a beeg butiful smile. I know you can!"

In the past, Rain has accused me of not being *fun* enough. I desperately want to show her that she's wrong, despite the not-so-fun things we have gone through. I *was* fun. At least, that's how I remember it. I fake a big toothy smile and immediately feel myself loosening up as a better mood starts to emerge.

Effortlessly, Rain leads the way as we clown out in front of the photographers. We stick out our tongues, turn our backs, wrap our arms around each other too tightly and pretend to sit on each other's laps. There are even rabbit ears. We run the whole gamut of childlike silliness.

The videographer's English is limited so he invites us, with his large hands, to look at the camera. Rain says, "Auntie Rene and Auntie Bethany, thank you both soooo much for inviting us. We had a fantastic time and we looooove you! Happy, Happy Wedding day!"

"Anyt'ing else?" he says.

Rain pauses for a second before she blurts out, "... *And*, my Mom likes your friend, Jaaaahn!"

Soaked in embarrassment, I snatch the microphone from her startled hands.

"Congratulations you two! Please ignore what Rain just said. Can we cut that out?"

The photographer eyes our spectacle with a hearty laugh.

Signing off with the rigidity of a Breaking News Reporter, I say, "So long and thanks again. Enjoy the Galapagos!"

The photographer takes the microphone from my tight grip. He says, "Thank you, Ladies. You two are pretty funny."

The camera light is finally off.

When we are out of earshot, I turn to Rain, taking her hand firmly into mine. "Rain, how could you? That was totally inappropriate what you said about Jahn. And, on camera!"

"Stop," she whines. "You're hurting me."

I don't want her to cry. Stopping under a swaying palm tree, I cup her face gently in my hands. "Rainy, I didn't mean to hurt you. You must learn not to be so impulsive. Think before you say things. And especially, things that you only *think* are true. I never said that I *liked* anyone!"

"You don't like *anyone?*" Jahn says from behind me.

Startled, I swivel, "You've caught me. That was totally out of context! I do like people! Look, it was really nice meeting you. Unfortunately, we have an early flight in the morning and we've got to get going."

Not taking no for an answer, he says, "Good thing, it's not even close to morning. Bethany said I could enjoy the last 30 minutes of the DJ. I have a very tight timeframe to drink, dance and munch on leftovers—all in about 27 minutes." He looks at his watch. "Would you mind sparing me a dance since, you do like people, after all?"

Rain interrupts my plan to decline. "Mom, you should dance with him."

This is my opportunity to show her that her mom is fun. After a breath, I say, "Sure Jahn, I'd like that."

The irresistible falsetto of Marvin Gaye blasts through the speakers, warming everyone with the timeless hit, "Got to Give It Up." Tossing my purse to Rain, I let Jahn escort me to the center of the dance floor where he twirls me around and gently positions me with my back to him.

He whispers into my ear, "I know it wasn't an easy decision, dancing with a strange man."

Over the thumpin' bass, Marvin sings, "*I got myself together baby and having a ball. As long as you're grooving there's always a chance. Someone's watching... gonna make romance...*"

Without shyness, Jahn holds me around the waist. He moves like one with sex on the mind. My body submits, doing what the bassline wants it to. I let the groove have its way with me.

"This song just never gets old. I love it," Jahn says into my ear.

My knees bend effortlessly and my hips sway from side to side.

"You're a great dancer, Girl," he observes.

"A little rusty, but good enough," I say with renewed confidence.

Jahn twirls me around again to get a full view. I take the opportunity to peek at him, as well. If I took my heels off, he'd be only slightly taller than me, but he is not fazed by my height, at all. His muscular hands are able and strong and I spin, weightlessly. A perfectly shaped goatee adds definition to his prominent bone structure. I revel in his hands and arms, covered with dark silky hair, gliding all over me.

Between dance steps, he asks, "Whatcha thinkin', Girl?"

I feel my body react to the heat of his touch. "Just thinkin'" is all I say.

Jahn takes my hand and twirls me again to face him. "That's *not* the answer I was hoping for."

I deflect, "What are *you* thinking?"

"I was thinking how nice it would be to have a way to contact you. What's this song called again? 'Got to Give it Up?' See what I'm sayin'?"

"Very clever, but I just met you."

"Morgan, come on now. I'm Bethany's best friend from high school. I've known her and the Ricci's since we were both 15 years old! Longer than you both have known Rene. That has to count for something. You already know me by association. Loosen up. Let me get you a drink. What would you like? It's on me," he teases.

"White wine. Riesling, if they have it."

I can feel the woman in me emerging. She's been sleeping for too long. While he's gone, I do a sequence of quick yoga breaths to calm my nerves.

With a chilled glass of Riesling, a beer in a fancy bottle and Rain by his side, Jahn delivers, as promised. My leather purse drags on the ground behind them.

"Mom, I was hanging out with some cool kids. I saw Jahn at the bar. I knew he was probably coming back to you. I just came to say Hi. Can I go back, now?"

"Rain, don't go too far. I'll be ready to go, soon."

"No, you won't! You're having a good time, I can tell," she says.

"OK, go have fun!"

To tame the silence, I ask, "So, Jahn, what do you do?"

"I'm a high school gym teacher."

It's obvious. His body is firm, chiseled and trim. Fighting the urge to comment, I say, "Really? Tell me more."

"Not much to tell. It's not that glamorous, but it's work that means something to me. There are just too many young men who don't have a male figure in their lives. Single mothers aren't enough. No offense to single mothers, of course..." his voice fades. "Morgan, I hope that didn't offend you. Don't get me wrong, a single mother—I mean a single grandmother raised me."

"I'm not offended at all. And, I must say, you turned out pretty damn well."

"If you don't mind me asking, where's Rain's father?"

"We're divorced," I say curtly, admiring his face. Scanning it, my smitten eyes finally detect a minor flaw, tiny red bumps near his jawline.

"I am always sorry to hear that," Jahn says. "Now, please escort me down off my soapbox. What do you do, Morgan?"

"I am a Production Supervisor at a recording studio."

"That sounds like a pretty cool job."

The DJ's final wind down song is Heatwave's classic wedding anthem, "Always and Forever." It oozes out of the speakers and all of the couples around us meld into each other. Jahn remains the perfect gentleman, not pressing me into an awkward slow dance between strangers. His extended arm is the invitation. My body fits easily with his, engulfed in every inch of him, so close I feel his humming vibrate through my chest. I am surprised when I blurt out my phone number, "404-346-2252."

"Finally! You've come to your senses," he laughs, heartily. "Too bad my phone's in the car. Just give me your email address. I'll remember it."

Fearing that he will slip out of my hands, I say, "I could find a piece of paper and a pen."

"It's cool. You can just email your number, when we connect online."

My voice slows down as if distorted, hoping he'll retain it, fearing that he won't. "My email address is: motherofrain@gmail.com."

"Cool. By the way, I don't have a personal email account. Expect it to come from my .edu address from school."

"Maybe you should get a personal email," I suggest with unexpected friskiness.

"*You* would be a good reason to do that," he says as he gently kisses my hand.

His back turned; he is already in motion.

Insatiably, my heart dangles in mid-air.

JAHN

The Doctor said revealing yourself will free you.

I have done most of what is required of me.

- ✓ Be seen by MD or PhD—Dr. Winston
- ✓ Two letters of recommendations from therapists—Dr. Peterson, Dr. Winston
- ✓ Start on T

(It's all very strange and mind fucking. The curves of my body have melted. I'm all angles and lines. Goodbye softness…)

- ✓ RLE (Real life experiment)

(Got a part-time job at the community center as an assistant coach. Passed. No questions asked.)

- ✓ Change name and pronouns
- ✓ Change gender marker and get new birth certificate
- ✓ Top surgery
- ✓ Got hired at Holly Crest High School today

Bottom surgery—*Not yet.*

Momba used to say that "a watched pot never boils," so I try to keep the lights low, so I don't fixate on the absence of meaningful change.

CHAPTER

2

AUGUST
Mid-air

Giddiness tickles me, making it impossible to sit still or sleep. The flight back to Atlanta is not smooth, but most of the turbulence is within. The sun dances on the wings of the plane, warming me through the window. At the mercy of chance, I've hedged my bets on a handsome man who has somehow unearthed the lost pieces of me.

Rain sleeps beside me, snoring. Ear buds firmly planted in her ears, she's oblivious to what has just happened to her mother, after just one dance. I amuse myself by slowly rolling each moment over again in my head. Re-imagining it, playing it like a lost reel. How did his fingers grip my waist, again? Was it both hands or just one? Did he say goodbye when he kissed me or was it just the wind of his breath that I felt? Were there really sparks in his eyes?

Lost in my imaginings, the plane suddenly makes a noisy shift, the sound of possible mechanical failure. Breathing through it, hovering 40,000 feet above the solid ground that I've worked so hard to find, my eyes close, falling back into an unruly nap.

A bigger thump and bump of the plane startles me further. As the plane careens and jumps over another pocket of air, my jaw clenches. Rain, half asleep, is hypnotized by the music that fills her ears. Thankfully, she is unaware of the untimeliness of death. The sound of crying babies surrounds me… a young mother across the aisle pulls her baby to her breast, soothing him with shaky whispers. In the seat behind me, I hear the haunting gospel wail of an old Black woman. The flight attendant's voice pulls through the PA with scripted words of consolation.

Rain's limber body stiffens with the jolts, but not enough to wake her. My eyes remain closed, just in case. The heavy plane sounds deafen, as we hit more dense air. In the midst of the chaos, I suckle memories old and new. Above me, an overhead bin pops open. A lone shoe lands at my feet. At the pilot's request, flight attendants scurry down the aisle towards their jump seats. The rattle of plastic cups and bumping ice cubes fill my ears. The pilot takes one sudden turn to the left and the plane regains confidence, finally cruising on reliable air.

He says, "*Ladies and gentlemen, I do apologize for the bumps…*"

And just like that, the whole thing subsides. Rain remains unchanged as I suddenly realize how much I want to live. Once again, I replay being with Jahn all over again. He reminds me that I am still *here*. Laying my head back against the headrest, the only thing that soothes me is that there are only two weeks before I ask Rene if I can ask Bethany about her waiter friend, Jahn.

Waiting does damage. Sitting at work with my Gmail account as my launch page, each email that's not from him deflates me. The two weeks since the wedding stretch lazily like a rubber band that has lost its spring. Greedily, I have bitten my nails down to the nubs and have taken up a dangerous relationship with chocolate. A voyeur to my own demise, I have consumed sugar and gluten, letting them fog my brain. Living on the edge, I count the seconds.

The recurring memories of Jahn and me together taunt me. The strength of his grip… the way his mouth folds around my name… the beam of his smile. What a relief it was to speak his name aloud, even if only to my father, who didn't have a kind word to say, when I confessed that I met someone.

"You just don't need to get involved," he'd scolded.

I didn't argue, fearing that he might be right.

Finally, it is the 14th day after the wedding. It's 7:00 p.m. on the East Coast and 4:00 p.m. on the West. I dial their number.

To Bethany's sluggish answer, I say, "Is it a bad time to call?" knowing that it is.

Her voice drags. "Morgan, do you mind if I put you on speaker? We *just* walked in the door. It was a very long flight."

"So? How was the honeymoon?" I ask.

"It was great… Ya know? On second thought, it may be too late to talk. Rene and I are exhausted. If it's not urgent, I'm happy to have Rene call you back tomorrow. If that would be OK?"

"Bethany, it's actually *you* that I wanted to talk to," I say forgetting my plan to ask Rene first.

She stumbles, "Oh yeah? About what?"

To occupy my tense hands, I sit perched on the edge of my king-sized bed picking molecules off the comforter.

"You must be exhausted," I start.

"What is it, Morgan? Is everything OK?"

"Well… there is a small something… but it can wait."

Bethany remains silent.

"Uh… I just wanted to ask about something. I mean *someone* but it's really not important."

"Who? Can it wait? Let's catch up over the weekend."

Losing my footing, I say, "Good idea. Tell Rene I say, 'Hey.' "

"Sure," Bethany says as quickly as I hear the phone go dead.

Falling back on the bed, I reach for the Hershey Kisses stashed in my nightstand.

BETHANY

When the caller ID flashes a second time, I think, "It's Morgan again." Then I see it says *J. Booth*. I know Jahn means well, but I don't feel like talking. It's not the time for welcome back calls. *We just got home.*

I hesitate but pick up, because it's him.

With the phone cradled between my shoulder and ear I say, "Hello," as I lift another dirty shirt out of the suitcase and throw it in a pile. "We just got back from the airport a couple of hours ago. I'm kinda busy right now. Can I get back to you?"

"Bethy, I have a small favor to ask," he says, buttering me up with his old pet name.

"What is it, honey? You know we'll do whatever we can." I'd spoken too soon. With marriage, I've become a "we." Rene is not a fan of Jahn's. I switch the handset to speakerphone so I can continue to multi-task.

"Am I on speaker?"

"D'ya mind? I'm alone. Rene went to pick up dinner."

"Speaking of Rene, if her friend, Morgan, asks about me, could you just… keep it vague?"

"Actually, Morgan just called. And your name didn't come up. What the hell does keep it vague mean, anyway?"

Then, my heart stops.

With an apologetic sigh, he says, "I think I may have fucked up. I may have said too much."

Jahn is silent for a moment and then his deep voice booms out of the speakerphone. "If she mentions me, just say something positive. That's all I ask."

"*All?* What the hell happened between you and Morgan, anyway? Tell me."

"I just thought you should know that I mentioned that I've been your best friend since high school."

I try to catch my breath. "*What?* You told Morgan that? Why the hell would you do that? How *could* you?"

"Bethy, are you still there? This doesn't have to be a problem if we play it right. I know you've always got my back."

I release my grip as the soiled clothes fall from my fingertips, covering my feet. Stepping over them, I try to move out of the tight spot Jahn has just put me in. Everything on the floor is a blur. Sliding on plastic souvenir bags and luggage tags, I am desperate to get to the living room where I can sit.

My friendship with Jahn remains an issue for Rene. She thinks that he has taken up too much of my energy, already. Actually, he makes her furious. What if he tells Morgan *everything*, just to get close to her? What if Morgan asks Rene about the things Jahn says that I haven't told her? What if everything comes out? Rene would leave me. I can't let that happen.

As I fall onto the couch, trying to figure out what to say next, Jahn says, "B, you still there?"

Trying to change his thinking, I say, "Jahn, you *just met her*. Rene says that Morgan meets lots of guys. She probably won't even remember you."

The ticking of the clock reminds me of how time has sped. In all of my pre-marital bliss, I have lost track of him.

Jahn keeps pushing. "What if she *does* remember me?"

I don't give up. "She probably won't."

"B, why are you trying to fuck things up for me?"

Slumped against the back of the couch, I say, "You've already fucked yourself. I'm trying to keep us both from being ostracized. Didn't you and I agree to forget about the past? Didn't *you* say it would make life easier? Didn't you say that's how we could both move on?"

"That's what I told *you* to do. I don't have the luxury," Jahn yells.

It *has* been years. But I haven't forgotten any of it, no matter how hard I try. Every day, I still see how pain maims the face. The sight of dried blood stuck to plastic drains lives forever in my psyche. Cries of pain still disturb my sleep. It all happened so fast, but in slow motion. My hand pushes my belly down to silence my quiet groans.

"Would you just let me explain?" he begs. "I only mentioned the high school thing because I just wanted Morgan to know that I'm an OK guy... not a *stranger*. That's the only reason I said it. As soon as I did, I realized it was a big mistake. I just wasn't thinking."

"Bullshit, you *weren't* thinking... you *were* thinking, just with your dick!" I couldn't believe I'd said it.

Jahn's laugh is cynical and loud. "B, you got me there. I guess you could say that..."

"If Morgan asks me about you, which I highly doubt she will, you should know there's nothing vague for me to say about you. I've lied enough for both of us."

Jahn's breaths are heavy. "You don't have the *right* to say shit about me. And I don't have the right to tell Rene the things that I never told her, but could have."

"Jahn, listen to me. Morgan is *Rene's* friend. I never plan to speak to her about anything. You're the one who called our house looking for a favor."

Hoping he'll drop it, I say, "Just pray that she doesn't ask me anything."

"You know I don't pray," he growls.

"Maybe we should both start." I push the red button. There is so little time to clean up the big mess we've made.

CHAPTER

3

SEPTEMBER
Atlanta, Georgia

Rain startles me. The sun hasn't come up and it's still deep and dark outside.

"Mom, I can't sleep," she plops down heavily on the bed.

Without opening my eyes, "What's the matter?" falls out of my mouth.

"I had a nightmare, something bad happened."

"What?" I ask.

"I don't know, it was just bad. There was a monster. I couldn't see his face." She rubs her eyes. "I can't fall back asleep. I just want to be with you."

"I'm here, baby. I'll always be here. Don't you ever worry," I promise her, knowing that it isn't necessarily true.

"Come." She crawls into the bed. "That bad dream of yours is history."

Glancing at the clock, I fantasize about going on strike, just to see how it disrupts a mother's monotony. In only a couple of hours we'll be slammed with life's routine; rushing to get her up, feeding her and making her lunch. Some days it might be nice to leave work and bring her lunch from a restaurant. Maybe someone else's kid would perform an unexpected act of kindness and give her something out of their lunch box. Life is such a bore.

As she nestles underneath my arm with her head resting in the crook of my neck, I rub her back and say, playfully, "You're safe now, baby. But I need my beauty sleep."

"You have all the beauty the world can stand," she whispers.

"You too, Raindrop. So, for the sake of the world, let's both get some sleep."

At 7:15 a.m. the sound of the phone shakes us. Rain's bad dream has caused us to oversleep. I clumsily grab the phone to silence it and mistakenly push the green TALK button, instead.

Groggily, I say, "Good morning."

A man's voice says, "Morgan?"

"Yes. Who's this?"

"It's Jahn. Remember me from L.A? Jahn Booth? The gym teacher."

"I remember," I say sitting up, wishing Rain weren't in the room. "How did you get my phone number? And why didn't you send me an email, like you promised?" I immediately regret the thrust of my nature.

"I'm sorry about that. I got caught up with things and when I thought about it again, I figured you might not even remember me. I got your phone number from Bethany. Sorry to call you with some not-so-good news," he says.

Like a knife, the cut of another untimely death slices into me all over again.

Not wanting to know, I force myself to say, "What happened?"

"It's Rene's mother. She passed away late last night. Bethany called to tell me. She asked me to call you."

Without warning, tears pollute my eyes. "Oh Rene! No!"

My heart flashes back to the loss of my own mother.

He says, "Bethany said she locked herself in the bathroom for hours."

Just the thought of Rene going through this causes the blurry images of my own buried loss to pop up in my head. I can still see the NYPD officers draping my mother's dead body, while rush hour commuters look on.

"Are you there?" Jahn asks.

"Yes. Sorry. I was just remembering…"

"The mother thing is so complicated," he says, without elaboration.

"Knowing Rene like I do, I'm sure there's no funeral service. She doesn't go for things like that."

"Actually, there is a memorial service being planned. Bethany and her family convinced her that it's the right thing to do. She wasn't happy about it, but she gave in. It's actually Bethany who's taking care of everything. Rene is really counting on you two to be there, which is why I'm calling."

"We'll be there, just let me know when you have the details."

Gripping the phone tighter, we listen to each other's tentative breaths. My voice rushes to say, "One more thing… It's good to hear your voice again."

"Yours, too," he says.

"Jahn, unfortunately, I need to get started on my day. We're very late for school."

"Me, too. Gotta hit the gym. Have a good day, Morgan."

I tap the red end button to disconnect. I'm left with only a vision of Jahn in the gym, muscles flexed.

Momentarily, Rain has slipped my mind.

"Who were you talking to? Was that *Jaaahn*?" she says.

"I knew you were listening!"

"Hard not to. *So good to hear you*," she mimics, popping her head out from under the covers.

I smile while pushing her gently out of my bed. "We're late! Get outta here!"

———〜———

I dread the days that Jax is in the studio. He has a number one single that sold almost a million copies, called "Blood Bath." Although the beats are solid, the lyrics are abhorrent.

Back-in-the-day, I would've found Jax very attractive, no matter what kind of music he made. I would have convinced myself that Jax and I had a "connection," simply because he would have said we did. His Nigerian accent and the addicting beats of his songs would have put me in a trance. Running into him at some industry party, after a drink or two, we would have found ourselves comingled in some dark corner, hoping not to be caught but mutually titillated by the idea that we may. After our groping ended, he'd plant a final goodbye kiss on my chapped lips and the affair would be over.

From across the parking lot, I see his single red dreadlock and shiny baldhead (massaged with coconut oil), approaching. The loc dangles from the bottom of his scalp to the center of his back, like an obedient tail. Jax' Nigerian skin, smooth and luminous, is dark with reddish undertones. His cat green eyes scare and excite.

The intoxicating scent of his Indian Nag Champa incense follows him through the door. Always cordial but terse, I am aware that his knowing eyes can't ignore my sometimes, thickened skin and baggy swollen knees. No longer sensitive about invisibility, I expect to be ignored by him. For him, my only purpose is to make sure that lunch is on time.

"Good morning, Mor-gahn." Jax' voice is loud and raspy. He unpacks his suede backpack and packets of organic nuts, berries and endless device chargers spill out onto the floor. One of his lackeys picks it all up and puts it back after he finds what he was looking for.

Mr. Greenstein, my boss and the studio owner, says we should always compliment the artists as soon as they enter the door.

So, with my best professional face, I obey. "Hey Jax. The song is sounding really hot! They love it at radio. Will we be working on the club re-mix today? That's what's on the schedule."

"Nah," he says. "I'm bringing in a vocalist to make da joint a little hotta. You know how I like to mix things up. C'yant always go by da rules."

"Who's coming in?" I ask, dreading the additional artist paperwork.

"I'm not sure, yet. I jus' wait til dem show up."

"Your manager knows that I have to know three days in advance—"

"Mor-gahn, don't sweat da small stuff. *Is all good,*" he assures me with a slippery rapper's tongue.

The entire studio schedule that I worked on yesterday disappears into the ether with a single tap of the delete button.

My cell phone vibrates. As I pull it out, my favorite picture of Rene is on the screen.

Mr. Greenstein would kill me if he sees me on a personal call. A few more of Jax' ragamuffins spill through the door, making it safe to talk. Buzzing them in, and pointing towards studio E, I'm sure they won't look my way again until lunch.

"Please hold," I say into the phone. It's the code that Rene and I have developed for forbidden calls at work. When I reach the conference room on the opposite side of the building, I am able to speak freely. "Rene, I am so glad to hear your voice. I heard the news this morning."

All I hear are cries and sniffles.

"I'm sorry Rene. So sorry."

As if shards of glass are stuck in her throat, Rene's voice crackles, "I'm sorry that I feel the way I do."

"What do you feel? Can you describe it?"

"Furious at that bitch! She did nothing except try to talk me out of who I am. You know memorials are not my thing. Bethany is doing it, not me. She can have it. One thing's for sure. There will be no burial."

"Rene, what does that mean?"

"Her ass is going to burn. I'm just about to schedule it after I get off the phone with you."

I pace the small conference room. The death of my own mother is upon me again, making me strangely sensitive to the wishes of the dead. Too young to fulfill any of my mother's last wishes, it unnerves to think that Rene will cremate her mother knowing that she wouldn't want that. As much as I want to tell her that she shouldn't, I refrain. It's her mother, not mine.

Rene's fragile voice shakes, "Morgan, do you want to hear the last thing she said to me?"

"Yes. Tell me."

"I am ashamed to call you my child."

My stomach knots up. "Rene, you know that she didn't mean that! Forget it. People say things they don't mean. Life turns us cruel, sometimes."

Rene's tears return. "Just when I finally feel free, she's gone, no longer accountable for the pain she's caused. She'll never be able to see that I survived, despite her."

"What matters most is that you know."

RENE

Bertha hated that I never wore dresses. So, I peruse my closet with care to find something that she would have called, "manly." Letting my fingers gently dance over the assortment of colorful silks, the memory of her makes me weak. I've always been proud of my work shirts because they are professional, comfortable and subdued enough to keep people focused on what I'm saying, not what I'm wearing.

Standing back, assessing them, I remember the grimace on my mother's face when she saw me dressed for the office for the first time. I still feel the slap across my face that constantly lurked behind her eyes. My knees buckle.

I resume searching, pausing at a light blue chemise, that's usually worn slightly slouched over a pair of lightweight stretch capris with knee-high boots. I recall it's the only outfit of which Bertha ever approved. *Finally, a woman's color*, she said. Feeling the softness of the sleeve slip between my fingers, I keep looking.

Then, I see something that would be appropriate. A navy-blue long-sleeved silk T-shirt and charcoal grey fitted pants with mid-sized navy pumps with block heels. The grey and navy work well together; somber, yet stylish. I'll accessorize with my alligator belt, blue satchel and of course my diamond wedding band. I hear Bertha's words in my ear: *Why don't you grow your hair?*

I hear myself say: *because I don't want to*. Touching my shorn head, I feel the familiar bumpiness of the micro curls hugging my scalp. It's just the way I like it, which happens to be the way that Bertha loathed.

Standing naked in the mirror, the reflection of Bethany's quirky wardrobe signals how different my life is with her in it. She brings color and peace. Always on the thinner side, I can't help but notice how my disease has further trimmed me down turning me into a mere wisp of a woman. I have mastered hiding behind the foils of fashion finery, never making the truth of my flimsiness evident. So grateful that Bethany sees more to me than the loose skin that dangles from my muscle-free limbs, since I've lost my appetite and energy for the gym.

Stepping closer to the mirror, a burst of my breath fogs the glass. I am frightened by the resemblance to my mother, which makes me shiver. Like Bertha, my skin has reddish undertones. Our faces share the same backdrop perfectly made for our wide set hazel eyes and aquiline noses. Large, naturally crimson lips are our family's trademark.

Bertha Mae Harden had, at one time, been a beautiful woman. For as long as I can remember, the features she gave us triggered envy and lust in others. Our family's racial ambiguity comes from centuries of old pains and twisted privileges. Bertha never named the breezy island where her people were from and, as children, we pelted her with questions about her history, but to no avail. Fifteen years ago, it no longer mattered. That was when Bertha broke us all up, after I confessed the truth of who I was. Her last fit of cruelty left us all strewn about like missing puzzle pieces. At her instruction, my siblings distanced themselves from me.

I had no choice but to do the same.

Over the phone, Mr. Denton offers me choices. The basic cremation package is $1,890.00, but I choose to splurge on the Silver Lining Package for a little over a thousand dollars more, for the sake of proper closure. The rental option includes a cherry wood casket and a plastic insert that burns with the body. I choose it because it suits Bertha's flamboyant sensibilities and still satisfies my need to watch her roll into a sweltering inferno.

Mr. Denton wants to elaborate. "The cremation chamber is sometimes called a retort."

The word makes me chuckle. I can't help but be amused by the fact that it sounds so much like *resort.*

"Retort?" I repeat, also remembering the other meaning for the same word, a witty comeback. *How perfect.*

Mr. Denton says, "The word 'retort' describes any vessel that can be subjected to extreme heat. Mrs. Harden, I hope you aren't finding the facts of this process insensitive."

"I'm not sensitive at all," I say, stiffening my upper lip.

"Then would you be interested in turning the key?"

"Excuse me? I am not familiar with that term," I say, slightly annoyed that there is something else that I do not know.

"It simply means to start the fire. We offer this service for free."

My heart beats fast and hard.

Mr. Denton continues, "Cremation has a long sacred history in many cultures; only in America has it turned into an ecological issue, worthy of protestors. Can you believe that?"

Hoping that his trivia will stop, I say, "Interesting."

"Hindus, on the other hand, consider the person who turns the key to be of great honor. Usually, it's the eldest son." He pauses. "Of course, it can be the eldest daughter, if that is the wish of the deceased."

Bertha would have wanted nothing less than me turning her key. Buying more time to consider, "Can I give you my final answer when I get there?"

"Sure can. Mrs. Harden, you and your mother are all set for 2:00 p.m. Cremation can be difficult. Don't forget there's room for additional family members, if you change your mind. You may want to bring your husband for emotional support. Did your mother leave a widower or are there any other siblings?"

I decide not to correct him, knowing that having a "husband" is the easiest way when dealing with strangers who assume that everyone is straight. "Yes, there are others, but none that can attend."

"So, I guess it will just be you witnessing?"

"Correct."

"I look forward to meeting you this afternoon," he says, not knowing all that he has stirred.

Bertha always said that lateness is disrespect. So, I arrive an hour early, 12:55 p.m. to be exact. Only here, in my car, can I let my tears fall. She was a real mother, once. She filled me with the shameless adoration that only mothers can muster for their offspring. "We are two peas in a pod!" she used to sing into my ear as she braided my long tresses, piling them atop my head to match hers.

"Two peas!" I slam my fist on the steering wheel, remembering, regretting and repenting.

Bethany still doesn't know how I lost my mother. Always evasive, I've tried to dodge the pain and repetition of the story that had no end, until now. I still haven't processed how a small piece of personal truth could detonate a family. Bethany will never understand how I blame myself. Sometimes, I think that I should have lied to Bertha; weaving tales of false liaisons with imaginary men, just enough for her to feed on, while keeping the family intact.

In my rearview mirror, I see the ghoul that I have become; the drips of dried mascara paint my face. Wiping them away, there is no turning back. I do what I came to do.

Checking emails on my phone in the waiting room, I am interrupted by a pale hand that appears in front of my face. It belongs to a short, paunchy middle-aged man, with a pink balding scalp. In a neatly pressed suit, he stands before me beaming a counterfeit smile.

"I'm Harvey Denton," he says, his outstretched hand dangling. "You must be Mrs. Rene Harden."

I feel my body weaken, only able to offer a limp hand in return.

"I'm so sorry for your loss," he says with practiced refinement.

"Thank you," I say with my head bowed, restraining from saying, *your condolences change nothing*. Bethany had scolded me too many times for that.

I allow Mr. Denton to walk me down the long corridor in silence, staying five paces ahead of me. The only sound I hear is the bristle of his pants, which make a swishing sound. The thick carpet silences our steps and the walls echo with a magnified hush. As we walk, I feel watched by the eyes in the gold-framed portraits of the funeral home's founders. They all have matching pale skins, ruby red lips and dark, pitying eyes.

Mr. Denton stops in front of a black door. The sign reads: VIEWING.

Inside, I settle into the place where I will spend the rest of the day. The warm light of the table lamp is deceiving, making the room feel more like a cozy living room, not a crime scene. A large picture window faces directly into the crematory. The monstrous, all-metal retort has just an opening large enough for only one casket. The narrow 400-pound concrete hydraulic door opens only after a small button on a computer console is pushed.

Mr. Denton gestures for me to sit in the lone chair that faces the retort. In a moment he has disappeared and re-appeared on the other side of the glass. I watch as he mouths words to another man in a white medical smock.

"Ready?" Mr. Denton mouths at me.

I nod, not sure that I am.

He pulls an oddly shaped key from his pocket and dangles it for me to look at.

I stare at it, blankly, finally, realizing what he's asking. Shaking my head from side to side, he understands my response to the unanswered key question. I wish I could, but I haven't forgotten that this is *not* what Bertha wanted.

When I look up, Mr. Denton is in the room with me, again. "Mr. Ashfield will take it from here," he says.

On the other side of the glass, Mr. Ashfield rolls the rented casket toward the window for my approval. The casket seems so small, not nearly large enough to hold all that she was. I am disappointed to see how death shrinks you.

A text from Bethany causes my phone to vibrate.

I love you. Thinking of you.

I text back, *Trying not to think,*

Mr. Denton advises that it takes three to four hours for the average body to burn. Bertha was never average, so I will wait as long as I have to. As Ashfield approaches the button, uneasiness takes over my body. Suddenly, I need proof that it is really her in there, but my mouth is glued shut. Tears creep along the rims of my eyes. Denton hands me a scented tissue.

First the red button, then the green button and then a green light comes on. The large metal doors of the chamber slide open and all I can hear is a raging swoosh of air.

With one firm push of Ashfield's heavy hips, I watch the slightly scratched casket slide onto the conveyor belt. After going into the retort, it drops Bertha and the insert in perfect position to slide in between the flames.

Bethany texts again.

How are you feeling? Wish I was there with you.

I ignore her.

Another text comes in.

I can't imagine what you must be going through.

I power the phone off.

Mr. Denton and I can't actually see the body approach the heat but I turn away just thinking about it. He leans in and puts his arms around my shaking shoulders. I am surprised and flustered when my whole body falls into him. The scratchy wool of his jacket scrapes my skin, jolting me to remember who he is and what we are doing. I pull away.

The room spins.

He says, "Mrs. Harden, I hope you will find comfort knowing that your mother is in a better place now. The chapel is across the hall if you need more time."

I don't see him leave.

—————————～—————————

For six hours and fifteen minutes, I sit silently, miserably, drifting in and out of consciousness. I haven't left my seat all day. It is Mr. Ashfield's knock on the door that wakes me out of a dizzied sleep.

"Your cremains," he says as he hands the warm golden urn to me. His skin is ruddy, his face, neutral. "She took longer than I anticipated," he says.

Morbidly, I smile, amused by the word, *Cremain*, yet another bizarre word in the circus of death.

Quickly, I grab a warmed Bertha from his hands and flee, speedwalking through Founder's hall while what's left of Bertha bobs in my bag. I walk out into the darkest night, ever. The only light is from the gas station across the street. I leave my car and walk towards it.

A car full of boys raging with hip-hop speed pass me. They sing:

It's Raining Blood, Man

Better yours than mine

Better yours than mine

The savagery of the lyrics stops me in my tracks, reminding me of my own newly savage nature. My eyes wander until I see a homeless man stumbling towards several garbage bins, spilling over with trash. I follow him, but he runs.

Discreetly, I pull Bertha out of my bag. Pushing up my sleeve, my bared arm reaches through a swarm of buzzing black flies. I fight them off, determined to find a surface that is flat. Silence and closed eyes are my prayer. Gently, I place her down for the final goodbye. Now, she's safe, among all the things that the world no longer needs.

CHAPTER

SEPTEMBER
Atlanta, Georgia

M r. Greenstein is on the phone, where he always is on the rare days that he comes into the office. From his glass window, I see his chubby hand summoning me.

Without looking up, Mr. Greenstein's assistant says, "Morgan, go on in."

Inside the door, I see one of his stubby fingers point at the lush leather seat where he wants me to sit. He continues to growl at the person on the other end of the phone.

I do, as silently directed, moving slowly through the expensive silk trees that create his lavish environment. Three of the walls of his office are glass, allowing Mr. Greenstein to keep his eye on us from every direction, while remaining insulated enough to loud-talk.

The solid back wall holds a large picture window with a montage of old framed portraits surrounding it. Each picture features Mr. Greenstein and all of the hip-hop artists that started their careers at Greenbelt Studios and went on to fame and fortune. The photos have always made me want to examine them closer, giving me ample time to search for meaning in all of the bogus smiles fueled by greed.

In each shot, Mr. Greenstein's big belly is pressed up against a thug, a known criminal. Their gold teeth and red smiling eyes cuddled up with Mr. G. make me laugh inside. Under any other circumstances, the mere sight of these hooded men walking with an urban gait would have caused his short stumpy legs to flee the street in abject fear. Watching him in front of me caress his salt and pepper beard always reminds me how a-million-records-sold can make anyone forget anything.

In each picture, Mr. G. and the artistic thug hold a gangster's stance, saluting the camera and the world with raised middle fingers.

"Alright, Lou! My next meeting's coming in. I'll talk wit' cha later. Take me up on this deal. It won't last long," Mr. Greenstein says, as he slams the phone down on the large console of blinking lights.

"Asshole!" he says, meaning that he didn't close the deal.

Without looking up completely, he says, "Lovely Morgan, how can I help, today?"

Mr. Greenstein is also from New York, *Brooklyn*, to be exact. Years before, when he saw that I was from New York, he hired me on the spot.

"I'm doing well, Mr. G. Thanks for asking."

"What do you need from me?"

With caution, I say, "A couple of days off. My best friend, Rene, you've heard me speak about her…"

"The one who just got married in California? I remember."

"That's her. Her mother passed away. Rene doesn't have much family. She considers me like a sister. I *have* to be there for her. I hope you understand."

Quizzically, he looks up, "Where's her family?"

"Well… it's a long story."

"Gay?" Mr. G says with a droop in his smile.

"Yes… but it's more complicated than that," I say, wishing it were.

"The world needs to give the gays a break! I hate to think of all the families who are broken apart because of this thing. It tears me up. My own daughter is a gay. Me and my wife made peace with it when she finally got the nerve to let us in on it. We couldn't stop her. Who cares what people do in their own damned bedrooms, anyway?"

Mr. G. stands up and throws his chubby middle finger in the air as if he has a gangster standing at his side. When he sits back down, he continues,

"The people who don't like it are just jealous, because nothing's goin' on in their bedrooms. Ha!" he says with self-righteous glee. "Sure, Morgan, you go support your friend. She needs you. Keep me posted, Dear."

"Sorry to need more time off."

As he walks me to the door, he says, "Morgan, death has no schedule. We all just have to work around it."

———◦———

I'm not sure how to tell Rain about Rene's mother. I arrive at Thinking Leaf Conservatory (TLC), the small private school for gifted children that she attends.

As she bounds into the car, she offers me a perfunctory kiss to the forehead. Immediately, she fastens her seatbelt, so proud that her weight and age give her access to the front seat. After the buckle clicks, she says, "I'm starving!"

"Rain, I need to discuss something with you."

"Mom, whenever you use the word 'discuss,' it means something bad happened." Peering down at her new shoes, already scuffed with red Georgia clay, her mood slowly shifts downward. "What happened?" she says.

"Well, sweetie, Auntie Rene's mother passed away… and she wants us to come for the service. In a couple of days, we'll need to fly to California again. You'll have to miss school."

Keeping my eye on the road, so as not to be distracted by the tangle of her emotions, I add, "I know how much you don't like missing school."

"You mean go to a funeral? I don't want to go," she says with unusual certainty.

"Then, this is your lucky day because it's not a funeral. There's not going to be a casket or anything like that. It will just be beautiful flowers and nice people, saying nice things. And, lots of pictures of Rene's mother."

"Will Auntie Rene say something nice, too?"

"Probably not, baby. She'll be too sad. You know, when my mother died, I didn't say anything at her service."

"If you die, I'll have a lot to say," Rain says with a smile and an unsure giggle.

Not sure I want to hear, but I ask anyway, "Like what would you say?"

"I'd say how cool and funny you were. And that you were a good cook! I'd say you were pretty and sometimes, you even let me hang out with grown-ups."

As she speaks, I wish she'd stop. The road blurs as my eyes fill. My emotion is stirred, fearing that God could be cruel enough to let history repeat itself, stripping Rain of her mother, which is what He did to me.

Looking at the side of my face, Rain pauses and says, "Mom, I thought you said Rene's mother was a meanie?"

Playing dumb, I deny. "I did?"

"I heard you talking about it to Auntie Rene, once."

I push the hair out of my eyes to gather my muddled thoughts.

"Let's just say that Rene and her mother were from two different worlds."

Rain contemplates. "Then, how does that make her a meanie?"

"Mrs. Harden just didn't believe that girls could fall in love with girls or boys could love other boys. You know, like Rene and Bethany or Uncle Max and Uncle Caesar. Some people think that's wrong."

"I don't get it. Lots of girls fall in love with girls and boys fall in love with boys. Don't they?"

"Yes, of course they do."

The car slows as my mind swirls, not prepared for a discussion of morality. The driver behind me is heavy on his horn because my car has slowed and I am stuck at an ethical impasse. In response to his horn, I accelerate too quickly, nearly hitting the car ahead of me and slamming on the brakes. We both fall forward with a jolt, my hand flies across the seat to protect Rain.

"So what world was Rene's mother in?" she says as if nothing just happened.

I glance over at her and her face is scrunched up, trying to understand. "Maybe she wasn't a meanie… but she simply believed something different than we do. Sometimes, Mrs. Harden would say things that hurt Auntie Rene's feelings."

"Like what?"

"Things that are too mean to repeat," I say not wanting to get into the details of burning in hell, especially with the news of the impending cremation.

"That's weird," Rain says.

"All I can say is that everybody needs the kind of love that doesn't stop because of the things that they do. It's called unconditional love. Let me give you an example, Raindrop. I love you, even though your room is an absolute disaster. There's nothing you can do to change my love for you."

"That's good because I'm conditional, too. Nothing can ever change how much I love you. Even though you won't let me go to the bathroom by myself."

"*Un*conditional, you mean. Which is just a fancy way of saying '*no matter what.*'"

"Did Daddy love you, conditional? I mean unconditional?" Rain asks.

"Yes, he did… but then he didn't, anymore. But that can sometimes happen… only between grown-ups. But that never happens to fathers and their daughters. Your father will always love you."

Uncertainty paints her face. "I know he does," she says. She continues. "OK, I'll go for Auntie Rene. After all, she did send us to her wedding, which was epic. I need you to promise one thing, though. No caskets."

"Promise. No caskets."

With fluttering lashes meant to tease, she asks, "Will Jahn be there?"

My stomach somersaults at the sound of his name. "I'm sure he will. He's very close to Auntie Bethany."

"Will you go on a date with him when we're there? I'll stay with Auntie Rene and Auntie Bethany if you do."

"Rain, we're going to a memorial service for—"

"—a meanie."

"Rain, don't be disrespectful. We're going to a memorial service for Rene's *mother*. There'll be no time for social stuff."

Rain says, "You could kill one bird with two stones."

"You mean kill two birds with one stone?"

"Yeah. I guess that's what I mean."

JAHN

The Doctor says that life appears harsher from the other side.

The daily stench suffocates.

"Fuck dat holdin' out bitch! There's better skanks out there, any-ways," King says to his teammates as they pull their blazing red jerseys over their heads.

I watch them. I pity them. One day, I will be one of them.

"She didn't hold out on *me*, baby!" Timion jeers as he lightly fingers his swollen crotch.

Behind crumbling walls, I watch, listen and stall. The volume of their crackling laughter burns my ears. I feel for them, so aware of what we all must endure to be called men. As an observer, I am constantly pricked by their clamoring antipathy for women. I listen for things they don't say. Their verbal circle jerk continues while the vitriol turns me into a stalker, struggling to decipher which part of their cruelty is their nature and which part is simply the penalty of poverty.

My colleagues call them "animals." The insult is meant to disguise their disgust. If these old fuckers could see that I have turned these young men into champions, despite their primitive sheen. If only the white man could recognize what need really looks like.

As I listen to them, exasperation moves me to break it up. "Alright, fellas, that's *enough!* Watch what you *say*. Don't forget you came out of a *woman*. Gimme laps 'til I say stop! You'll thank me when the next trophy comes home with us."

They groan. Their sighs are laden with small curses that fall from their open lips.

"Shit."

"Mu-fucka."

"*Damn.*"

51

For just a few minutes, I hope that endorphins can distract them from their obsession with their largely overrated dicks. If Momba were here, she'd shake her head and call them, *"Niggas, raised by the cracks in the street."* They're no different from me—we were all born bastards with no men in sight. We've all been forced down the throats of unstable anchors, to whom we are tethered for life.

Trailing behind my young and twisted charges, we trudge past lop-sided lockers and dripping faucets while mold seeps into our lungs. No one can fathom that these scruffy boys have brave elegant men inside of them. They have won at the State finals for two years in a row. They are peacocks on the court, which is how I choose to see them, even in the locker room while they shit talk, erroneously thinking that their dicks make them men.

Like wild horses they rush onto the field pushed only by the forceful-ness of collective despair. I push them from the sidelines:

"Faster, Jackson…"

"You got this, Boone!"

"Signature move, Shaheed!"

Watching their bodies grind and flex, I yell to show them what I expect. However, my mind is scattered, trying to keep thoughts of Morgan at bay. She has whetted my appetite. Despite Bethany's lurid accusations, I do not live at the mercy of my flesh like men are wont to do. Morgan has pulled the man out of me.

Practice finally ends and I am eager to return to my four walls. On my desk, there is a note from Coach Blande. *Urgent: see me before you leave.*

His office door is open and a six-pack of sweating beers sits on his desk.

My eyes are stuck on the contraband. "Coach, you wanted…?"

Responding to my wide eyes, he says, "Don't worry, Booth. We're off the clock. Jahn, some new regulations have come down the pike and I just wanted you to be aware of them."

"What's up?"

He offers, "Beer?"

"No thanks," I say, sensing that he would use it against me, if there were ever a need.

His face is red. Limp, greasy hairs hang stiffly over one of his green eyes and he doesn't bother to brush them away. Speaking slowly, he says, "There's a new regulation and The Superintendent has made it an immediate priority. We'll be installing a new bathroom in the locker rooms in a couple of weeks. The construction work will be done after school, which may interfere with practice."

Trying to balance truth and protocol, I respond with care. "The bathrooms *are* in pretty bad shape. It could be a good thing…"

Blande's fist hits the desk with force. "Booth, we're not *renovating* the damned bathrooms, they're making us pull a *new* one out of our asses. We're taking the goddamned mop closet and turning it into a goddamned—" he picks up a crumpled memo from his desk and reads, "—*Gender neutral bathroom*." His face is red with anguish.

"I ask you, Booth, what the fuck is *that?*" He takes another swig of the beer. "I bet you need a cold one now. *Man!* What's this shitty world coming to? Do you know? I don't know what in the hell people are talking about, anymore. What does uh—*Gender Neutral* mean? You're just born one or the other. Right? It's nonsense. There's nothing neutral about it. Holly Crest doesn't have those kinds of in-between kids in this school. Do we?"

He closes his eyes to think and answer his own question. His voice raises, "We don't! These animals are too busy knockin' up their filthy little girlfriends for *that* stuff to be an issue. These animals are not confused one bit about what to do with their dicks."

My hands shake. My lunch starts to rise inside of me. My hand reaches for what the brothers would call piss beer, taking a desperate sip. The sting of the lazy carbonation hits the back of my throat. Twisting slightly in my seat, my hand goes to my mouth to muffle the sound of a rude burp as it releases. My face burns. The sting of the beer trickles out of my nostrils.

Blande's face is even redder than before. He reaches for another can.

A sneeze explodes from my whole head, relieving the pressure that builds in my skull.

"G'd bless you," Coach says, carelessly.

A shiver falls on my shoulders at the mention of the God I don't believe in. I place the mostly untouched can back on the edge of his desk.

A few stragglers outside of the door are desperate to make their presence known, with their thunderous laughter and cryptic jokes. Their clatter pulls us out of our stalemate. Their mouths are polluted with obscenities and Coach Blande neither hears nor cares.

"Jahn, what the *hell* is this world coming to?" Blande whimpers. "They say we have no choice in the matter. I say we do. What kind of law can change the way the world has been since the beginning of time? How could this even be *a law*?"

I say nothing.

He continues, "I just called you in to tell you, we have a meeting at 7 a.m. sharp. It's also a law that Administrators must meet with their staff to inform them of this bullshit, which pisses me off to no end. This neutered shit is simply not a problem we need."

"I'll be there," I mutter, rising from the seat.

Walking towards the door, with a slight slur, Coach yells, "Hey Booth, you forgot your beer."

I don't respond.

Behind me, I hear his words have gone sideways. "Suit yourself, Man. Just more for me."

———————

The 500 square feet of my basement squat is not impressive. Bethany's friend, now my landlord, cut me a sweet deal because I agreed to clean and paint the place myself. Every penny counts. The best part of the place is that it's just a short jog away from school so I don't have to get involved with the men's bathrooms at all. It's that last stall in the bathroom that fucks it all up for us. A whole bathroom filled with a row of urinals and just one lonely stall, the one we're supposed to use. If they see your feet pointing the wrong way, you're done.

Slipping the key into the lock, my weight pushes against the steel door and I fall in. The walls are the color of black coffee, with a splash of cold milk. The scrubbed cement floors and the 215 books that line my shelves are what make it home.

My head is heavy, filled with the burdens of my truth. Taking Doctor Winston's advice, I fall onto the futon, pen in hand. '*Writing helps,*' he'd said. On paper, I bleed all of the things I can't say.

———————~———————

I arrive at the meeting on time, but it feels as though I'm already late. Caution is being observed all around. Fresh bagels and new cream cheese packages sit in a basket at the corner of the table. The strong brew of cheap coffee permeates the room.

Somberly, Coach Blande takes his position, sitting with his ass hanging off the edge of the conference room table, as always. "Alright guys, you all know why we're here."

The two female coaches in the room have accepted being one of "the guys." Neither of them corrects him. Only I feel the slight.

There are three coaches lined up for the free food, which is the only way that 7 a.m. meetings can occur. No one speaks; it's too early for civility. Clearing his throat to hurry me, Blande waits, as I am the last to open my bagel and smear it carefully with cream cheese. My hands shake slightly.

I hear the unfamiliar voice of the new tennis coach among the rumblings. "Why is this an issue now? A student must have complained. But who? This District has enough problems as it is. Like dated books and not enough computers."

"—Or the shitty wages," complains the soccer coach.

"This bathroom thing should be low on the priority list. It'll just sit empty, anyway. Whoever needs it won't want to be seen using it."

The swim coach says, "Where will we get the money from? We need new uniforms! Ours have seen better days."

"Do we even know the number of *gender-neutral* kids in this school?" the volleyball coach asks.

"There can't be any here, considering six girls pregnant and sixty beasts lined up to make even more."

A collective laugh showers the room.

The distant ringing in my ears persists. My heart is beating outside my chest. My mouth opens, but no words come out. I think to myself *some kids may just need a little more privacy than others.* But only shallow breaths escape from my mouth.

Coach Blande starts the meeting with, "As far as I'm concerned, bathrooms have always been the same. Girls go in one bathroom and boys go in another. Those were the only choices we've ever had. Any other configuration is make-believe. This generation has too many choices."

I manage one word. "Perhaps..."

"Perhaps what? Booth?" Coach Blande dares me with his furrowed brow.

Perhaps the animals, as you call them, wouldn't feel the need to use their dicks so much, if they weren't constantly on display.

"Well?" Coach Blande waits for me to finish my unspoken thought.

"Sorry, Coach, I forgot what I was going to say. It wasn't important, anyway."

He slowly takes his glare off of me.

The gymnastics coach chimes in. "Exactly who will use this special rest room? Boys or girls?"

Someone else speculates, "Maybe it's girls dressed like boys and boys dressed like girls."

Chuckles ensue.

I haven't forgotten what I want to say, but am aware of the damage it will do. *Maybe you're the animals, the perverts, teaching men that their dicks are their highest prize.* I hear myself trying to catch my own breath. Their air is no longer mine.

Blande attempts to gain control with a rapid tap on the table with his coffee mug. "THAT'S ENOUGH!"

The buzzing of the fluorescent lights intensifies. The ruckus in and outside of my head is excruciating. I slowly rise from my chair with no destination.

Coach Blande's eyes catch me. "We're not done here. Where do you think you're going, Booth?"

"Nowhere," I say, sitting back down.

CHAPTER

5

SEPTEMBER
Atlanta, Georgia

"And now, let us pray," Rain says as she conducts our bedtime ritual. The intrusive chiming of the phone sounds from the other room, but we pray straight through it.

Rain's blinking eyelids dare an interruption. The phone rings and rings until it finally stops.

She prays her usual prayer, thanking God for me, the flowers and her distant father. Once again, I pray for health, happiness and something new to be grateful for. When we conclude, I rush to kiss both of her cheeks before I attempt to make the crossing to the other side of her pre-teen mess. Stepping over her books, game pieces, earphones and drawings, I recognize the landmines of my existence.

Safely reaching the other side, I whisper into the darkness, "Good night Raindrop. Sleep well."

"Don't let bugs bite the bed," she warns. I still smile at our inventive turn of phrase.

In an instant, her door is shut and I am already down the hall checking voicemail, hearing Jahn's voice.

"Hi Morgan. It's me, sorry to call so late. Please call back. 818-543-2201."

The second message is: "Morgan, I didn't leave my name. It's me again, *Jahn.*"

I like the sound of "It's me." and "Again." Hitting re-dial, his deep voice answers with unexpected gruff.

"Yeah?"

"Hi, it's Morgan," I say softly.

"Hey. How are you? Sorry to sound like that but it's been a bad couple of days at work. Haven't gotten much sleep and I took today off to clean out my turtle's tank. It's a pain in the ass! I'm literally wading through shit. Let me turn down the music. Be right back."

"When you called, I was putting Rain to bed. You'll have to tell me about your turtle another time."

"For sure. Just called to give you the information for the service, as promised." He reads from a paper that rustles in the background. "The service is next Thursday night at 7:30 p.m. ... Oh, yeah, Rene hopes that you and Rain will be able to stay for the whole weekend. And I was told to tell you that she'll send a car to the airport if she can't pick you up, herself."

Phone in hand, I am completely naked as I get ready for bed. I frown at all that sags in the mirror, thinking how I must correct it before I see him again. "Could you pick us up?"

There's no reply.

Trying to recover I say, "Sorry to ambush you like that."

"Nah, you're good, I was just checking my calendar. I *can* pick you up on Wednesday night."

"That works," I say, evenly. "Jahn, I can tell that something's really bothering you. Care to talk about what happened at work?"

"Like I said, I'm just wading in shit. Seriously, it's just the same ole' work stuff. You know how it is... not being able to say what's on your mind 'cause you don't want to get fired... that's just how it goes when you work for other people. Someday, I want to work for myself. Don't we all? That's about it. Not much more to tell."

"Sorry to hear that. Try not to let it get you down, too much."

He says, "Sometimes work just sucks. I just gotta do what a man's gotta do."

"And, what might that be?"

"I'll let you know when I figure it out," he groans. "It's getting pretty late where you are, isn't it?"

"I'm used to it. I'm a night person. But seriously, Jahn, if you ever need to talk about whatever, I'm here to listen."

"Thanks, Morgan. Someday, I may just take you up on that."

Anxious to peel away his thick layers, my body yearns to know him better. Wishing the call wasn't over, I listen as he disconnects. In the dark, I tell myself, it's much too soon for thoughts like these... thoughts that will only leave me adrift...

———————~———————

4 DAYS LATER

Jahn meets us at the curb, as he said he would. The airport bustles with the 24-hour sparkle of a city fueled by pipe dreams. The passenger window of Rene's familiar Black Mercedes SUV is rolled down and Jahn calls to me from the driver's seat, "Hey, Atlanta!"

He pronounces the word, as if it is *Lover* in another language. His perfect lips hug the L; his tongue lingers at the roof of his mouth. I want to respond with an open mouth kiss right then and there. I find myself addicted to his face. His dark blue sunglasses, worn at night, make his face more angular and more complicated than I remember. He wears an oversized "slap cap" that hugs his head tightly and droops down in the back. He wears it low on his forehead, letting the edge of the cap lay right above his thick eyebrows, drawing attention to his eyes. The hat is sexy, adding a flare of millennial grit.

An airport patrol car slows and the officer inside glances at Jahn. The car drives about three feet, and then reverses to get a closer look. Jahn notices it too, but chooses to ignore him.

"Hi, Jahn! Grrrreat to see you!" Rain says standing on her tiptoes to peer into the window, blocking my view.

Jahn laughs and says, "What's up, Rain? So glad you could make it." He comes around to open the back of the car and effortlessly heaves our cumbersome Italian designer luggage into the back.

I'm slightly embarrassed by my expensive bag that does not reflect my taste. We only use it when we're seeing Rene. She could never know that stuff likes that means nothing to me.

The officer continues to stare at Jahn, as if trying to place his face. I read the name on his badge, *Officer Douglas*. His eyes study Jahn, knowingly; as if there are pieces of him that he owns, from some other time, some other place. Jahn pivots his body and turns his head to resist the officer's intrusive gaze.

"Asshole!" Jahn mutters under his breath. "Shitty pigs! No respect for a Black man. Always looking for something to pin on us," he snarls.

Opening the back door, he ushers Rain into the plush backseat. "So, Rain, how was the flight?" he says as he helps her buckle her seatbelt.

"It was great," she says to the air as Jahn still moves around the car, getting us situated. "There was good weather and Mom let me watch a movie. It wasn't like the last flight when Mom and I thought we were going to die."

Jahn helps me into the front seat, teasing the boundaries by placing his hand low on my back.

I do not resist.

When he gets into the driver's seat, he winks at me. "How was the flight for you, Mama? How'd you pass the time?"

Visions of shameless kisses, random hands and impromptu gestures of affection cross my mind. Sitting next to him reminds me of the days when I was young and libidinous.

"Mainly, I slept," I say.

The car in front of us finally moves.

"Did you dream?" he asks.

I smile, knowing that lately my dreams only involve him. "You could say that."

Jahn confesses, "Actually, I hate to fly. It's impossible to relax in the air."

"There *are* support groups for that," I tease.

"Touché," he says with a finger pointed at me.

Playfully, I reach for his long, hairy finger and hold it for a little too long. Then, I let it gently drop into the space between us. Remembering why we are here, I snap out of it, changing my tone. "How's Rene doing? I was actually hoping that she'd come, too."

"She said she had something urgent to do tonight… something having to do with the service tomorrow. As always, Bethany had to work. New film."

"That's Hollywood for you. I'm glad this worked out."

"How's the savings going?" I ask, sensing that Rene may have asked him to pick us up so she could add to it.

"It's goin'," he says without turning his head.

For the rest of the drive, the three of us ride wrapped in a cozy silence. Only short, private breaths pass between us. Without his notice, I pull myself a little bit closer, trying to take in as much of him as I can. The steady buzz of Rain's cheap headphones and off-key singing lull the silence, pulling us through the dark of night, the clamor of Los Angeles and the hopefulness that exists when standing on the edge of connection.

PART TWO

JAHN

The Doctor asks, "Are you ready?"

"How are things?" Dr. Winston asks from his chair that faces me. He looks at me and right through me. The air in his office is humid like human breath.

"What *things* are you referring to?" I say, my eyes drawn to the renderings of the human brain on the wall that always suck me in. They are non-scientific drawings, almost drawn with a child's hand. There are murky colors meant to represent the lobes of the brain. I am always curious about them, having stared at them for the last few years, dissecting every brush stroke whenever conversations become too difficult. Today, I am slightly on edge, actually offended by the images, seeing how they insult. I resent that the brain can somehow be seen as something to be toyed with, manipulated, even gawked at for personal interpretation.

"I'm just checking in with you. Anything new come up since our last session?" he says.

"No. I'm good. Excellent, in fact," I reply.

"Jahn, you do seem somehow, different. What's happened?"

"Doc, with all due respect, I think this will be my last session."

Dr. Winston's face turns red. He sighs with exasperation and then says, "Jahn, needless to say, I'm very sorry to hear that. Tell me why you've come to this decision? I thought we were making excellent progress."

"I just think it's time. I'm ready."

"What has changed? We've missed a couple of sessions. Catch me up," he says with new alertness.

"Things at school are tough. The district is demanding a gender-neutral bathroom and my boss is pissed."

"Well, it's about time," Dr. Winston says. "It's 2020 for God's sake. How does that feel for you? Proud or paranoid? Our community has finally arrived. They finally see us."

"They're all such idiots. You should have heard what they were saying. They were laughing at us. I wanted to shut them down, so badly. I almost did."

"So, what stopped you? You have nothing to lose. The new laws support us. You really can't get fired. And if you do, you can always sue."

"I'm not the suing type. You know I just like to stay below the radar. And the other thing that's happened is Bethany's wife, Rene's mother, just died."

"Jahn, I am sorry to hear that. That's a lot to contend with. My condolences to the family. Did you know her?"

"I didn't, but I hear she was a bitch. She gave Rene hell." My head is down. My attention is on scraping off a spot of shaving cream that I hope he doesn't see.

"It's not our responsibility to teach people to be decent. How does the news of the death impact you? If at all?"

"Well, the fear of death is always imminent but especially when I think of… all that's ahead. But I can't start worrying about the surgery because I just need the money, first. Then, I'll worry."

"Right. And there's nothing to worry about, really. Just remember that 1.78 million have gone before you and they all lived. Yes, there are many complications, but death is usually not one of them. With that being said, what are you most afraid of when it comes to the surgery? Pain? Blood? The need for revision?"

"All of it, but I don't want to talk about that now. There's something new that helps me forget all of that stuff. It's something and makes me want to live."

"What is it?"

"You mean, who?" I whisper.

"That's great news, Jahn. Cis or Trans?"

"Cis woman, of course. I'm not looking for men."

"There'd be nothing wrong if you were," he says, nonchalantly. "We blur gender lines all the time."

"Not me."

"So, tell me more. What's her name?" Dr. Winston asks.

"Morgan. She's coming to Los Angeles for a few days for the memorial service. Bethany is already pissed. She says I shouldn't try to get involved. She says Morgan can't take too much stress."

"Is Bethany insinuating that you are stress? Being alive is stressful. Does this Morgan know your status?" he asks, with a raised eyebrow.

"No. Not yet." I don't want to think about what revealing myself will entail.

Dr. Winston shifts in his seat. "Jahn, what are you waiting for? If you don't tell her, she'll eventually find out since you have close friends in common. It's inevitable that one of them will say something. I'm surprised she doesn't already know. You know that people love to tell other people's business, don't you?"

I am paralyzed by the truth of his words. He smirks at my surprise.

"Have you forgotten how this thing works? All human beings are run by their sexual yearnings and curiosities." Dr. Winston says softly. "Let me help you with this. Give me an example of how you would disclose to Morgan."

I resist, "But it'll only be the second time I've ever laid eyes on her. It's just not time. I don't want to rush her into this stuff so fast."

"Don't you think you'd be more comfortable being your whole self with her?" Dr. Winston reasons.

"I just don't want her to…"

Dr. Winston waits for me to finish my thought.

And then, he says it for me, "… Reject you without giving you a chance? Jahn you are not the first trans man to ever meet a cis woman. From my experience, rarely does it *not* work out. The world understands, more and more. We have to give them the same understanding that we expect."

"Doc, I think I could really feel something for this woman."

"Make me understand, then. What is it that you feel? Love? Lust? Loneliness? There *is* a difference. It's hard to tell with the increased sex drive that testosterone sometimes causes. If T does have that effect on you, that alone could change your perspective," Dr. Winston says.

"I just want her to get to know me first."

Sliding into shrink mode, he says, "Apparently she already likes what she sees. How do you think she'll react to the truth? What's your greatest fear?"

"I have none—that's why I want to be with her. She seems accepting… open-minded. She's been through some rough things," I say cobbling together what I know of her and what I wish I knew.

He pins me in. "What would you say to her? Give it a try now."

I start slowly with my eyes closed. "Morgan, I was born a…' 'I am a… but…' I can't do this! What the hell am I paying you for? Help me, dammit!"

The doctor leans in. "I've been here all along to support you on this path. Long gone are the days that we have to keep our truth a secret. We're here and they have to live with us. We are still human beings which is our most cogent argument. Now, try it again."

My hands form fists. I stare out of the window, imagining Morgan, not Dr. Winston, sitting across from me. With eyes closed and an even voice, I say, "Morgan, I have something to tell you."

"Excellent. That's a good start. Now, tell her."

"You've got to let me think about it some more. You've caught me off guard. Jesus Christ! I didn't come here to talk about this, today. I came to say goodbye."

Dr. Winston shifts in his seat. "Yes, you did come to talk about this. You said earlier that she makes you want to live. Jahn, I can't force you to tell her. That's not my job. My job is to get you to think about how you'll feel if you don't tell her."

A wave of bad memories stream through my mind, flashing like lights. I brace myself for the flood of emotions that will soon turn into a public drowning. I see it all over again: cute girl, too much to drink. Me, young and confident dealing sloppy kisses in an alley. She invited me in… Kissing her felt so good and then in an instant, I'm running out of a house, a father and two brothers chasing me, calling me vicious names, hurling rocks and bottles at my head. Blood drips from my brow. I touch the scar that never healed.

Dr. Winston hands me a pack of tissues.

"I see some things came up for you. Do you care to talk about them?"

"Can't."

"That's alright. I simply urge you to remember those sensations when you want to resist revealing yourself."

I get up from the chair, needing to pace. I take long, deliberate strides across the spacious office.

"How does the thought of having a love interest feel to you?"

When I reach the other side of the room, my gaze is on my boots. "It feels like I always knew it would." I walk back towards him. "I feel like it *should* feel. Like my heart actually works." I feel my face filling with warm blood.

"Ahh. She makes you blush," Dr. Winston observes. "Why does Bethany object to this, anyway?"

"I don't know!" I walk towards him with frustrated hands. "It's like she doesn't want me to have what she has. *Love*. It fucks with me when she acts like I don't deserve love. Like, I've done something wrong."

"Make no mistake. *Everyone* deserves love. It is our entitlement as human beings."

"I just have to go for it with her, no matter what happens."

"All we know for sure is what our heart tells us. We just have to listen. We all deserve to slide into our skin with ease. There's no risk, really. There are only realities. Jahn, will you allow me to give you the worst-case scenario?" Dr. Winston adjusts his glasses and leans in, again.

"Give it to me," I say.

"Here's the deal. There's a chance that Morgan will say no to you… that she can't accept you. That… she doesn't want a man like you. Don't forget she has the right to choose, which doesn't make her wrong. She may say that she's afraid of being seen with you or it's against her religion or bad for her health. She may even say that you *disgust* her. Who knows what people come up with when they are dealing with fear. Perhaps she has no biases. Maybe, you're just not what she's looking for, which is fair but—"

"Enough dammit!" I feel the tears but I don't want them.

The air is stagnant and I need water. Bending down to fill the flimsy paper cup, Dr. Winston says one last thing...

"Jahn, there's also one more scenario that I'd like you to consider... That Morgan will say... *yes*."

I stand at the water cooler and let that sink in.

After a pause, Dr. Winston says, "Is there anything else that we need to discuss, seeing that this is your last session? Remember, you can always call me when you need to. If something comes up, don't ever hesitate."

"Thanks. I guess I need to thank you for getting me this far. Wish me luck."

"Jahn, you're a good man. You don't need luck, only the courage to love and be loved. Just be who you are. Forget what Bethany or anyone else says. This is your path. Unfortunately, our time is up. Be who you are."

Standing, I reach for the doorknob but Dr. Winston grips my wrist. "Remember, there's no such thing as a last session for us. I'm always just a phone call away."

Heading out of his soundproof office, I see a slumbering body in the waiting room. Their lean collarbone protrudes from the V-neck of a soiled pink sweater. The owner's perky breasts seem out of place on an indigent's body. The angular face is mannish, yet demure. The lips, hastily smeared with a shade of pink, are too pale for the dark canvas on which they sit. A muffled snore falls from them.

Two startled eyes apologize as they settle upon me. Long arms gracefully pull things together as the wearer theatrically tightens the knot of the scarf, bringing it closer to the neck, covering an estranged Adam's apple.

Awkwardly, I rush by with my eyes down, afraid of breaching patient privacy, theirs and my own. My appointment has gone over and they have fallen asleep. Perhaps, this was the safest place for them to sleep.

When I am on the other side of the door, I overhear Dr. Winston's soothing voice. "Sherrie, so sorry to keep you waiting."

Doctor Winston always asks his patients, "Are you ready?"

We never really are.

CHAPTER

6

OCTOBER
Los Angeles, California

Without Rene, Bethany drives us to the church in silence. Concerned with her wife's whereabouts, she has little to say. At my insistence, we arrive at Rise Up at 6:00 p.m., 90 minutes before the service is to begin. Like Rene, I, too, was raised to believe that tardiness is sin. Bethany feels it's too early, but she doesn't argue. The only words that Bethany speaks are, "Rene was out all day yesterday and didn't come back until very late and then left again at the crack of dawn."

My best friend has unraveled. Rain and I expected to see her last night, but knew she had been at the crematorium all day. She didn't even leave me a voice message to tell me how it went. Jahn dropped us off after midnight and the key was under the mat. We made our way to the guest room and settled in like we had done many times before. Exhausted after the long flight, the sounds of Bethany's sobs lulled us to sleep. In the morning, the house was still with only a note from Bethany: *I will pick you up before the service.*

Rise Up Missionary Baptist Church stands tall amidst a modest working-class neighborhood of miniature ranch houses all positioned on micro plots of land. Weathered palm trees and leash-less dogs populate the avenue on the Southside of Los Angeles, as the sun starts to set.

Large faux marble columns and an Italian fountain announce Rise Up, before we even reach the front door. Inside the elaborate foyer, the first thing you see is an oversized portrait of the Honorable Bishop White. His long chemically straightened hair is neatly tucked behind his ears. Two large flat screen TVs sit on both sides of the portrait, flashing idyllic meadow scenes. Piped-in gospel softly pours out of every wall.

Bethany takes Rain to help with the flowers and she suggests that I hand out the programs as the mourners file in. Standing alone, I pick up a program to make sense of this woman that I never met but had been already trained to hate. Bertha's smile is stingy, without a glimpse of porcelain. Her eyes hold the deep, thick hum of an old Negro spiritual; ire with grace. It is obvious that her life was built on difficulty and doctrine.

The scripture beneath her picture reads:

But our citizenship is in heaven, and from it we await a Savior, the Lord Jesus Christ, who will transform our lowly body to be like his glorious body, by the power that enables him even to subject all things to himself.

Philippians 3:20–21

My eyes wander to my watch. Rene is still not here. As the crowd starts to trickle in, all I see are Hats. They are vibrant oranges, reds, blues, greens and yellows. The hats are decorated with bows, flowers, ribbons and buckles, which are sewed on, stapled, embroidered and pinned. The bright colors match the snug fitting dresses of the ample women who model them. Their color choices have no regard for the somberness of the occasion. Their husbands, all dressed in black or blue, merely serve as backdrops against which the wives can shine.

On the cover of the program, Bertha Mae's hat is the most formidable of them all. Almost styled like a cowboy hat, hers is black and oversized with a veil in the front and hundreds of tiny rhinestones wrapping the band.

People slowly start to gush through the stain-glassed double doors. As I hold the programs, my stomach aches with the lost opportunity to properly eulogize my own mother. I wish I could have written her obituary or chosen her photo. I wish I could have said something, anything, to show that I was hers and she was mine. *I hope that Rene does not do something that she will regret.*

The mood in the sanctuary is frantically upbeat. At 7:15 p.m., the Hats still hug each other, laughing and chatting as if at a party. Their powdered smiles seem to know something about death that the rest of us don't. Robotically, I hand out about one hundred programs and still, no Rene. Behind me, I feel a breathing body, too close to mine.

"Howya doin,' Lady?" whispers Jahn, catching me off guard.

I smile, only pretending to be angry. "Jahn, don't sneak up on me!"

"Is Rene here yet?" he asks.

"No. Which worries me."

His whisper and position are deliciously inappropriate. Pushing the Hats aside, he suddenly appears in front of me, dressed like he was at the wedding with a tie replacing the bow tie.

"Don't worry, she'll make it," he assures me with a wink. Glancing down the aisle, he says, "I do see the pulpit *is* sorely missing something..."

"Exactly."

"Well, the worst is over. Bertha has already reached her final destination.

Gotta go find Bethany. Is that where Rain is?"

I nod.

Jahn leans in to me as if he were going to kiss me. As his face gets close to mine, he lingers, smelling my perfume. My lips quiver at his audacity.

A couple of Hats overhear his rude comment and snatch the last of the programs out of my hands.

"See you in a minute," he whispers as he dashes through the throng.

It is 7:25 p.m.

Eerie moans from an elderly woman at the back of the church startle me. Several Hats refer to her as "Mother," as they pat her humped back and pass her to find seats in the front. At last, out of the corner of my eye, I see Rene. Her gait is unstable as she stumbles towards me. The fire of whiskey seeps out of her every pore. It is clear that her hellish night has mutilated her designer garb into a soiled canvas of misplaced wrinkles and stains.

Rene struggles to carry the heavy tin box that has jellied her body. Her voice is as watery and shaky as her posture. She pushes the box towards me, "Can you take this to the front. I can't hold it any longer."

I trip over the box that holds the remaining programs. "Of course, Rene, anything… Follow me. Bethany and Rain are already seated."

The church is fully packed with seated mourners and Hats who still gather in the narrow aisles, talking and catching up like they have no place to be. I grip the handles of the weighty trunk, struggling not to drop it. I stagger down the aisle in my high heels, ankles twisting and turning.

Rene staggers behind me.

Hesitantly the Hats stop talking briefly to stare and create a narrow path. The Hats show no recognition of Rene. I care that they don't see her.

Bethany, Rain and Jahn summon her and she stumbles into the pew. I still have about 15 feet until I reach the empty space on the draped, table. The heavy trunk of faux gold lands on the table with a thud. I notice the top of the trunk is unprofessionally sealed with a store-bought epoxy but there is no time to question its strangeness. The service is about to begin.

The sanctuary falls silent. The organ has ceased as the Honorable Bishop White saunters across the stage in a black robe with purple crosses embroidered on the stole. I hurry to take my seat between Jahn and Rain.

His voice booms. "We have come to this holy place to celebrate the life of a strong Christian woman, Bertha Mae Harden. She was once a wife, a mother and a friend to all."

Muffled sobs fill the air.

Perhaps, Bertha was not a monster after all. Or, maybe this is all just the smoke and mirrors of being a believer. The sweet voices of the choir rise with repeated wails of "Hallelujah." My visceral longing for my mother takes me by surprise. Hot tears gather in my eyes.

After the minister finishes his welcome, the pianist plays a slow jazzy tune, intended for the mourners to read the obituary silently to themselves. Hungrily, I read the single page that chronicles Bertha's life, desperate to know her on my own terms. It says that Bertha was born in a place called Holetown, Barbados. *Rene always said that she didn't know which island her mother was from.* Bertha was a school bus driver. *She never told me that.* Oh, it was *Ayanna,* the niece that should have been in the wedding. *Rene had never used her name.* Stumbling over the next sentence, I don't comprehend the words as they are printed: *Bertha's greatest joy was her three children and grandchildren, Martin, Suzanne and the eldest, Rene.*

My eyes skip over the long list of grandchildren and then get stuck on the next sentence. *"Rene Harden is married and lives in Hollywood with her spouse, Miss Bethany Ricci."*

I read it again: *"Rene Harden is married and lives in Hollywood with her spouse, Miss Bethany Ricci."*

The rest says: *Bertha Mae's biggest regret was losing contact with Rene, of whom she was extremely proud. In lieu of cards or gifts, Bertha has requested that all monetary gifts are sent to The Human Rights Campaign. Bertha's citizenship is in heaven.*

Looking down the length of the pew to catch a glimpse of Rene, she has already slipped out of her seat. Behind me and up the aisle, I see the back of her shaven head, bobbing up and down, as she stumbles.

In a snap decision, stumbling over a mountain of knees, I pursue her. My steps hasten up the aisle. She stops and glares at me as if I were a stranger. I grip her thin arm and she lets me walk with her into the chilly marble foyer.

As soon as I turn my head, Rene slips out of my grip and heads toward the women's bathroom. Not knowing what to do, I follow slowly behind her, but she is quick and is already inside. Peeking my head into the bathroom, I see her sitting on a faded velvet chair in the corner. Her shoulders are slumped and her face is blank. I don't know how to approach her, so I stand still, waiting for her cue.

Bitterly, she says, "Don't miss the show." Her voice is heavy and hoarse. "Did you read that bullshit in the program?"

Startled by the look on her face, I say, "Didn't Bethany write it?"

"Hell no! All of it's lies. She was never proud of me, no matter what I did. Her only acknowledgement of our relationship was saying that the two of us would both burn in hell."

I'd never seen Rene so wrong and strong. I want to believe that she's grieving, as alien as it appears.

The bathroom door creaks open and Bethany sticks her head in. "Babe, it could be true…"

A purple Hat suddenly emerges from a back stall. She keeps her eyes down, knowing of what we speak. She quickly splashes her hands under the faucet and rushes out without drying them. I follow her out the door now that Bethany is here. Rain and Jahn are waiting outside.

Rain looks frazzled and confused. "Mommy! What's wrong with Auntie Rene?"

"I don't know, Rain. Grief looks different on everyone."

Jahn touches my shoulder, lightly. "You OK, Morgan? You ran out of there, like a crazy woman."

"I'm OK. Just a little blindsided by all of this." I look at both of them and say, "Auntie Rene says, 'We're missing the show.' Let's get back inside. Bethany's with her now. She'll make sure that Rene does the right thing."

As Jahn opens the door of the sanctuary for me, he whispers, "What is the right thing?"

I pause. "It all depends on the variables."

There are scriptures, prayers and a lot of tears. It has been nearly two hours and Bishop White is just about to begin his home-going sermon. The topic is forgiveness but Rene is still in the bathroom with Bethany.

Like Mr. Greenstein said, I wish they would "leave the gays alone." Bertha missed out on her daughter and Rene missed out on a relationship with the woman who gave her life. As I mourn the glaring absence of Rene, Rain's words echo in my mind, "*I'd say a lot if you died.*"

JAHN

The Doctor says that gender dysphoria is not mental illness.

Inside the cavernous limousine is quiet. The driver swerves and we all hold on to whatever we can. Shit, we almost hit a dog. Seeing his startled gaze, I marvel at how life straddles the fence. It is only a near miss that lies between life and death.

Rene starts to doze off, resting her head on Bethany's shoulder. Rain clutches Rene's free hand, while staring at the tattered program in her lap. Morgan sits beside her daughter with her eyes closed.

They all sit in a row before me, the only man, closest to the door, in case of an emergency. The wet bar is untouched, although unlimited drinks are included in The Package, the driver previously explained. A single empty glass of wine shakes on the ledge behind Rene as the car pulls away from the curb.

I can't help but stare at Morgan, sitting directly across from me. Her face is intricate, beautifully imperfect. Her coal black eyes sit on a peculiar angle with one eye slightly larger than the other; the smaller eye is puffy. Her long locs frame her cocoa face, shielding it from the harsh elements of which only she is aware. Her lips, curvaceous, her nose, unobtrusive. Her black dress clings to her bountiful breasts and falls to what would be considered a respectable length. The thin slit on the side suggests a woman, not a girl, with yearnings, perhaps as deep as my own. Her well-fed thighs ignite a surprising warmth below.

Discreetly, I lick my lips at her bare legs, which are devoid of sun. Those legs will never be photo-ready. They bear too many random discolorations, scratches, bruises and places that have been sorely overlooked, due to a life filled with more pressing concerns. Nevertheless, her skin arouses a new hunger in me. I want her. My insatiable eyes lead me down to her ankles, which are a little bit swollen, perhaps due to her shoes: costly and uncomfortable.

I fantasize, nonetheless. Her with me, up close and alone. Her, breathing in my air, me, breathing for the first time... I picture her on my couch, filling my empty space with only a turtle's tank light to illuminate. Our blind hands will fumble to find what we are both missing. Just the thought of her there shakes me. The thought of being myself with her, like Dr. Winston suggests, could liberate me, if I could only trust her to take me as I am.

Then, an insidious thought reminds me that if I take her there, trust her there, *allow* her there, she will discover that I'm not good enough. My frugal little life will cause her to smirk on the inside, while she politely smiles on the outside. Asceticism is unappealing to girls like her, with shoes like that. Who am I kidding? When we met, she'd assumed that I was *engaged* to someone, stashing cash for a ring… Imagine that?

Bethany snaps me out of my thoughts. "Whoa Jahn, where'd you go?"

"I'm here," I say, embarrassed. "Just thinkin'."

"J—What are you going to do about your car? It's still at Rise Up, remember?" Bethany says. I had briefly forgotten, as the car whizzes further and further away from my only decent possession.

I suggest, "When we get back to your house, maybe the driver could take me back to pick it up. Would that be cool?"

"That'll work," Bethany says, barely moving so as not to disturb Rene's heavy head.

We have become people whose words have been absconded by grief, but I take my chance, anyway. "Morgan, would you ride back to Rise Up to get my car and then maybe we can pick up something for everyone to eat?"

"Can I go, too?" Rain jumps in.

Morgan shoots her a harsh glance.

Bethany's eyes bore into me. Her teeth slightly clenched as she turns to Rain, "No sweetie, you stay with us while your mom goes on a very short ride with Jahn." She then turns her attention to Morgan. "You'll be right back. Right?"

Morgan is caught off guard. "Sure. Yes," she says.

Bethany's face softens as she turns to Rain again. "Rainy, you can help cheer us up. We sure need it. Your Auntie Rene would really like that."

Rain says, "OK. I can cheer you up with my funny faces."

I ask more directly this time. "Morgan, so are you up for the ride?"

She silently nods. I think that means, yes.

CHAPTER

OCTOBER
Los Angeles, California

I am stunned that Jahn just asked me out in the limousine, in front of everyone. I can't bear the righteous looks of disgust that I deserve, which is why I keep my head down for the rest of the ride. I only peek and see that Rain is smiling. Rene sleeps through the whole ride. Sitting across from Jahn, I can't help but imagine what it would be like to be alone with him.

As the limousine rounds the circular driveway, Bethany nudges Rene to wake her. Being helpful, Rain gathers up the crinkled programs. Once the driver opens the door, I head out first. My wink at Jahn is to tell him that I won't be long, only needing to do one thing: change my shoes. The ticking of my nerves builds with every step that I take towards the front door.

Getting involved with him seems ambitious or ridiculous; I'm not sure which. I fear that I am suddenly out of my depths. I want it to be right, even though so much about it is wrong. Our first date is a funeral. We live on opposite sides of the country. We won't be able to see each other often. And, after all these years, I have forgotten how to be with a man.

Rene leans on Bethany, like a lush, while Bethany fiddles with the key, trying to hold her up and open the door at the same time. I refrain from knocking her aside so that Jahn doesn't have to wait too long. Once the door is open, I push past them all, kicking off my heels on the way to the guest room. Once there, I reach for my flats. The details of how it happened so fast have already gone over my head. All I know is that I will be alone with Jahn in just a few minutes.

Staring in the mirror, I see all that has to be done. I brush my teeth, spritz more perfume, gargle with a swig of harsh mint and gather my locs into a tighter ponytail. *It has been so long.*

I rush past Bethany and she says, "Careful, Morgan, Rene will wonder where you went."

"Bethany, it's pretty late already. I won't be long. Thanks for staying with Rain," I say as I inch towards the door, hoping that she won't mention this betrayal at a later date.

"Rene and I could certainly use some cheering up," Bethany says loud enough to remind me of my sins. I blow Rain an air kiss and shut the door behind me.

When I get outside, Jahn is standing in front of the limousine waiting for me as I bound down the stairs.

"Get in, my Lady," Jahn says with his feigned British accent.

I smile. "Thank you, sir."

"How was it in there? How's Bethany?"

"She's as fine as she can be… in a very awkward situation."

"Is she pissed?" Jahn says as we get situated on the huge two-toned circular seat.

"What *is* it between you and Bethany, anyway? Did you date her or something?" I ask.

"No. We just have some history," he says, already touching me. "None of it matters now because, finally, you and I are alone."

Laying my head against the padded headrest, my eyes stare at the ring of lights on the ceiling. Mingled perfumes linger in the muggy limo air.

"Are we all in?" The driver yells over the divider, reminding us that we are not really alone.

"Yes sir!" Jahn squeezes my hand.

"I'm glad you're here," I admit.

His eyes look at me with curiosity. "Morgan, what about me makes you glad?"

"I'm not sure. You feel really familiar to me, like someone I already know."

The driver has put his window down to flip off another driver. "L.A. assholes!" he screams.

The breeze from his window sends cool air to the backseat. I shiver.

Jahn searches my eyes and puts his jacket around my shoulders. "I don't know, Girl. There's just something about you that I can't get enough of."

"I feel the same way but to be honest, I feel torn. I'm glad to be with you and I realize it wasn't my mother, but…."

"How old were you when it happened to you?" Jahn asks, as he lightly strokes my arm.

I stare up at the ceiling to avoid his eyes. My head sinks deeper into the plush leather as I rattle off the CliffsNotes of my sorrow. "Bertha's memorial service was like a flashback to a very difficult time. I was only 15 when my mom died. I feel a little guilty being with you tonight."

"No regrets, Morgan," he says with urgency.

A strip of moonlight shines through the open sunroof as we speed underneath it. His face is sculpted and handsome.

"You are being in the moment right now and I like that. It's sexy," he says pulling both of my hands into his strong grip.

"I wasn't expecting you to ask me out… in front of everyone. Not tonight, at least. You know I'll be here for a couple more days, right?"

He sits up, dropping my hands in order to make his point. "If we don't listen to our hearts in the moment, where does that leave the future? It's never worth it to do what's comfortable for others."

I love how he talks with his hands. "Yeah… I guess you're right. Switching the subject, what are we going to eat? I'm starving."

"It's your choice but I'm buying."

"I appreciate the offer but I know that you're saving up for something. I thought we were taking food back for everyone else, anyway."

"That, I admit was a teeny tiny lie… I just said that just so they would go with it. Look, you're doing me a favor by coming back with me to get my car. Buying dinner is the least I can do. I am saving, but some things, I mean, some *people*, are worth saving a little less for."

"I'm not so sure about this. We should probably head back after we get the car."

"What are you so worried about? Bethany? She sent me a text right before you came out of the house."

"I don't believe you. I was only in there for five minutes. Let me see it!" Playfully, I reach for his phone.

"You were actually in there for eight minutes and 23 seconds. No, really. She sent me a text, giving us her blessings!"

"Stop playing with me. That doesn't even sound like her."

"OK. You got me. But, what can she do? We're here. 'Act now, apologize later,' that's my motto. What did I tell you? No regrets. Believe me, Rain will not miss a meal. You see who they are, Brentwood dykes, all disposable income and no responsibilities except to indulge. Making everybody jealous is like their job. I'm sure there's all sorts of gourmet grub in that house. Angus Beef, Lobster Tails and microwaveable duck."

"Still, it doesn't feel right... Rene flew me and Rain across the country to support her and instead of consoling her, I'm out on a date with you. I don't want to be rude but I've lost my mother and me sitting here with you is not right. I'd be hurt if Rene did that to me."

"But you'd eventually forgive her, right? Like my therapist says, 'There are no risks, just realities.'"

"The reality is that Rene is hurting. I don't know what's come over me... it's *you*... You see a therapist? You seem so together."

"It's the L.A. thing to do. Out here, we're all working on being 'self-realized,' he says with his famous imaginary quotation marks. "You know that's some ole' Hollywood shit," he says with a sparkle in his eye.

I don't quite buy his answer, but understand it's none of my business.

He has already changed the subject. "Rene's mother is already dead. What's a few hours? Rene's probably fast sleep, anyway. She slept the whole way back to the house. Remember?"

His hand has found its way to my bare leg.

I concede, "You're probably right. Rene is probably sound asleep; dinner has been served and Rain is probably making silly faces for Bethany and she is actually laughing."

"Morgan, you're thinking way too hard about it," he says.

"Will you do me one favor. Just let me check in with a quick text."

"Whatever you say," Jahn folds his arms.

As I text, Jahn hangs over my shoulder reading each character as I type.

Rene, how are you? Do you mind if I hang out a little longer?
We'll be back soon. Hope that's OK.

In seconds, the return text reads:

This is Bethany. Rene's asleep. See you in the morning.
The key is under the mat.

I smile at him. "Looks like you were right. It's done."

"Told you. You're a grown woman." His smile confirms our collusion. "It's been a trying day. Let's just grab something quick to eat and we'll head back. I promise."

"OK," I say, feeling torn and turned on.

"Whatever you want to eat, I can take us there."

"How about Thai? I'm in the mood for something hot, spicy and delicious."

"Damn, Girl, I thought you were describing me for a second," he says fingering his perfect goatee. His mouth is wide with a smile and his eyes light up. "L.A. has the best Thai. After we pick up the car, we'll grab takeout from my favorite spot."

The air feels different than when he picked us up at the airport. Already, we are deeper in.

The driver finally says, "Final stop, Rise Up!"

The parking lot glows under the street lamps that illuminate the last cars left.

Bertha's mourners still trickle out of the social hall.

"Which car is yours?" I ask.

"It's the yellow Mini Cooper over there, at the back. It's an older model," he adds.

"What an unusual color," I say as we walk towards the tiny sunshine yellow car with black racer stripes on the hood.

"It gets me where I'm going. It was the cheapest car on the lot. I had an F-150 truck but it died on me and I couldn't afford to get the transmission fixed with my new budget."

As he speaks, he walks me around to the passenger side and unlocks the door. Still teasing the boundaries, his hand falls lower on my back than before. A scented paper pine tree dangles from his rearview mirror, filling the car with a strong pleasant smell.

"Sorry, radio doesn't work," he says as he puts the key into the ignition. The dashboard lights up and he pushes a button and the sunroof slowly glides open. "But I do listen to music. I am really into music, you know—something else we have in common. I just use my phone's Bluetooth and an auxiliary speaker. The clock doesn't work either. I never bothered to get it fixed. I hate knowing how fast life ticks away."

Rene would be mortified at how poor Jahn is, but I don't really care about those things. She'd say that I could do much better. The old motor of the Mini chugs us onto the freeway while luxury cars whizz by at top speed. I marvel at the millions of stars that twinkle with endless possibility.

"Jahn, you said something the other day, something like, it's possible for someone to *not* mourn the death of their mother? How would you know?"

With slight exasperation, he asks, "When did I say that? Do you really want to talk about that, now?"

He chews the inside of his lip and his mouth forms a tangle.

"I do want to because you said it and I want to know why."

Jahn's frustration is evident as he re-pushes the button and the sunroof glides shut. "Damn, Girl, after a funeral, I was hoping for some lighter convo."

"Is talking about your mother painful?"

"Talking is never a problem for me. You've been hanging out with the wrong dudes, if you think we don't talk. What do you want to know?"

"Jahn, there's one thing you should know about me. I can't stand light conversation. If it's light, it's not conversation, it's just… nothing, really."

"I guess what I was trying to say is, you can't mourn what you've never had. I think that's what Rene is feeling. Her relationship with her mother was fucked up."

"And yours?" I ask.

"Mine, too. It wasn't a relationship at all. It was just a void. As far as I know, she's alive. She didn't raise me, my grandmother did."

"Where was she?"

"I guess mothering wasn't her *thang*," he says. "She put me on the school bus one morning when I was six and that was the last time, I ever saw her face."

"I'm so sorry," I say, wishing for stronger words.

"It's not your fault."

Trying to hold the fragile conversation together, I say, "What happens to us is no one's fault. It's just *life* that happens and we can't do anything about it. Were you close to your grandmother?"

"Momba? I guess you could say that. She's all I had." Flashing a smile, he says, "Changing the subject, if you don't mind. You mentioned that you want to go dancing with me? Did I hear that, correctly?"

"Yes, you did," I say, still wanting to dig deeper.

"Let me check out what's happening this weekend. Maybe we can go tomorrow night, if Bethany will let you out," he smirks and rolls his eyes back in his head.

The car slows and Jahn says, "Damn!"

We have stopped in front of a small shack with a carved wooden sign that says Coconut Milk. The OPEN sign is dark.

As he shifts the car into park, I say, "What are we going to eat?"

"We'll figure it out," he says. "It's L.A., something's always open. If you don't mind, there's a song that I want you to check out first." He pulls out a small black cube from the glove compartment. As he reaches over me, the weight and smell of his fragrant body are suddenly all over me. I inhale, not knowing how to handle his closeness.

"This song has been haunting me for weeks. Check it out. One of the kids at school was playing it. I haven't stopped listening to it since."

Jahn fiddles with his iPod. His fingers are long and hairy. Once the Bluetooth activates, there is a moment of silence and then an atmospheric intro fades in. The sounds are haunting and they chill me. Then, a melancholy instrumental oozes out of the cube. It's a song that I don't recognize but Jahn knows every note. He moves his head slowly from side to side, waiting for the first strum of the acoustic guitar. His moist lips and whole body are animated as his head bobs to the beat. As the song builds, he closes his eyes, bracing himself as he transcends. Parts of his body are synchronized, moving and gliding over every measure. The guitar builds and other instruments come in, creating a flawless space for the final christening, the vocals.

I am amazed at Jahn's intimacy with music. I recognize it. I am a willing audience as I bear witness to his sacred ritual that he effortlessly performs. As the guitar chords layer, Jahn's soulful soprano mixes perfectly as he mimics the singer. Their voices become one. I am so taken by what he's doing that I can only grab snippets of the lyrics as they come at me.

I'm driving fast… don't think I know… go slow.

Beads of sweat. How hot can I get… I'm not there yet.

When the singer's voice resumes, it is strong and sensuous. Jahn takes the singer's cue, joining him, first in falsetto and then digging deep into a shameless scat. As the song reaches its climax, suddenly the bottom drops out, leaving a partial silence so the vocals can attack again, this time driving deeper into the scat.

Jahn finally remembers that I am beside him. "Here it comes," he warns, "Listen!" The guitar comes in hard and the chorus comes back.

I don't know you

But I want you so bad....

A shrill falsetto comes in followed by three high notes. As the song winds down, Jahn closes his eyes just for a second, as he gently falls back down to earth. "Damn! I love that shit! That white brotha is crazy soulful. I'm feeling him."

"Wow. I love how you just shared that with me."

"Morgan, you get me," he says reaching over and moving a loc out of my face. "What are the songs that do that to you?"

"There are too many to name," I say.

"I'll wait for you to share one of them with me when you're ready."

"Deal," I say, already thinking of the millions of songs that have possessed me throughout my life.

"I know you're starving but my apartment is close by. I need to go home just for a second. Do you mind stopping with me? I'll make it quick."

———

When he hits floor B in the elevator, we sink down to the basement, which reeks of settled garbage. The two-tone green and grey paint peels. I am daunted and intrigued by the subterranean danger. I feel my old fearlessness creeping back up on me like an old friend. I assure myself; *he is safe.*

When we arrive on level B, he heads for a small spiral staircase in the corner of the basement, which takes us down even further. Suddenly, in my mind, I see my father's eyes rolling back in his head as I go down the winding staircase. I stumble hearing his scold, *"Where the hell do you think you're goin'? You don't know this man! Have you lost your mind?"* The shrillness of his voice almost causes me to miss a step. I pull back as Roy's voice follows me, close.

"You OK?" Jahn asks me as he notices the change in my pace and face.

"Yeah. I just remembered that... I should call my father."

As we reach the oversized black door of his apartment, he says, "You should know that I never bring anyone here."

"Why not?"

"It's too small for visitors."

"Why me, then? I'm a visitor."

"No. You're not," he says.

There is a peaceful silence as we walk through the door into darkness. The only light comes from the turtle's tank across the tiny room. His house *is* made for one. In the shadows, all I can see are hundreds of books lining the walls like wallpaper.

"Make yourself at home," he says as he rushes into the bathroom with some urgency.

My eyes go right to the tank, which is full of murky water. There is no sign of life, only a mild reptilian scent.

Above the tank, there is a large poster that reads, "I AM SCIENCE FICTION." The words are scrawled in an artistic script, as if he could have written and framed it himself. The small island that divides the kitchen from the living space is his dining table. A paperback book with the cover torn off sits there. My fingers itch with curiosity, so eager to know what he reads and how he thinks. A worn leather bookmark peeks out from the tattered pages. I hesitate before opening to the marked page. The only words I have time to scan are: *The mind is the substance of humanity. Mind is deeper than matter.* I don't want to get caught turning pages without his permission.

Jahn's space feels confidential like his air. I want to understand all that I don't. There's no time. Just wondering about his book feels wrong. The flush of the toilet reminds me that I am in violation. I prepare a quick apology in case he asks about my wandering eyes and itchy, uninvited fingers.

"Ready to go?" Jahn says as he emerges, not seeing me toss the book back how I found it.

"I like it here. You're pretty tidy... for a guy," I say.

"I don't know if that's a compliment or an insult to guys."

"It's a compliment. And, an insult to guys," I say with a friendly poke to his firm chest. "Obviously, not all guys."

"I just needed to check on Berd and hit the bathroom real quick."

"Did you check on him? I don't even see him."

Jahn laughs. "He isn't going to greet you. He's a turtle, not a puppy." He wraps his hands around my waist, turning me slowly towards the tank.

"Can you see that dark brown mound in the corner? That's Berd. He's hiding," he says affectionately. "That's where he hangs out. And that," pointing to a futon, "is my hang out spot."

"Your turtle's name is Bird? B-i-r-d?"

"No B-e-r-d. It's short for Berdache."

"What's it mean?"

"It's a Native American word. It means Two-Spirited. The Berdaches were the shamans of the tribe. Ready to go, now?" he says, heading for the door.

I stay still, not ready to leave.

"I'm thinking of a place called Kogi to eat, but we have to get there soon. It's a food truck. Korean food, L.A.-style Burritos stuffed with extra meat and Kimchi is the main flavor. It's goooood," his lips form an unusual shape. "It's not like that stuffy grub you get from Rene and Bethany. You said you wanted something *hot*, didn't you?"

I gently touch his face, "I think I may have found it."

The dimmed ceiling light brings a warm glow to his face. "You keep sayin' stuff like that and I'll have no choice…"

"I'll keep my mouth shut, then," I say looking straight into his eyes.

"But I won't," he says as he comes towards me.

All day, I have felt his eyes, leading us to this moment. His open mouth paints a kiss on my eager lips. Breathlessly, I fall into his firmness. Every part of me remembers what to do. My moist tongue playfully licks his top lip and then sinks down to the bottom, before inhaling his mouth. My hands linger on his back, feeling the bulk of pure muscle. Jahn's hands rise towards my face, slowly turning and pulling it closer so he can taste more of me.

He kisses me as if my mouth is his own, as if he knows exactly where to go and how long to stay. His kisses are intoxicating, more like anointings. The carefulness of his hand on my breast makes me shake. Effortlessly, my arms wrap around his trim waist. His bulky leather belt is where my fingers want to play. The silver of the buckle is cool to the touch. Beneath his loosened suit, my hands roam the alleys of his back's complex musculature. He leads me to the futon.

This time, I kiss him, first on his neck. Then my lips travel up to his mouth. Jahn toys with the fabric of my skirt, sliding his fingers in and out of the slit. His fingers climb my leg. He has slid my lightweight black dress upward. I feel his bare skin next to mine.

I lose track of the details. Eyes closed, all of my senses piqued, his fingers tease my warm skin. I let him play. When I move closer, he pulls back. I wait with my eyes closed. *Nothing.* Finally, he places a last kiss on the tip of my nose.

Pulling my body closer to him, I want more. I am overcome with this man and all of his light and darkness... this man with hundreds of books and a turtle named Berd.... this man who, with one look, seems to know the rest. This man, Jahn, spelled with an "a," is softly bringing me back from the dead...

BETHANY

The door slams and thunder pulses through me. The last time this happened, years ago, the emergency room doctor explained to Rene that, in clinical terms, I suffer from something called Intermittent Explosive Disorder. And, I do. Much like the Improvised Explosive Devices of the military, something in my brain blows at the slightest provocation, chewing away at my sanity each time it happens. It happened again as soon as Morgan slammed that door to go on her date with Jahn.

I wanted to scream and hit my head against the wall, but it was not the time. Rene had fallen asleep on the couch and Rain needed something to do. She asked if she could watch television, mumbling under her breath that Morgan doesn't allow her to watch at home. My hands shake but I try to be gentle, placing them around her fragile shoulders, careful not to press too hard, as I lead her to a place where she will be out of my sight, with a new playmate, the remote control.

Skulking into the bathroom for the last resort, I cringe at the heavy bags beneath my eyes, evidence of the wear and tear of rage. Am I jealous of Morgan or disgusted by Jahn? He is a fool to think that he can trust her. She's just another desperate woman who's been destroyed by the recklessness of men. Morgan is a woman whose only fix is a man.

I swallow the round yellow pill without water, hearing the clutch of my throat as the dry pill sinks without the luxury of buoyancy. In case Rene is listening, the only sound she'll hear is the intentional flush of an empty toilet.

Eyes closed; I wait for calm to come on the cool tile floor. My mind sees Jahn charming Morgan, telling her what she wants to hear, seducing her with his eyes. He's doing what he does, making her believe that he's the man she's been waiting for. And, she does what desperate women often do… *believe*.

I can almost smell Morgan's suffocating floral perfume burning my nostrils. Envisioning her telling him that her heart is strong enough for whatever lies ahead makes me want to kick something. They both lie. No one can be as strong as me, who has been there from the start of him, knowing, seeing, counting every step it took to get her here. He is not a man with a past that is easily told. Transition doesn't go over well in crowds. It creates too many whys.

In my head, I still hear his plea; "I *am* a man."

How did I let myself get so attached to her? I asked him what was wrong with just being a dyke? Why was that not good enough? *It's not good enough for me*, she had said over and over and I listened, but never understood. She promised to always love me, no matter what. I told her that I would be her forever girl. Damn! These are things that children say and can never mean. I just never thought that she'd go through with it...

If only Morgan knew that Jahn's treasure chest holds none. If she's had as many men as Rene says, she'll be sorely disappointed to find that there's no way around it; a man either has balls or he doesn't.

For hours, my mind blows while I lay on the cold tile floor. Silence keeps me while my storm passes.

CHAPTER

8

OCTOBER
Los Angeles, California

I can feel her presence pulling me out of sleep. My eyes struggle to open but the tension in her voice jolts me.

Bethany towers over the bed. "Morgan, did you have fun?"

The sun blasts through the sheer curtains and right through her hair like a laser beam.

Bethany's black curls are a blur, piled on top of her head in a sloppy bun. Her cat eye reading glasses complement her young, flawless face. Steam from her coffee mug rises and the sound of her blowing to cool it off, disturbs me.

I hope that she can't see Jahn's hands all over me. I pull the sheets up tighter to hide all of the sweet places, the hickeys that always are visible the morning after.

"Yeah, it was fun. Thanks for leaving the key. How's Rene doing, today?

Where's Rain?"

"Rene took her out for breakfast. She feels better after a good night's sleep. Thanks for asking," she says, with a tepid smile.

"Why didn't you go, too?" I ask, rubbing the sleep out of my eyes.

"I told Rene I have a migraine." She steps closer to the bed, standing where my feet rest underneath the blanket. "But, I don't," she says pushing my feet out of her way, almost sitting on them. "Actually, I wanted to talk to you, alone." Her hot coffee sloshes against the side of the mug as she sits. I curl my body backwards against the headboard.

"What's up?" I say, dodging the inevitable coffee spill.

"Just get up, Morgan, there's not much time. I'll make you breakfast. We'll talk then."

In the mirror my face looks different. The muscles around my eyes have relaxed. My lips now part with ease; my jaw is no longer sealed with tension. Re-living his hands enveloping my waist, I feel him in every nook and cranny. Showering would negate the proof of him, so I don't. I brush away the red-hot swirl of his tongue's motion, watching it slide down the drain. Splashing cold water on my face snaps me out of the haze. The fluffy guest room bathrobe will cover all that needs to be.

A colorful bowl of fresh fruit and a platter of smoked salmon await. "How'd you like your eggs prepared?" Bethany asks with her back to me.

"No thanks, I'm not eating eggs these days. My Chinese herbalist told me to stay away from them."

I don't know what to do with myself standing in the center of her large gourmet kitchen. There are so many drawers, filled with costly things. All I want is to find napkins and silverware.

"Anything wrong, Bethany?" I say to her back.

She's almost violent when she turns around. "What are you thinking, Morgan? You tell *me* what's wrong. Is it OK that you went out on a date the night of Rene's mother's service? She says you're like her sister. She needed you here for a reason. She fucking *flew you* both here! I know that you're an only child, so you don't have a clue what a sister would do, but going on a date is not it." Her eyes twitch with wrath.

I speak quietly while my heart thumps loudly. "Rene said she needed sleep… I figured it wouldn't be such a big deal. She slept all the way home from the funeral. Did Rain do something wrong?" I place two placemats directly across from each other on the round table, paying special care to fold the paper napkins as if they are cloth.

"Rain was not the problem. You are. I just don't know what you're doing."

"What do you—"?

"Morgan, you've been acting like a teenager with a first crush ever since you met Jahn."

"What do you have against him, anyway? Some best friend you are. Why are you meddling in this?"

Her voice hits a strange high note. "Ohhh! How many times have I asked myself the same question? The truth is, I don't want any part of this. Rene always makes such a big deal about you and Rain and I'm just trying to look out for you both."

"Maybe Rene makes such a big deal because we're real friends. Not like you, who has nothing nice to say about Jahn, your supposed best friend."

"This is bullshit. None of this should be happening." She throws a fancy dishtowel into the sink.

"Don't you judge me! Bertha's service was hard for me to take. It was like me reliving the whole thing all over again. I just needed to clear my head. Jahn was a welcomed distraction."

"Morgan, if the service was painful for you, think about how it must have been for Rene. This isn't even about you or your damned mother— who's been dead for 30 years, I might add. When will you get over it?"

I don't attempt to answer a question that is unanswerable. I spit, "Let's talk more about it when your *damned* mother dies."

Bethany gasps at the thought. She covers her open mouth. "Morgan, I'm sorry. That didn't come out right." Her posture softens. "I'm just under a lot of stress. Ever since we heard the news about Bertha, it's like the life has drained out of Rene. It scares me." With that, Bethany crumples into the chair. "Morgan, there's something going on with her. She won't talk to me. I need you to find out what it is."

I dare to reach out to Bethany. She stiffens as my hand approaches. I settle on touching the fabric of her shirt. I comfort her with, "Rene loves you. I promise I'll find out what's up. I'll take her to lunch today."

Beginning to eat, the fire of Jahn still smolders. Forgetting where I am and with whom, I turn ravenous as the sweet watermelon juice trickles down my chin. I savor his memory.

"Morgan, are you there? I picked up some fresh-squeezed juice at the market. Let me pour you some." She rises again, returning with a large glass of juice.

She wastes no time. "Morgan, what is it that you see in Jahn? I find it so interesting that you seem to have so much in common with him. And, so quickly."

Feigning interest in food, Bethany cuts her omelet in half and then quarters and then eighths, without taking a single bite. She has moved her chair a little closer.

"Actually, we have a lot in common: music, books… lots of things," I respond. "He has an artist's sensibility, even though he's an athlete. He has two sides. I can't explain it, we just hit it off."

Bethany stammers, "D-d-don't you find anything strange—I mean *different* about him?"

"Like what?"

"I bet he's not like the other guys that you've been with." Bethany puts her fork down and pushes her plate aside.

"You're right. He's not. That's probably what I do see in him," I say as I take a sip of the juice, saving the rest for my pills.

The whistle of the teakettle startles us. Bethany jumps up again, her messy bun, falling further into her face. She rushes to turn off the fire and pull a mug off the shelf for herself.

"Want some herbal tea?"

"No thanks."

"So, what'd you guys do last night?" Bethany asks from the pantry, where she is selecting her tea.

Trying to keep my mouth full, I mumble, "Not much, really. We tried to go out to dinner but the place was closed. It got late so we just hung out a little…"

I walk to the cabinet where she said I could leave my pills. Returning to the table, I start to sort them out, separating the prescriptions from the supplements. Blood pressure pill. Cholesterol pill, Hematinic Folic-Acid,

Anti-inflammation. Kidney supplement. Fish oil. Iron supplement. Vitamin D, Vitamin C, Lysine.

Bethany's eyes widen in disbelief at the number and size of the pills that keep me alive. "Rene doesn't have so many. Do you need a little bowl?"

"The napkin is fine."

Bethany sits down with her tea, holding the steaming mug with her bare hands. Not at all bothered by the heat that seeps through the ceramic, her tightly wound fingers redden. "So, where did he take you?"

"His place. But we were just there for a few minutes. It's a cool spot. Have you and Rene been there?"

"Of course, I have, Morgan. I got it for him and helped him move in. Rene hasn't been there. Jahn says she's too uptight."

My smile is insincere. "That's funny. You seem to be the uptight one."

"Morgan, it's just there's a lot going on. For this to happen to Rene's mother right after our honeymoon is not exactly a fairytale. I'm worried about my wife and don't know how to help her."

"She just needs time," I say.

Sitting quietly sipping her tea, Bethany watches my pill ritual in silence and awe. After a decade, I do it mindlessly. While she watches, I think of Jahn. Delirious after our last kiss, my mind wanders to how we left it. Was he supposed to call me or was I supposed to call him? I lick my lips.

Bethany's face temporarily lightens as she says, "Oh, I just remembered, I got some passes to a kid's screening. I hoped that we could make a night of it and go out to dinner before. I hope Rene will come out with us."

Her fingers are red from heat. Finally, her mug hits the table. She looks me up and down. "Or, do you already have plans for tonight?"

"Actually, Jahn suggested that we do something but...?" I stop speaking, jarred by the rapid change in her face.

"Bethany, you don't know how much I crave adult time. Raising a kid on your own is not for the weak."

"Are you weak?" she asks.

"We're all weak when we're willing to admit it. Even you. Hanging out last night just reminded me that I still have some life left."

"Just don't do something that you'll regret," she tells me.

Jahn's words spill out of me, effortlessly. "No regrets."

Bethany starts clearing the dishes.

I feel more comfortable speaking to her back. "Bethany, what's your problem? You've known Jahn, forever, right? This is the second time you've warned me about him. Is he a pedophile? A rapist? Does he have a computer full of child porn?"

She turns slowly. "Nope. But people change, Morgan. That's all I can say."

———⁓———

Rene takes driving seriously and always has. I've had to get used to the fact that she never speaks while driving. With a pilot's confidence, she navigates through L.A. traffic, absent-minded pedestrians and eight lane highways without having to think. Her expensive cars seem to change her inside and out. Classical music always swirls throughout the car, swallowing up all possible conversation.

I marvel at the lights and energy of Los Angeles while practicing how to broach the difficult topics on my mind. When Rene finally turns into the driveway of Café Malibu, the valet recognizes her and the convertible. He smiles and Rene flicks him a crisp $20.00 bill.

The restaurant is opulent. Flanked with palm trees and flowers in bloom, we walk down a long bamboo walkway to the hostess' stand.

"Reservation?" the pretty hostess asks.

"No reservation. I'm a regular. Rene Harden. Is Monica, here?" Rene always has a name to drop.

"There's a table out on the veranda overlooking the garden, Ms. Harden? Would that suit you?"

Rene corrects, "It's *Mrs. Harden*. And yes, certainly, that will work. Thank you."

As she walks ahead of me, her head is regal, once again.

"Can I get you ladies something to drink?" The server asks as we sit down.

"I'll have a French Connection—Cognac and Amaretto," Rene says.

"I'll have a glass of Riesling, please. And a glass of water."

Hoping for a benign start, I say, "Rene, I really planned to take you to lunch, today."

"But I beat you to it," she says with a feigned pout. "What did you want to talk about?"

Rene's eyes dart around the room looking for her drink.

Two glasses of water appear on the table and Rene sneers at the busboy who brings them, "Where's my *drink*?"

"Sorry," the busboy says, rushing away.

"Rene, I owe you an apology. I'm sorry about last night. It wasn't cool for me to go out, socially, after your mother's service. It was insensitive."

"Girl, I was fast asleep. It's OK. I heard that you and Jahn hung out. How'd that go?"

"It was good. Surprisingly good," I say feeling myself warming up again.

Rene's meticulously tweezed eyebrows raise. "Uh-huh. Your face says it was much better than good."

"Bethany was not too pleased. She nailed me about it this morning. *What is it* with her and Jahn? Did they date in high school? Did he break her heart? Or seduce one of her girlfriends? She acts so strangely whenever his name comes up." I take a sip of my water to stop myself from saying too much more about Rene's new wife.

"I don't know him that well. He's a pain in the ass, really. He used to take up a lot of her time. He just needs a woman in his life, so he can leave mine alone. Bethany says she's like his big sister and you know how that goes…"

"Actually, I don't. Bethany reminded me of that, too."

"Don't mind her, Morgan. You make her a little nervous."

"Why would *I* make her nervous?" I ask.

"Any woman that I respect makes Bethany nervous. One day, she'll get used to our relationship and then she'll lighten up on you, I hope. Fingers crossed."

"Please remind her that I'm totally straight," I say with a laugh.

With mischief in her eyes, Rene says, "Being straight hasn't mattered much in my life and Bethany knows that, too. That's probably why she's so suspicious of you. It's *different* with women. *Some* women, that is… their hearts and bodies speak louder than their… claimed sexuality."

"Enough about that," I say, not wanting to lose sight of what I have come to talk about. "Rene, how are you doing? I am so sorry about Bertha. Talk to me."

"Let's start with that insane memorial service. I'm still trippin' from it," Rene says, sitting back in her chair.

"Despite what you've said about Bertha, I was surprised to see how much those church people really seemed to love her. And I noticed that they didn't recognize or acknowledge you, at all."

"That's because I've never stepped foot in that ungodly place before yesterday. Those people have no idea about the Bertha that I knew. Those lies in the program were just words on a page, paint on a canvas to make a pretty picture."

"You don't have to hate her anymore. What confuses me is that, if she was such a gay basher, why did she want to make a donation to the Human Rights Campaign?"

The waitress waves her hand, apologetically. "Your drinks are coming right out."

Rene frowns and finishes off her water. "I don't have any idea. That's a weird one. Rest assured Bertha didn't ask for that."

"You'll never know for sure. Maybe she did. Being bitter is no good for us, you know that. She's gone. What will you do now?"

"There's only one thing left to do. Live… without apology."

The drinks arrive and Rene takes hers down like water. While the server is still setting down my wine and the breadbasket, she orders a refill with just the point of a finger at her empty glass.

Looking at the menu, I say, "Bethany wants to take us all out tonight. Would you be pissed if I skipped it and went out with Jahn, again? He invited me dancing."

"It's fine with me. Besides, you know my old ass won't be taking you dancing! So, go with him. What matters to me is that you were at the service. By the way, thanks for being here. The Christians are a tough crowd."

"Rene, why did you say that Jahn's a pain in the ass? Do you think I'm crazy wanting to get to know him?"

"Not at all. He's a loner, sort of an unusual guy, just how you've always liked them. Over the last few years, he has taken up a lot of Bethany's time. That's all. He's harmless. I hope tonight goes as well as last night. It's been nine long years for you, Girl. You deserve whatever action you can get."

I raise my glass and she raises hers.

I say, "Here's to deserving... *and* action."

Our glasses clink and Rene drinks hers down in one swallow. Then she says, "Switching the subject, if I may... I have something to talk to you about."

"What is it?"

"Morgan, you can never share this with anyone. It's strictly between us." Her voice and eyes lower.

I take a sip of my wine and pull myself to the edge of my seat so I can hear her.

The liquor has loosened her up. "Morgan, you look really great, by the way. I haven't had time to tell you that."

"Stop stalling. What the hell is it?"

"You may need another drink. Let me get a server." Rene's eyes roam the room again.

"Tell me whatever it is! You're making me crazy."

"OK," she breathes deeply. "I threw Bertha's remains, I mean *cremains* in the garbage."

A splash of wine shoots out of my mouth. Rene moves back to avoid the sprinkle.

I quickly wipe up the spill with my crisp cloth napkin. A waiter looks to see if I need help but I motion him away with my hand. "I got it," I mouth.

After I compose myself, I say, "How's that possible? Is that even legal?"

Rene's expression turns muddled and then she rears back in her seat. Jagged and labored laughter spills out of her mouth like broken teeth.

People turn to stare.

My stomach turns.

Rene wipes her tears on the pristine white linen. "Let me explain. After the cremation, the funeral guy hands me the expensive gold inlay urn that I purchased for almost $3,000.00, for her remains, I mean, *cre-mains*. Anyway, it suddenly dawned on me that Bertha didn't deserve any of it. It just wasn't worth it for me, to have those church ladies think that she was a good, loving person. I didn't want to be an accessory to her lie. I realized that there is no Heaven to go to. Her last stop was the fire. She'd never know the difference between the gold urn or that tin piece-of-shit that I got at Wal-Mart."

My mouth falls open.

She continues, "I just needed to get one last 'fuck you' off my chest. This was my last opportunity, so I took it."

Finishing off another cognac cocktail, she puts the glass down hard on the table. I am shaken by the sound of the ice tumbling in the glass. Rene stares out the window behind me. As if her words are not coming from her, she says in a voice I have never heard before, "Fuck you, Mama. You're right where you belong."

As she speaks, my heart pounds. I bring my wine to my lips and drink it down, greedily.

There's more. "At the gas station, after disposing of her, I then remembered Bethany. I knew my wife would want to see the urn as soon as

I walked in the door. It was too late. While I was placing the urn in the garbage next to an crumpled Wendy's bag, I wasn't thinking straight. I had read that remains have the weight and consistency of sand. I hopped in the car and headed for Wal-Mart for that piece-of-shit trunk, some sand, a shovel and some Gorilla Glue."

At this moment, I regret not knowing what a sister would do.

Rene's face changes. "I guess you had to be there. It all seemed funnier at Wal-Mart."

"Rene, you will always be my best friend. That's all I can say."

Her eyes redden as she holds back tears.

I offer, "My best friend, there must be a better way to deal with all of this pain and anger."

Her eyes grow fierce again. "Can't you see that there is *no* better way? If what I did makes me feel just a little bit of peace… if it makes me feel that I got back just some of what's she's taken from me, there is no better way." Rene's face collapses. Her head rests in her hands.

I watch her weep.

Finally, she looks up at me, her face swollen and red, "Morgan, you can never tell anyone what I just told you."

"Rene, there's no reason to ever repeat it. It stays between us. Everybody has to do whatever it takes to get them to the other side."

JAHN

The doctor asked what kind of man do you want to be?

The bi-monthly sacrament calls. Every two weeks, without fail, I step out of my jeans and kick them away. When my boxers finally hit the floor, I am one step further. My supplies are neatly arranged: surgical gloves, a Band-aid, a pre-sterilized needle and a cotton pad, soaked with alcohol. From the back of the drawer, I pull out "the juice," as the brothers call it. The label on the small but sacred bottle reads: 1 cc, (200 mg), T.

Testosterone, that is.

In the mirror, my spine twists and turns trying to locate the perfect site on my ass. The endocrinologist warned, "You must avoid the build-up of scar tissue." This game of injection site switching has become my inside joke, as I try to add levity to that which will always be my life's burden. I smile, imagining a hopeful future, an older and fatter me, with a little more skin to spare.

As I survey my backside, I spot an undisturbed parcel of real estate on my left cheek. *Bingo*, I say aloud, assaulting it with rubbing alcohol, in a circular motion. I still feel my palms sweat and my heart race every time I do it. My hands are eager to push me over the threshold of manhood. The clear barrel of the syringe slurps up the oily elixir. My body quivers with anticipation. I inhale and countdown: 3, 2, 1… stick and plunge. Into my muscles, the needle dispenses a measured dose of liquid power. My head falls back, orgasmically. The rush of the hormone causes my body to shudder in ecstasy.

And, it's done.

My hands work fast to break it all down, shoving the balled-up prep pad and unused Band-Aid into the glove and tossing them. My little red biohazard box, the needle graveyard, accepts my used deposit.

I pose and marvel at my nakedness. Proud how the T stopped the flow of blood and grateful for the gifted hands that removed the cumbersome breasts that hung around my soul like a noose. Foolishly, I impressed myself thinking that losing two vestiges of femininity would be enough. The final step remains out of reach, as I stand trapped between two worlds; unable to shake Bethany who knows all and Morgan who needs to know something.

Although my progress is evident to the naked eye, my pride is short-lived. From the outside, my maleness consists only of a bearded face, thick hairs that blanket my extremities, a flat upper torso and a semi-deep voice. I remain impatient and incomplete. The truth shames me with the reality that these minor victories still won't count enough to *count* with her.

Tonight, I'll be more careful, not letting my hunger get the best of me. Telling her the truth is my last resort. It's the only angle I haven't worked.

CHAPTER

9

OCTOBER
Los Angeles, California

Waiting for Jahn to pick me up, I nibble on my freshly painted nails. I have thought of him all day. After that lunch with Rene, I need another distraction and he is my favorite kind. He called saying he needed to see me, immediately. I don't know why but he didn't sound happy.

Jahn honks his horn like a wayward teenager picking up an easy date. He doesn't ring the doorbell, doesn't come in to greet Rene, Bethany or even Rain, like we expect. Instead, he *texts* me that he is outside, waiting.

Rene gives me a hug and hands me a spare key dangling from a small gold keychain. Bethany's eyes refuse to meet mine.

Rain hugs my waist. "Have fun, Mommy! Tell Jahn we say hello!"

"I will, Raindrop," hating to think that I will have to tell her what I sense will be the case—that Jahn won't be our "new friend" after all.

When I slide into the car beside him, he's unshaven and rough around the edges. The darkening sky dims his face, his eyes are weighted down with worry. When I lean over to kiss him on the lips, he turns his head, offering only a stubbly, impersonal cheek.

"Jahn, what's wrong?"

"Nothing is wrong with me," he says, as if I have already missed something. "We just need to talk."

"We haven't known each other long enough to have something wrong between us."

With his eyes intensely on the road, he says, "Morgan, I beg to differ. Were you there last night? There's things that you need to know about me."

"OK. Tell me, then."

Here they come... those feelings that blast up in my chest, right before my heart enters harm's way. I feel my hands tense into a fist. A moist gaze falls to my lap. This is where we'll say goodbye before we've even said hello.

Jahn seems to ramble, muttering to himself. "We shouldn't apologize. What's done is done." He says louder, "I just should have told you..."

All around us, LA is caught up in the lather of Friday night. Looking out the window, watching the cars whiz by, I say, "You should have told me what?"

His hands grip the wheel. "We need to go to a private place where I can speak freely."

From the side, my eyes see all of him. His black baseball cap is backwards. His black jeans have greyed. I can barely read the faded letters on his t-shirt. I think they say: *We dream and call it truth.* I'm afraid to wonder what that means to him or to us. I feel control slipping fast. "Jahn, you're upset. What's happened? Just tell me..."

He has turned into a stranger, his neck is stiff, his eyes stuck to the road. "So much has happened. Where should I begin?"

My stomach tightens anticipating his words before he even utters them. *There's someone else...*

I beg. "Whatever it is, just tell me." I take a final gulp of air, "Is there another woman?"

He doesn't answer, just glances over his shoulder, peeks across my lap at the mirror on the passenger's side and takes the chance. Effortlessly, he darts through four lanes of traffic, navigating only with one tense hand. The blaring horns of road rage deafen us as we head for the ramp. He is fast and furious.

The night air, cloudy and dense, hangs over us like a tarp. I can feel the jagged pieces of him, sticking out all over. For the first time in his presence, I feel afraid. Hot tears snake along the rims of my eyes, gathering into the corners where they pool. I fight them with all my might, preparing to hear what he has to tell me.

Jahn swerves into a space inside the nearly empty MacArthur Park. The walking paths that begin at the edge of the lot lead into ominous darkness. The empty park is littered with only left-behind Frisbees and a single abandoned basketball underneath a bench in the distance. The pungent stink of marijuana permeates, stinging my nostrils. There are a couple of night joggers emerging out of the darkness. They stretch and cool down from their run, trying to catch their breath. A lone mother, out too late, walks with multiple babies, one in a stroller, one harnessed close to her chest and one who totters, sloppily, beside her.

Through the windshield, I spot the bench where Jahn will sit me down to say what he has come to say. His movements are slow and careful. He unclicks his seatbelt, slowly opens his door, gets out and then closes his door without slamming it. I can't take my eyes off him. I watch him as he crosses in front of me, trying to detect what is going through his head.

He tentatively opens my door and crouches down beside me. "We're here."

My mouth has dried up. I don't recognize my own hoarseness. "Just tell me what it is."

He says nothing, only offering a strong hand to pull me from the car. Just the mere touch of him makes my clenched fist unfurl. We sit on the same wooden bench where blissful couples have carved crudely drawn hearts with their initials inside to declare their love. I wish we were here to do the same thing, memorialize what we feel. Sadness comes upon me, yearning for my youth when "falling in love" required nothing greater than infatuation.

"You asked me if there is another woman?" His eyes lower. "Yes. The answer is yes. There is a woman that you should know about."

"Is it Bethany?"

"No. It's actually me... the me that I once was."

I can't grasp what he is saying. My nerves are all tangled up trying to understand his cryptic confession. I say nothing, waiting for more.

"When you asked me why I am in therapy, I blew off the question. I wasn't ready to tell you all of this."

We sit side by side. Our gazes are set, looking out over the lake that is only a black hole at night.

Both of his hands are knotted into fists that rest on his jumpy knees. For the first time, Jahn struggles with his words. "It's really not a big deal…"

But his twitching body says it is.

"I'm listening," I say, nervously re-twisting a loc of my hair.

Without turning to face me, he says, "Morgan, I was born female. I have been undergoing transition for eight years, which requires therapy to confirm that transition is what I really want. And, it's to make sure that I am ready for all that being a man entails. I had top surgery four years ago and I have been taking male hormones for almost three. I will eventually have bottom surgery, which is… what I am saving for."

My face is blank. I do not hate him for this news, although this unveiling confounds me, forcing me to question my own desires.

He turns to face me and my eyes meet his startled gaze. Still, his liquid eyes take me to a place of no return. Grappling with what to say or not to say, I can only blurt out a regrettable question, "What was your name?"

"Morgan, what I have just disclosed is not an invitation to dig up a forgotten past. You deserved to hear this from me, so I told you. My life's story is not gossip. I told you out of respect. If you want to know me, you must know where I come from. But my past is no longer relevant. And neither is my dead name."

My head aches trying to grasp these new words and ideas. His eyes are wide open, hungry for my acceptance. Mine are closed, searching for words that won't further offend. "Why won't you tell me your old name?

"Because it no longer belongs to me. It's not who I am anymore. Consider her dead. If it will make you feel better, choose any name that you like and fill in the blank. Amy, Martha, Sally, Mary for Christ's sake! I am not any of those names. The only name that I answer to is Jahn. But if it makes you feel better…"

I feel slightly dizzy, confused by his impatience and sudden anger. "So, how do you want me to feel?"

"The way that I still feel about you."

I don't answer, not being completely sure what any of it means. "One more question," I say despite the countless questions that are populating in my brain.

He waits.

"Why didn't you tell me this? Why didn't you trust me enough to say something before... we kissed?"

"I didn't tell you because I care about you. I wanted us to get to know each other without the taint of my complications. If I disclosed this last night, or when I picked you up at the airport or even at the wedding, I guarantee we wouldn't be here today. Revealing this simple truth often makes people smile politely, listen intently and then create an excuse for why I'll never see them again."

Suddenly, I'm mad. "Jahn, I am *not* some people. I am a woman that you know and you say you care about. I am a woman like Rene, who carries around a chronic disease that is invisible to others but each day, our minds and bodies are forced to bear the painful, uncomfortable, unrelenting truth of it all. You think I am going to run away from you? Where could I run? You've already brought me here."

Silence buzzes around us.

His face turns apologetic. "I didn't know that you have Lupus. I'm sorry to hear that."

"Don't be sorry. And I will not be sorry for you. I was going to tell you but didn't, I guess, for the same reasons that you didn't tell me. I didn't want you to judge me before learning who I am. Like I said, I am not some people."

"Morgan, all you need to know is that I *am* Male and always have been. It's my body that wasn't quite right at birth."

He gently reaches over to touch my face. His touch, so familiar.

"I have no doubts about the man that you are," I say.

"Most people reduce my manhood to some sort of costume... something I wear to deceive others. When actually it's quite the opposite. My manhood is the truth."

117

There are only awkward breaths. There is no ready response for what we have both shared. Words only tangle us. So, I do the only thing I can, reach for him.

There is nothing to declare just yet. Promising him safety without abandonment is what I want to do. When I choose him, I want it to stick. Time is needed to grasp the slippery nuances.

Abruptly, he says, "Morgan, tell me what's going through your head right now?"

Above us, thick murky clouds release themselves, sprinkling us at first and then pelting us with cooling rain. We don't run. Instead, we let the waters come down, like our truths, baptizing the moment. When he reaches for my hand, I cover it with both of mine. We sit that way for several moments. In those moments, my fears slip away.

Jahn pulls me up and together we splash through the rain towards his car. We are moving in slow motion as our shoes fill with frigid water droplets that leap inside our shoes from all sides. As we splash, my head starts to clear. More questions attempt to choke me, but I swallow them. While Jahn fishes for his keys, I lean against the car, drenched. He slides his hand behind my back and pulls me into a tight hug. I gently pull away wanting to study the angles of his face, once again. His prickly skin grazes my cheek, reminding me of the man he is.

I am lost in the moments that lapse between his last embrace and sliding me into the car. Releasing all doubt, sinking into this moment, I want to lose control; unsure of all of the moments before and after this one. In his car, we sit and savor dryness while courage unfolds.

He breaks the silence again. "Morgan, have you ever met a person like me before?"

"No. I mean, yes. Just once."

"Was it a trans woman or man?"

"Trans man," I say tentatively… "A man dressed as a woman?"

He rolls his eyes. "Then it was a trans woman. Where did you meet her?"

Shame comes over me. I shouldn't have mentioned it. I am not proud of who I was.

He waits.

I find myself pleading. "Don't judge me. I didn't know any of this back then. No one did."

"We've always been. We are not news... only to all of you. Dammit, just tell me the story." He turns away from me, bracing himself for the worst.

Dragging this unfortunate incident out of my past is like reawakening a parasite that once lay dormant. Now fully awake, it eats away at me once again. Telling him this truth will solidify my unworthiness.

"I don't like to talk about this," I say.

"Why not? Finally, you can talk to someone who gets it."

"It's just not a great story."

"None of them are," he says with a tinge of resentment.

"I went to a yoga retreat with my best friend from college. When we were there, everyone was buzzing about someone named Alice. They spoke about her with such kindness, tenderness and perhaps, maybe even a touch of pity-"

"Oh no, here it comes," Jahn moans.

"Please don't interrupt me! It's hard enough to talk about..."

His face is neutral.

"Anyway... We started guessing, thinking this Alice must be elderly, disabled or something like that. We expected her to arrive in a wheelchair with an aide. We had no idea of what else could invoke that tone amongst the other yogis. At silent dinner that night, he was the first person I saw. There he was, a man dressed like a woman wearing a nametag that clearly read: Alice."

"Surely that's not all. Tell me the rest," he probes.

"Alice was 6'5" in heels, wearing a mousy brown wig with red lipstick and a blue caftan. He sat alone, eating carefully, reflectively, like all of us were supposed to do."

Jahn says, "Go on."

"The facilitators had warned us how difficult it is to be silent for any length of time but how necessary it is to go deeper. Rebecca and I weren't deep. We just couldn't help ourselves. Muffled giggles and hidden gestures were how we communicated with each other throughout the meal, much to the dismay of the other yogis."

"That's unfortunate," Jahn says.

"That's it. You keep interrupting me. Story over."

"Sorry, Morgan. But it's difficult to hear. You're not just talking about Alice, you're talking about *me*," he says. "I'm sorry. Go on."

"I'm not proud of it. When we got back to our room that night, Rebecca and I laughed like we had never laughed before. We imitated and mocked everything about Alice that we remembered."

A nervous smile forms on my lips, remembering the strangeness of it all, briefly forgetting my audience.

Jahn's face reddens.

My confession continues. "The joke turned into a bet… one of us would talk to him before the weekend was over."

Jahn winces at my pronoun use.

"The winner would get ten dollars. Rebecca said she knew she couldn't do it, without laughing in his face. We decided to withdraw the bet as we tumbled onto our cots and laughed about it some more."

Jahn's face is grave. "Dammit, Morgan! Alice was a *her*, not a him. It's disrespectful to refer to her with the opposite pronoun of what her clothing indicates."

I want to scream back at him. *Your world is not for me! How should I know all of this stuff?* I want to say this but I can't when I see the hurt on his face. "I'm sorry Jahn. That's just how it was. You asked me to tell you. That's my story. I told you I don't like to talk about it. It was a very long time ago."

He says nothing for several minutes.

Dryly, he finally says, "So much for yoga's enlightening qualities. I see why you didn't want to talk about it. It makes you and Rebecca sound like idiots. So, laughing at her is all you did?"

"Yes, I was an idiot. Yeah—we just laughed, which is stupid, I know."

What I can't tell him is that Rebecca and I made Alice into "a thing," a game, a skit. We became a mob, using code language and hand gestures every time she passed us. Our laughter kept us safe from seeing the human being behind the wig. I actually remember wishing that Rebecca wasn't there, so I could have properly met her. Rebecca would not have understood my curiosity about who we'd always considered "freaks." We laughed until our stomachs hurt. Which turns my stomach, now.

He says, "Laughter is what we do. Contempt keeps us safely on our sides." He puts his hand on my knee. "It's OK, Morgan. Thanks for telling me."

The rain finally stops. Jahn turns on the car and rolls down the fogged windows. The refreshing scent of after-rain wafts into the car.

"So, when did you start being a boy?" I am surprised by my own thoughtlessness.

"I've always been male," he corrects me, again. "You mean, when did I stop wearing girl's clothes?"

"Yes, that's what I meant to say," my head is dizzied by the details of transition.

"When the blood came, the charade was over. I couldn't fake it any longer. Male clothes were my only resistance to the lies that my body was telling. I just couldn't bear to see myself the way the world saw me."

"Did your grandmother understand what you were going through?"

"She knew, but didn't know what to do with it. She laughed at me. But in the early mornings, it was crazy, I'd catch her down on her knees, tears streaming down her wrinkled old face, praying for me."

He starts to mimic his grandmother with eyes closed and clasped hands, "*Please, please, please, Lord, help my girl, Lord.*"

My heart breaks while Jahn laughs at his own poor joke.

I look out the window at the dark parking lot, hoping to find answers there.

"Seriously, Morgan. You deserve to make your own decision. Like I said, last night, it wasn't the right time to talk about this. I was getting pretty heated." He smiles briefly at the memory. "There's never a right time." He continues. "No one should have to discover that I'm... incomplete, in the middle of... intimacy. I know that I may never find a woman who's comfortable with my body as it is now. I can only wait for the world to make room for me."

Sadness pulls me as I say, "I think that if two people really care about each other, nothing else should matter."

"If it were that simple, the world would be full of happy trans people, blissfully in love. We are finally becoming visible, despite the fact that the trans 'celebs' give the wrong impression, making it look so easy, which makes it harder for those who are not famous or rich. It's not reality. They can afford the surgeries and specialists so that their transition is seamless. But for those of us who can't afford it, a life in-between is not easy."

"You know, Jahn, people don't have to know," I say. "You look like a—"

His eyes change. "—I *am* a fucking man. Of course, *they* don't have to know, but somehow, *they* think they're *entitled* to know. Haven't you figured out that the world is obsessed with the male phallus? We yearn for the *certainty* that a penis creates. Sadly, *nothing* is certain anymore, so people feel vulnerable. Hatred is what they reach for."

"Jahn, I need time to think about all of this. I have to think about Rain and how this may confuse her."

His hands grip both sides of his head in frustration, "What the hell are you saying? You're confusing *me*. What would you tell Rain about me, other than what she already knows?"

"Jahn, I admit, I'm afraid! But I know how I feel."

"Morgan, getting involved with a man like me has to be your decision. You must know for certain that you can love a man whose heart is in the right place, but who's betting his life on an expensive surgery that he can't afford. Look at me. I am a black trans man who is more likely than others to be harassed, hurt and unemployed. The odds are not in my favor. And, you'd be agreeing to love a man without a penis."

I feel my eyes tearing up, not sure how to handle his complexity. "Is that what's this is all about? A *penis*? Is that what you're saving money for? Did you ever think about men who are impotent? They still find love. Some people are not obsessed with the male phallus. They've learned that there are more important things. You just have to stop fighting and let it happen."

"This *is* about a penis. I'll never feel like a man until I see it dangling between my legs. That's not how all of us feel, but *I* do. And it *sucks*. I guess I'm like the rest of the world, obsessed. I can't give you what a man is supposed to and that destroys me."

"Jahn! Maybe, I don't want what I'm supposed to want. I want the things that you still don't know are inside of you. Don't I deserve the same freedom—that you're asking of me? Can't I be different? I've had my share of worthless penile sex—the kind that men give away without even thinking. Sex has never served me the way I've been taught it should. Believe me, I tried."

Jahn's face is blank. "Morgan, you just don't realize all the *shit*… This life makes it so hard to focus on anything else besides my own faulty wiring and other people's fear and disgust. Joy eludes me. Daily, my existence gets all swallowed up trying to prove that I'm human. But when I saw you, something in me shifted. I realized then that I wanted the chance to care about someone more than I care about myself."

I whisper, "That's also what men do."

JAHN

The doctor said these procedures are complicated.

I often wonder, will we all be remembered as a fickle generation, unwilling to accept the bodies we were given? Will history accuse us of being restless, confused, insane and insatiable? Will our journey to affirmation become an indictment, despite the purity of our intention?

I am aware of the dangers and rewards of that which I seek. Transitioning means my body will shed its organic nature, stepping out of a given skin in order to become the properly assembled man that I have always been. The very act of transition relies on audacious will, trust in others and the skill of strangers in white coats. I understand that my sex will be but a craft, *handmade*, sculpted by steady hands that have been charged with the task of fulfilling a young boy's wet dreams.

Damn! How complicated it has been to wear two sides, knowing that I deserve what others have, a singular and perfectly aligned *self*. I will go to my grave trusting that a self-made manhood is better than a life gagging on a woman's blood.

Scanning the tattered brochure again, my eyeballs hit the high points:

… insurance companies… exclude… sex reassignment surgery… many costs… indirect costs… loss of employment, loss of housing, etc.

The Options:

Metoidioplasty in simple terms enlarges the clitoris through the use of the hormone testosterone. Surgically, it is the removal of the ligaments surrounding a testosterone-enlarged clitoris (Phallus), allowing it to protrude further from the body. The clitoral hood then acts as a foreskin and silicone testicles are implanted in the larger outer labia. The enlarged clitoris is inherently shaped like a small penis. With this procedure, the new organ remains sexually responsive and becomes erect without prosthetic assistance.

Phalloplasty *is the construction of a penis using a skin graft from another part of the body such as a flap of skin from tissue harvested from either the forearm, the side of the chest, the pubic area, or the thigh. A prosthetic device is implanted and after a complex surgical procedure, the new penis can both urinate and become erect. Silicone implants in the outer labia serve as testicles. Men sometimes first undergo a metoidioplasty and then later undergo a phalloplasty.*

Men often elect to do other enhancement surgeries:

- ***Urethraplasty/Urethral lengthening, Scrotoplasty*** *(constructing the scrotum)*

- ***Glansoplasty*** *(constructing the head of the penis).*

Surgeries that pertain to the removal of original internal sex organs:

- ***Hysterectomy*** *(removal of the uterus)*

- ***Oophorectomy*** *(removal of the ovaries)*

- ***Vaginectomy/Colpectomy*** *(removal of the vagina)*

- ***Mons Resection*** *removes external pubic fat so that the genitals protrude further*

Surgery is permanent and irreversible.

CHAPTER

10

OCTOBER
Los Angeles, California

Driving with the certainty of a man, one of Jahn's hands is on the wheel and the other rests on my thigh.

OPEN says the blinking red sign as we pull up in front of Coconut Milk, his favorite Thai restaurant. Jahn drives around to the back of the simulated grass hut and parks the car. He opens my door and offers his extended hand. When I stand, he takes his finger and runs it along my collarbone, playing with my diamond pendant. He studies my neck as though he has unearthed the last erogenous zone. His eyes are magnetic and feel good on me. As his fingers pull my diamond to his lips, he gets close, his citrus scent overwhelms, pushing a heavy sigh out of me. His mouth is suddenly under my chin, my eyes close, my neck arches backwards while his lips pull my dangling diamond into his mouth. When he releases it, the diamond lands wet on my skin.

He plants a last kiss and whispers, "I'm starving."

"Me, too."

Entering the restaurant, I am swept up in the colors, the smells and the seductive sounds of the lounge music that embraces us as we enter. Everyone in the room seems to be in unison, bobbing their heads to intoxicating beats that are just loud enough to captivate.

"Mr. Yahn, Mr. Yahn, welcome back," says the hostess.

Her nametag reads: *Sukanya*. She wears a traditional satin skirt and fitted tunic in bright orange. Her face is meek and pretty. The only distraction from her classic beauty is the gold septum pierce that clasps her nostrils together, like a bull's.

Jahn hugs her warmly, "Good to see you Su, meet my friend, Morgan."

Sukanya is polite despite her limited English. "Nice uh meetchew," she says clumsily.

"You, too," I say, still dazed by all the things that I am thinking, fearing and feeling.

A body flanked in a black feather boa rushes past me, tickling me with their haste.

We follow Sukanya to our table. As we walk through the colorful crowd, raucous laughter comes from a group of short stocky girls dressed in button down shirts with ties, baseball caps and multi-colored high-top sneakers. Sitting around the next table is a celebratory group of young, dewy males. Their skins are varying shades of brown hailing from many places. What they all share is an ineffable beauty. They tussle loudly with each other, calling each other "bitch," pointing, jeering and snapping fingers in each other's faces. They all wear body jewelry, earrings, studs and hoops that dangle extraneously off the sides of their perfectly shaped heads.

The smallest of them wears a red skirt with black leggings. He is a boy but doesn't mind if you think otherwise. His long hair is pulled into a shiny bun so tightly that his eyes stretch upward. I turn to look at him again, but he has pivoted back to his friends.

Sukanya seats us at a table behind a beaded curtain in the rear of the restaurant. She lights a decorated candle and leaves two thick menus on the table. A fast busboy with elaborately hennaed palms places two glasses of ice water at our plates and disappears. His flaming pink hair is a blur as he darts in and out.

Inhaling deeply, I absorb the elements of our impending liaison. If only I could have a moment of peace, without Jahn's anxious eyes begging my acceptance, it would give me the time I need. The strange air of Coconut Milk pushes me like a tornado's winds, swirling me around, leaving my senses dangling. I tell myself, if this is his place and these are his people, I must learn to feel safe amongst them. I wish it were that simple. The oddities of the space feel somewhat familiar but distant at the same time. As a young club kid in New York City, I had seen these faces before, but after being tamed by Georgia and having a child, it is again strange and curious. How would I feel if Rain was one of those girls in sneakers and a bow tie?

Shamelessly, my eyes dart from side to side. Then, I freeze on a single object that my eyes can't totally comprehend. All I see is the black boa draped around a long, lean body bursting through the beads, taking a seat in the corner. The complexion of this person is smooth and dark like a bar of exquisite chocolate. I notice the subtle glistening of deep berry hues that lie beneath the skin. Short kinky jet-black hair hugs a perfectly rounded epicene skull. The spectacle wears a yellow ball gown, which hangs effortlessly off of a stunning physique. The heels are impossibly high, the waist is small and perfectly hugged by a small sequined belt. The makeup is flawless; lips bathed in a bold shade of red and irresistible almond-shaped eyes are flanked with long, delicate lashes. The only dissonance is the Adam's apple that jumps and vibrates as the wearer greets the crowd warmly, doling out double-cheek kisses and winks only for a selected few. A fluorescent smile lights the distance between us. My inability to take my eyes off of this formidable human embarrasses me.

"Morgan, stop staring!" Jahn hisses. "That's just Brix."

I notice that the other gazes in the room are irritatingly steady. I am the only outsider, sneaking peeks.

"There must be a pageant tonight," Jahn says, his head buried in the menu. He looks up, "You know what pageants are, right?"

Afraid to show the fool that I have become, I say nothing for a moment. Then with caution, I say. "*Beauty*—pageant?" not understanding how those two words could have a place in this conversation.

"Brix is saving up for bottom surgery in Serbia at the end of the year. I hear it's 40% cheaper."

Looking at the crowd, I ask, "Does everyone do pageants to pay for their surgeries?"

"Not everyone. Mostly MTF's which means Male to Female, if you were wondering. I am FTM—I know you know." His eyes are glued to me.

Losing confidence in my apology, my voice fades, "I didn't mean to imply that…"

"Don't knock it. For some, it's the theatre that keeps trans life possible. People love to be entertained." Snidely, he adds, "It's the least we can do."

"Do you know Brix personally?"

"They're a part of a local group that I belong to called Transexpression."

"They're?"

" 'They' is his preferred pronoun. Brix likes to be referred to as 'They' instead of him or her. Gives him the freedom to exercise both sides."

Jahn's head is buried deep in the menu, again.

"I guess that makes sense," I say as my new expanded mind stretches further than it's ever been.

Desperate to change the subject he says, "So, what looks good to you on the menu?"

"You look good to me."

Taking a gulp of ice water, he says, "I hope you can still say that after you've seen all of me."

His eyes are firmly planted on me but my head dives into the oversized menu to avoid his stare. I ignore his lewd comment.

Sukanya returns. "Anything drink, Mista Yahn?" she asks.

He looks at me, "Morgan, wine?"

"Yes. You pick."

"She'll have a glass of Riesling and I'll have a Singha."

"OK. Ready to order now?" Su asks.

Again, I defer to him, only able to point at the first dish under the heading FISH on the menu.

With an accent to rival a native, Jahn looks up at Su and says, "My lady will have the Pla Sam Rod. And I'll have my usual, Kao Moo—"

"Dang," Sukanya finishes his sentence. "Thank you, Mista Yahn. Be right back with drinks."

He looks at my expression. "Morgan, you ok? What's up? You're from New York. You should be used to these things."

"*I was* from New York. Clearly, I am no longer."

"What's it like in Atlanta, anyway? I've never been. Never wanted to go 'til you," he smiles.

"Well, the traffic is as bad as LA. There are just miles and miles of freeways that separate the races, the income levels and the sexual orientations. Everyone has their own suburban bliss and as long as they keep it to themselves, it works out for everyone."

Jahn looks up at the ceiling and rolls his eyes back. "The way you describe it, doesn't sound that great. There must be something good there, besides you and Rain."

I feel a twinge of overprotection of the banal suburban existence that I painted. "They call Atlanta the Hollywood of the South. You may even like it," I say. "Especially since you love music."

Brix' insistent glow still shimmers in my peripheral view.

Jahn waits for me to say something, pulling my hands into his.

I fumble, "So, tell me about your students. What's it like being around teenage boys all the time?"

He pauses, cutting to the chase. "Are you wondering if my students *know* about me?"

"Of course not! Well, sort of… It did cross my mind, fleetingly but I really do want to hear about them."

"My students don't know and why should they? They have always known me as Coach Booth. That's all they need to know."

"What if they ever found out… would you…?"

Letting my hands go, a sticky tension pulls him close. "—lose my job?"

Pink hair sets our drinks down and flees again. We keep our eyes on his blur as it disappears.

"So, tell me more about Transexpression?"

"There's not much to tell. It's just a group, part support group, part activist, part social. We trans folks get lonely, too, you know," he says with a sarcastic grin.

"After the surgery I won't have much need for them, but for now, they're something to keep me busy."

Jahn's talent for discarding the past stings me. It's another of our sore spots but tonight I decide to concentrate on his handsomeness and the way his eyes paint me.

He interrupts my wandering thoughts, "Be honest. Morgan, tell me what's on your mind. It's not too late, you know."

"Not too late for what?"

Taking a final gulp of his Singha, he says, "For us to chalk this all up to a lit weekend in L.A. and say our goodbyes when you leave on Sunday."

"Is that what you want?" I ask him as I wonder if it's what I want.

Looking directly into my eyes, he says, "No. Yes… Maybe…"

Shared stress holds us together. I know I don't want to lose him to discomfort. I resent the tired version of what life is supposed to look like but I'm frightened by the weight of his. His eyes wait for me to say something. I take my time. If I give in to what my body is telling me, his complex life will soon be mine. He is *a different kind of man.*

Finally, I respond, "Jahn, it's complicated. I do know what I feel. I just fear that I won't know how to do all of *this*," I wave my hand around the restaurant.

"Just love me like any other man. That's all I ask of you."

I want to respond but Sukanya interrupts us, carrying hot plates with steam rising.

Pink hair trails behind her, carrying two bowls of piping hot rice.

"Pla Sam Rod," Su names my meal as she puts it in front of me.

The sweet, fragrant basil is the only familiar sensation my body has had all evening.

"Kao Moo Dang," she continues, as she sets the other dish down in front of Jahn.

"Khob Khun Club," says Jahn as he slaps his hands together in prayer position, a gesture of gratitude.

"Khob Khun Kah," Sukanya says her hands also praying.

"Jahn, how do you know the language?" I whisper after she leaves.

"It's just a few words… a gesture of respect," he says digging into his meal.

The plates sweat. My fish smothers in a rich red sauce. I empathize, also preparing my whole self to be devoured. I watch Jahn spoon out a heap of brown rice. He separates the wilted basil leaves from the thick gravy and places them at the center of the rice mountain. He carefully pours the dark brown sauce and large pieces of barbecued pork over the rice. He adds extra spicy chili sauce and it drips from his red lips.

"This is so good," he raves at the first bite. He orders another beer while my original glass of wine sits idle. I cover the glaring eyes of the fish with a few grains of rice. As the delicate, flaky fish hits my tongue, a smile comes across my face.

"Good?" Jahn asks with his mouth full.

"Mmmm, mmmm…" is my answer.

The only sounds at our table are the sounds of chunky silverware clanking against heavy china plates adorned with dragons. Jahn is unapologetically ravenous, scraping the bottom of his plate, trying to get all of the gravy onto his fork, leaving the plate empty and begging to be filled again.

The heavenly taste of my fish excites my tongue. Although I have finished my first small serving, I want more, but am self-conscious of my once-accused un-lady like appetite. Ever since Rain was born, my emotional appetite has grown, only to be quelled by ethnic delicacies, which have become a perfect stand-in for sex.

"Morgan, hope you're not ready to go home yet. I have an idea."

"What is it?" I say with a full mouth and spoon in hand as I discreetly reach for a second serving.

With a slow smile he says, "Confession: I don't want the night to end. It feels good hanging out with you."

"I don't want it to end, either. But just for your information, that was a confession, not an idea. So, what do you suggest?"

His eyes turn mischievous. "I want to take you to a place you've never been before."

"Sounds scary," I say. "But I'm up for it."

"What time is your Bethany imposed curfew tonight?"

"Instead of a curfew, *Rene* gave me keys. Told you, I'm a big girl from New York."

As we drive towards Jahn's "idea," his car already feels like home. The questions keep coming up in my mind and I ignore them for now, trying to remember all of the sticking spots at the same time. I look at all the lights of Hollywood as they blur around us. There are so many things that I should and shouldn't say. I am bewildered and intrigued by him, never knowing what lies ahead. I know that the most important thing is that I am going wherever he takes me.

So many things swim around in my head. I break the silence. "Are there pictures?"

"Pictures of what?" he asks.

"You. *Before.*"

He asks, "Morgan, how can I move forward if I'm constantly looking back."

"Jahn, I just want to know all of you, that's it."

"I haven't asked to see pictures of your past. I just want to know you as you are now."

I feel my stomach slowly drop when we pull into the parking lot of his building, which was his "idea."

"I hope you don't mind," he says. "It's just the most comfortable place for us to hang out, without a waitress interrupting us every five minutes. And we don't have to spend a lot of money. Hope that's cool with you…"

Feeling slightly duped, I hear my father ranting in my head. Willing myself to trust him, I say, "Yeah, it's cool."

"Morgan, I want us to get comfortable with one another. I don't want there to be so many unanswered questions. I want us to feel safe to be ourselves."

Again, I keep a neutral face, despite the stink of the basement.

He keys in to the big black door, takes my hand and leads me into the darkness. We both remove our shoes.

"Can I offer you something to drink? You barely touched your wine at dinner," he says.

"Too much excitement, I guess. Sure, I'd like a glass now."

"Morgan, just relax. I don't want this to feel strange."

I worry about what the "this" is.

I want to move towards him, but I'm afraid. "Jahn, do you think we can really pull it off?"

"Pull what off?" he asks.

"A real relationship. Think about it. We live so far away. I won't be able to get back to California for months and I can't afford another minute off of work. My boss has been amazing, but I can't ask for any more time off for years. I'm surprised he hasn't fired me yet. I know you are saving and it would be expensive for you to come see me. And—"

Jahn's twisted look causes me to stop rambling. He takes a swig of his Singha and puts his fingers over my moving lips.

"OK, I'll stop. Where's the bathroom?"

He points, "It's the door to the right of Berd's tank."

"Be right back." Arriving at the front of the closed bathroom door, I realize I should have gone at the restaurant.

Carefully, I open the door, preparing to be ambushed by smells of manly rituals to which I should not be privy. Much to my delight, the bathroom is immaculate. The toilet seat is down but when I lift it, the bowl is sparkling white.

I sit.

When I stand to wash my hands, in the mirror, I am disappointed to see the plain, make-up-less face that stares back at me. Less sleep than I am used to has given my eyes a sunken look. My skin is parched, almost ashy; lipstick completely gone, leaving only the unattractive pinkish-brown hue of my bare lips, now chapped from too much activity.

As I critique myself, I realize that behind the mirror lies a medicine cabinet. Antsy and afraid to look inside, there is a fear of discovering the secrets of his manhood that are not meant for me to find. But I can't help myself. I close my eyes and reach out for the knob that opens the medicine cabinet. Fearing that he will hear me opening it, I leave my hand on the knob and think again. Pulling my hand back, I am reminded that snooping is such a dirty habit.

Above the toilet there is another strange piece of framed art. It is a crudely drawn symbol representing male and female. The arrow of the male shoots out of the head of the female, making it one abstraction. Underneath it reads: *Meld.* My eyes linger, wishing I could ask him what it all means, but I sense that would also be a sticking point.

"Are you OK in there?" Jahn yells from outside of the door.

"Coming right out!" I yell back. "You know how we girls are!" I say these senseless words trying to buy a few more seconds, realizing that he *does* know and wishes he didn't. I can't believe I've said such an asinine thing. I reapply my shimmering lipstick just to sooth the dryness and to, once again, draw his lips to mine.

When I emerge, Jahn has topped off my wine again. I thank him and kiss him softly on the cheek, which is scruffy and manly. Arousal takes over me like a fever.

"So, what's next?" he says.

"You're the one with the big idea. You must have had something in mind," I flirt.

"You asked me why I stopped so suddenly last time. Let's put it this way, I can't let that incident go on the record. I won't stop this time, I promise," he says.

I do not recognize this newly confident version of him as my own feelings of vulnerability start to creep in. The thought of revealing my body to him sends a chill through my bones. My body is owned by my disease, forcing me to relinquish all control. No longer a candidate for intimacy, his gaze feels slightly traumatizing.

Reluctantly, I loosen my body and allow him to pull me close, trusting that if I want him to stop, there's still that safe piece of him that will hear me.

After a brief embrace, he turns the music on. It's that song again. The song from the car. The song is called *Secret*.

To interrupt what is inevitable, I ask, "Where's Berd"?

"He's where he always is. Maybe if he feels your vibe, he'll come out," Jahn says, playing with a loc of my hair.

I ask, "Can *you* feel my vibe?"

He takes the wine glass out of my hand and sets it down on the island next to his beer. Grabbing me around the waist, he moves my hips to mirror his. We move slowly to the mid-tempo.

Hearing the familiar melody, my body seamlessly sinks into the grooves of the guitar line. Jahn holds me with his eyes closed, singing the words into my ear. His cool breath feels like wind. He twirls me around in his personal space, not letting me get too far. I reciprocate, throwing my arms around his neck. As the chorus begins again, we sing "Secret" together:

I know that I don't know you but I want you so bad.

Everyone has a secret, oh can they keep it? No, they can't.

Our lips move in sync wrapping around each of these seductive words. The music holds us and suddenly I am aware of the profundity of this entanglement. With every moment that passes, we are shape shifters, busting down the walls of all that has ever been. I feel his strong grip on the small of my back and I know that I can't let go of the earth as it shifts.

As the song ends with a long soulful note, Jahn performs the finale with a dramatic ending that leaves him down on one knee in front of me. I admire his whimsy.

Reaching for my glass, he steps away, pulling his t-shirt over his head. As he does this, my body feels a wave of nerves and excitement. His well-defined chest comes towards me. I reach out to caress the dark bushy hair. The embers of my body heat, allowing him to unbutton my shirt. His hands are warm and sensitive, speaking in tongues that my body has never heard. My breaths are long and deep as he then unbuckles his belt.

When he reaches for my zipper, I back away, moving backwards to the couch, knowing that he will follow. His hands are energetic and frisky, his kisses slow and syrupy. My jeans open and he slides his hand around my waist, gently bringing my jeans down. With my hips' movement, I shimmy them down to my ankles. I kick them off and they land in a heap at my feet. Jahn comes closer. With his hands, he holds, almost controls, my waist gently pushing me onto my stomach to shield my eyes from seeing him.

I resist, also not wanting to reveal the evidence of my unbearable disease, marked by years of endless scratching, only thought complete at the first sign of blood. My scarred back is my greatest shame. Naively, I thought I had my body to myself. Cold doctor's hands are all my back has come to expect. I never imagined that someday there'd be a need to apologize for this which has left me undesirable. I am on the verge of tears as Jahn moves forward.

Firmly on my back, he feels my resistance. He loosens his grip, taking another tack, gently kissing my stomach from the waist up. Each of his kisses feels like an angel has landed. When he finally reaches my tight lips, he stops.

"Babe, what's wrong?"

I admit, "My body's not ready for this."

"But are *you* ready? Because that's all I want, your heart and your mind to be ready. The body will follow. I really don't care how your body looks. I only care about what's inside."

"I could say the same thing to you," I say.

"Say it, then. I need to hear it."

I shake and he holds me steady. "So much is going through my head, Jahn."

He says, "Let it all go. Do you know how many of my brothers didn't make it this far? To hold someone in their arms that they care about? Too many of us put ourselves in danger, drinking and doing drugs to ease the pain. For them, dying is easier than living without love. I've wasted too much of my life trying for perfection, causing myself unnecessary pain."

His eyes look down on me. I see him from another angle. His hands are alive with emotion. They move and point and direct the earth, always holding on to possibility. His hands make me love him more.

"We can't be ashamed," he says and stands up.

He unzips his jeans. His expression has become unfamiliar and newly erotic.

I take a deep breath seeing his open fly. His black boxer shorts and six-pack abs make me feel like a teenager, causing juices to flow that I can't contain. I want to feel his rough skin against mine.

He stands back to display himself and says, "You do the rest. Morgan, don't be scared of me. This is who I am, for now," he whispers.

I leave my T-shirt on the bed where he left it in a heap. With only a half-cocked bra on, my long locs are the only thing covering my exposed ample breasts. I take three steps towards him. My hands go directly to the wide waistband of his boxers. I slip a single finger inside and let it linger. I feel heat coming from him. Pulling the waistband towards me, I peek inside. There is a hairless flat abyss that is much like mine.

A lone tear rolls down his face. His body tightens, bracing for rejection. Veins are popping in his neck. When he steps out of his boxers, I'm still there. I am neither repulsed nor afraid. Instead, I stand in awe of the beautiful contrast; the amazing strength of his top and the vulnerability of what's below. I appreciate the softness of his floral folds, seeing small slivers of pink bursting from his seams. I am curious to unfold the possibilities of his strange yet familiar flower. It is simply *him*, the way that he is, much the way that I am *me*.

Both of our bodies have been medicalized, sent through a system of torture and taint. We are both changed; neither one of us still in the bodies to which we were born. Struggling to make peace with what is, we are safer together.

Jahn and I spend the rest of our precious night, merging hands, kisses and caresses. We spend countless hours exploring each other's bodies, exposing ourselves inside and out. When sleep finally comes over him, I lay awake in the darkness, my head resting on his flat, virile chest. My hand lightly brushes over the barely noticeable indentations left by chest reconstruction. He is what he says he is.

Berd rustles in his tank, finally emerging from his shell. I shift again in our spoon. One of my hands protects Jahn's flatness above and the other cradles his delicate swollen clitoris below. He is whole. There is nothing missing.

PART THREE

JAHN

The Doctor says, being human is elusive.

She has a hold on me. I let her see all of me, but it can't happen again. All I have left is my resistance.

It *was* amazing how our bodies were finally able to meld without shame. Now, I watch her sleep. Her speckled nakedness blinds me with sorrow, but not pity, as she feared. Her imperfect skin reveals the injustice of chronic illness. Her body speaks, telling the story of a body's betrayal. I saw the many places where scratching was her only relief. Dark spots, scabs and dried blood are all that's left of what was once a perfect canvas. Life has drawn on her. She is as vulnerable and fragile as I, only leaving me one choice: to love her broken pieces that much more.

CHAPTER

OCTOBER
Los Angeles, California

My eyes stay closed as he whispers over my supine body. His whispers feel like breezes. "Babe, it's late. I need to get you back to Rene's."

Wishing for his touch, I admire his unshaven beauty with my hungry eyes.

In response, Jahn does that incredible thing to my neck that I never want to end. Wrapped up in his jumbled sheets, I hear the percussive rhythms of gravel hitting glass signaling that Berd is also awake.

Although the ringer is off, my phone *could have* at least vibrated, but it hasn't. It's almost noon and there have been no missed calls. Neither Rain nor Rene have missed me, or they are just being generous, allowing me to get my fill.

"Good morning, babe," he says trying to get my attention in a more straightforward way.

I groan as I peer at the time on my cell phone. "Oh! It's late, Bethany must be beside herself… But on second thought, as you said, 'I *am* a grown woman.'"

"A grown-*ass* woman," Jahn says as he pats my naked bottom.

Finally, the buzz of the phone and Rene's image out of the corner of my eye prompt me to sit up so I don't sound so hung over after our night of bliss.

Clearing my throat, I answer, "Hello?"

"Are you lost?" Rene says with a chuckle.

"No, I'm not lost," I say, peeping at Jahn, rubbing his chest. "When do you want me back?"

"Well, Rain and I are hungry *again*. We've already had chocolate chip waffles this morning and Bethany is just now getting up and preparing for a late brunch for all of us. Can you be here within the hour?"

"Sure," I say tentatively as Jahn plays with my locs, trying to pull me back into bed. Into the phone, I struggle to not giggle or breathe. His touch tickles.

"Rain, remember her?" Rene teases, "She misses her Mom!"

"Tell her I'm on my way. See you soon." I hang up the phone feeling as though I have been away for years, not a day. After this time with Jahn, nothing will ever be the same. I am no longer sure who I will be when I meet their eyes again. Everything I thought I understood and believed is now outdated. Life itself has taken on new colors. Will Rain be able to see the conundrum of Jahn as I wear him on my skin?

With a kiss, he says, "I'm going to jump into the shower. You coming?"

"Sure, and will you come to the house and hang out for a while? Rain really wants to get to know you better."

"I'm down. I'll chill for a while. Besides, I'm starving," he says.

With warm water spraying our bodies, my hands and gaze admire his firmness. Jahn washes himself quickly, still self-conscious, he monitors my eyes. To gawk is not my intent; I just want the truth of his every inch to sink into me. His warm kisses keep me standing while slight vertigo makes me want to go back to bed. My knees shake from exhaustion but I pick up a long back scrubber that hangs from his showerhead and turn him around.

He allows me.

His back is smooth and mocha brown. Carefully, I scrub. Then, I apply liquid soap with a body sponge and it foams up into a cloud of delicious citrus. I wash it all off with the handheld sprayer and he groans with gratitude.

Between water droplets, he says. "Your turn."

With hesitation, I turn myself around for full exposure. He delicately washes my back as if it is flawless and smooth. I wonder if it was wise to give so much of myself when I may never see him again. Old habits from back-in-the-day have re-emerged and I regret them. My eyes start to water. Panic sweeps over me while water spills down the drain.

"Whatcha thinkin'?" he catches me off guard.

"I'm thinking about missing you."

"Don't. There's at least four more hours. I'll hang out with you guys for as long as I can."

I say nothing.

"Morgan, I can't say exactly when, but we *will* see each other again soon. You know, I can't do without you for too long."

I ask, "What will you be doing all day tomorrow, without me?"

"I've done nothing since you've been here and there's a Transexpression event coming up. I've got stuff to do."

He reaches over me to shut off the water. We stand before each other, naked and dripping. Stillness and the echo of gurgling water draining out of the shower are the only sounds.

"I'm sorry and not so sorry that I took you away from everything... I hope it's been worth it."

"You're exactly what I needed," he says grasping my hands. "Like I said, there will come a time that I won't need them anymore, but not yet."

"Jahn, why do you say that? Why won't you need them? They're your friends, aren't they? You've all been through so much together."

"It's complicated, Babe. Some of us just want to move forward with our lives. After surgery, I'll be a fully accepted man and I'll no longer need them."

My teeth chatter at the mention of him throwing away another past. I wonder, will he do that to me once he's on the other side?

"You cold?" he says seeing me shivering. He hands me a white towel that hangs on a hook that smells good, like him. I wrap myself up in it.

"Jahn, I hate to tell you but you're already fully accepted. Rejecting the others is just you doing to them what you feel has been done to you."

"Morgan, you just don't get it and I don't expect you to." Frustrated, he turns and steps out of the shower. The door locks me in. I am a wet bird in a cage. I watch a trail of water slide off of his carved buttocks.

In a minute, he returns with another crisp white towel wrapped around his waist. His body is dry, but droplets of water still gleam out of the forest of his chest hair. We don't say anymore.

When we arrive at Rene's, it's been much more than an hour. I use the key that Rene gave me. As it turns in the lock, I am not aware that Bethany stands behind the door and it nearly smacks her face as I enter. She visibly stumbles but plays it off with a fake welcome smile. Her hand covers the red spot on her cheek. But I see it. Behind her, vibrant sun rays burst through all of the windows and I hear Rain in the background, "Mommy, Mommy, My Mommy is here!"

I hate the way Rain's voice makes me feel; twisted and out of sorts. Over the past hours, my heart has shifted. In this moment, the only love I thirst for is Jahn's.

Weakly, I yell into the kitchen, "Yes, I'm here and I'm coming for my hug in just a second."

"Hope you enjoyed your evening," Bethany says, recovering from the near-miss door slap. "We've waited for you. Rain set the table a long time ago, mimosas have been poured and the food is now cold. I'll attempt to warm it again. Get washed up so we can eat." She speaks only to me.

"We are washed up, Bethany. We just took a long hot shower together," Jahn interjects.

Surprised at his candor, I grab his hand and he follows me down the hall. Stopping when we are out of sight, he plants a reckless kiss on my ready lips. Quickly, we kiss and I go to my room. Looking in the mirror, I see that my makeup has grown faint. I worry that if I linger, he will plan his escape to avoid Bethany's rancor.

When I see him standing at the table, I am relieved. Rain is already pouring herself more orange juice. Ever so carefully, she handles the heavy crystal vase that holds the fresh squeezed orange juice. Without incident she puts it down. Into her wine glass she drops several strawberry slices. "See Mom, this is what Aunt Bethany showed me. The strawberries make it more like a fancy drink. Not just plain ole OJ."

"That sounds very grown up, Raindrop. Auntie Bethany really knows how to dress things up and make them look pretty."

Rene tries to hide a knowing smile.

"Where should I sit?" Jahn says and Rene directs him to the seat next to mine.

Silence nags us all as we try to find comfort in our seats.

Jahn breaks the menacing silence. "So, Rene, how are you holding up? My condolences again. I know it's been a tough time."

"I'm slowly feeling like myself again." Rene smirks, "And, I apologize in advance." Cleverly, she often uses self-deprecating humor to soften the arrogance.

"That's good to hear," he says. "How are things going at work? What happened with that big case you were working on... before your mom and everything?"

"From what I can tell, we're set to win..." Never afraid to talk about work, Rene takes the floor, explaining, clarifying and posturing about the firm's success rates.

As she speaks, I don't listen, suddenly overcome with how striking she is. I admire her words and how she adds a little lilt to the end of her sentences. Her Island background paints her speech. The faint freckles that sprinkle her warm brown face are unusual and intriguing. Her eyes are a deeper hazel than I remember.

Jahn's eyes stay on mine for a second too long, as if begging me to help him out of the obligation of listening to her talk about work any longer.

I rescue him with an interruption. "Rene, I'm excited to spend the rest of our time with you."

Bethany glares at me and says, "Isn't that nice of you to find the time, Morgan." She almost slams down the platter of re-heated chicken sausages. The skin is wrinkled and burned around the edges.

"What are we going to do tomorrow, Auntie Rene?" Rain says, her smile wide and bright.

Bethany audibly groans.

What is that thing that Rene said about straight women and their "claimed sexuality?" Was she telling me that to educate me or to test her own irresistibility on my naivete? Watching her now, I can see how in another life, another circumstance, I might have been caught off guard by my intrigue. Rene's attractiveness is a fact. To anyone with their wits about them, intelligence, humor, beauty and strength are hard to ignore, no matter who it is.

I continue to watch my best friend with eyes of intimacy, knowing things of her body that even Bethany will never know. Eternally bonded through illness, we have become accidental kin. How many nights have we both stood alone in our bathrooms staring at our naked selves with shock and dismay, remembering who we once were? We have seen our skin turn grey, our mouths go dry and our spirits wane. We have both been touched, too often, too intimately, by the cold hands of doctors who prodded and probed. We have both endured biopsies, steroids and toxic meds. And here we sit, grateful to have survived.

In between her stories and anecdotes, Rene looks back at me. It's as if she can see the fire in me that Jahn has ignited, she feels the new heat that warms my skin. She looks at me as if she knows that something has changed.

Jahn smiles longingly, noticing the mutual admiration between two old friends. It is a sharp contrast to what has happened with Bethany, right out in the open, for all to see. Sipping our mimosas, the room gently revolves around us. Rene speaks, Rain tries to keep up, Jahn listens, Bethany seethes. My eyes watch bodies, minds and hearts all jumbled together, fighting the past as we all hurl into an uncertain future.

My shoulders loosen and my head falls onto Jahn's shoulder. I accept the warmth of his protective arm draped over the back of my chair. My body revels in his hands as they gently stroke my neck.

BETHANY

Politely, I get up from the table.

Throughout the brunch, I have tried to focus on Rain. Trying to distill her pastel innocence through my drunken eyes, hoping to conjure up some peace. I marvel at her childlike ways, so effortlessly happy, not all tangled up in the misery of maturation.

From the moment Jahn and Morgan walked in, the stink of sex emanated from their pores. I find myself strangled by a peculiar jealousy. I pour mimosas, excessively, to relieve the tightness that forms in my throat.

Rene even asked aloud, "Really? Hon, *another* drink?"

Ignoring her, my attention is only on the disturbing question at hand: *How could he love her with such ease after all Jahn and I have been through?*

I listen to Rene take over the conversation again, telling endless work stories. She comments on the elections, Israel and the suicide epidemic. As always, my wife poses a simple question for the table, "Could it really be that the masses suffer with mental illness or are those who commit suicide just exercising the freedom to leave this life when they tire of it? Who's to say this life is for everyone. Why is it illegal or insane to reject it?"

Rene shoots me a quick, knowing glance and then turns away. She has briefly forgotten that hers is not a hypothetical question.

Jahn surprises me when he jumps in. "Sometimes the cruelty of life weakens us to the point of no more options. I agree with you, Rene, the majority of people couldn't possibly all have mental illness; they are just tired of treading water in a harsh sea. Maybe they are the sane ones."

Morgan rubs Jahn's back, obviously blindsided by his cryptic confession of his own suicidal moments. When I see her touching him again, her eyes meet mine and she quickly drops her hand. Bored and annoyed with all of them, I am unwilling to participate in a philosophical tête-à-tête when there are real issues that need to be tackled. Seeking air and time, I excuse myself. Mesmerized, I leave them all in Rene's capable hands.

Standing in my garden, I gasp for air.

Am I the only one sitting around that table who can see it? Is it just me who is pinched and pricked by the lies? I already know that he'll come looking for resuscitation after Morgan has crushed him, but he will soon discover that he's not the only one who's changed. I belong to someone, now, too.

When I injected that first shaky shot of manhood into her thigh, I never realized that I would be sending her off to a manly planet where I would no longer be needed. Does anyone care that it was my bare hands, covered in blood, caring for her when no one else would? How easily everyone forgot when I turned nurse, changing pus-filled drains, removing post-surgical binders and administering endless sponge baths. I doled out pain pills and spoke saccharine words of encouragement so that she could sleep through the night. I wiped away every drop of the salty sweat brought on by the hormonal gymnastics of transition. Does anyone care about that?

Clearly, I have not been successful masking my resentment of Jahn's new incarnation, but I am the one who helped her morph into this stranger named *Jahn*. The minute she donned his new male skin, she discarded both of us: the stiff, awkward short-haired girl that she was and me, the girl that saved him from death with unconditional love.

I'd feared that she would desert me one day, even though I was the one who watched her learn to strut like a man, patiently waiting for her to get it right. How dare Morgan barge into our lives, playing sister to Rene and toying with Jahn's unformed manhood? How silly she is, making him feel like he could ever be accepted into her monotonous suburban world. He's a transsexual, for Godssakes, and she's not even queer. How dare she step into my home, glowing from Jahn's misplaced affections? How dare he look at her with eyes that once looked at me?

Upon my return to the table, I see that now Jahn has become the great orator. As I take my seat, I pour one last mimosa and listen to his eloquent toast to "love," "loss" and "moving forward." I watch him, the entertainer, graciously thanking Rene, Rain and me for sharing Morgan with him for the past few days. He confesses the many things he has not accomplished because of her. Finally, he offers Morgan back to Rene for the last day of the visit so he can "get back to his life."

I despise his every word.

What is it today that is giving me new eyes for him? The gentleness with which he touches Morgan's skin makes mine warm with memories. I can't just stand by and let her take up all of the air.

I watch Jahn's hand slide up the bell sleeve of Morgan's blouse. She smiles with caution attempting to avoid my eyes. But I see all.

Rene's eyes light up at the news that she will have Morgan and Rain all to herself on the last day. Rene's mention of a trip to the beach causes Rain to erupt like champagne, leaping from her seat, kissing Rene's face and hugging her neck.

I sit on the outside, anchorless, worrying that I will float away in the night, while my wife fawns all over *"Morgan, her best friend from Atlanta."* No longer do I know where I belong in the grey mist that has obscured everyone's vision.

The endless brunch lingers on for thirty more minutes until all that remains of the bagels and muffins are hardened crumbs. Rene is alarmingly lenient with Morgan's autonomy in our house, leaving her alone with him to say their last pathetic goodbyes.

When it's time for Jahn to finally go, Rene and Rain hug him and leave the room. When Rene tries to grab my limp hand, I pull away. Dawdling, I notice a small scrape in the hardwood floor. I pause to examine it but the pressure of my touch makes the scrape worse. I frown at the new damage that I've caused.

Secretly, I use the extra moments to take in the view from across the room. I can't help but admire Jahn's new style; the goatee and his swagger that he wears like a new hide. He no longer needs or sees me, blinded by the haze of impossible love. They don't even know that I am standing here.

Straining to hear her voice, my steps are slowed. My ears can only hear the strident tone of the dirty little promises that she'll never keep.

CHAPTER

12

OCTOBER
Los Angeles, California

"Mom, what's the matter? Why can't you sleep?" Rain asks as I change positions beside her for the tenth time.

The moon shines brightly through the guest room window and the LED clock says 3:37 a.m.

Hoping that my angst wasn't so obvious, Rain's voice offers relief from my tossing and turning.

"That's a good question, Raindrop. But it happens sometimes… even to you… Remember that time before your play last year when you couldn't sleep? And, every night, for a week, you'd come into my room and I couldn't sleep, either."

"Did I really do that? Sorry, I don't remember," she says.

"You were understandably anxious."

"What does 'anxious' mean?"

"Anxious is how we feel when we're about to do something that we've never done before. Being anxious means that we worry that things won't go like we want them to. By the way, your play went very well and there was nothing to worry about, after all."

"So, if there's nothing to worry about, why are you understandably anxious, now?"

"I think I get that way when I really care about something."

Rain sits up and says, "So, what are you caring about now?"

She waits for my answer but there's nothing in my head that would make sense to her. I've regressed. I thought I'd outgrown being tantalized by a man. With Jahn I've fallen backwards into the grip of insatiability. Saying goodbye to him with Bethany overseeing us was not exactly how I'd imagined our goodbye would be. And then there was that horrid look in Bethany's eyes that has spooked me. There was steam coming out of her. I just need to get to the bottom of whatever it is between her and Jahn. No one will rest until I do.

Rain nudges me and whispers. "Mommy, are you still there? You were going to tell me what's bothering you."

"Sorry, Rain, there's nothing to tell. Maybe it was one too many mimosas at brunch. Instead of relaxing me, it kept me up."

"I don't get it," she says, "If grown-up drinks are supposed to relax you, how can they keep you up all night?"

"Rain, that is just one of the great mysteries of life…"

Too tired to pursue the conversation, I feel her droop as energy escapes her.

"Going now," she announces. Her heavy eyelids succumb to the weight of sleep.

I plant a tiny kiss on her ear.

As she pulls her body closer to mine, her last words are, "Are we really going to the beach tomorrow?"

Before I can answer, deep breathing snores are all I hear.

Jahn and the great mysteries of life rattle me to the core. The warmth of his touch confounds, stretching me in ways that I never thought possible. I marvel at how he has seduced me, despite the fact that his body is not yet that of a man's. In the darkness, I've become twisted; a woman whose barriers have melted and vision has changed. From now on, everybody I meet will spark curiosity and a craving to know what lies beneath them. No longer believing in "face value," I panic, not knowing how I will survive the old world with new eyes.

Sliding my body, ever so carefully, under the covers so as not to disturb Rain, thoughts of the beach wash upon my musings. I drift, drowning in all of my fears that somehow comfort me.

I am awakened by sun and Rain asking, "Is it time?"

The clock reads 8:30 a.m.

"Time for what?" I say, my eyes still closed and my mouth mangled in a morning's scowl.

I feign sleep as she tugs at my shoulder. "We're going to the beach!"

A tinge of dread comes over me. "Rain, we have to wait for Auntie Rene to get up first. We don't want to wake her."

"Sorry, Mom. I'm just sooooo excited," she whispers.

Throwing the fluffy white guest bathrobe over my pajamas, I peek out to see if anyone is awake. Rene emerges at the other end of the long hallway. Her legs are long and lean in white sleep shorts. A black tank top hugs her long, boyish abdomen. Her short curls stand on end and she sweeps her hand over her head to tame them.

Without any trace of decorum, Rain runs down the hall like a freed animal. Rene crouches down to catch her and give her a boisterous hug. Over Rain's shoulders, Rene looks at me approaching.

Rain jumps up and down with glee, shouting "Beach! Beach! Beach!" with a childish sing-songy melody. For a small moment, I wish she weren't there, surprisingly irked by her joy. I feel strange and formal when I greet Rene, "Hey."

"Good morning to *you.*" Rubbing Rain's back, she says, "We really don't have much time for the beach, but I always keep my promises..." When she stands, she touches the tip of Rain's nose with her fingertip and then unfolds the plan. "I figure if we get in the car by 10:30, we can head to the beach, have some lunch, be back for dinner and make your red eye flight, tonight."

Looking at Rain, I say, "I guess we need to do all that we can... she's suffered enough grown-up madness this weekend to last a lifetime."

Rain dashes away from Rene, yelling, "I'm going to wear the purple bathing suit. Hope that's OK!" Her voice fades as she gets further away.

Amused, I yell after her, "Sure thing!" I whisper to Rene. "It's the only bathing suit she has."

"I can't believe I suggested taking her to the beach. What the hell was I thinking?" Rene says with a snort.

We both trail behind Rain, back to the guest room. Rene shakes her head and suddenly bursts into a combustible flame of laughter.

"What's so funny?"

"You and me..." she says. "... going to a beach? You don't find that funny?" Rene's giggle creeps into her voice again.

I pause for a second and then recognize the irony of the two of us plagued with a disease that prohibits sun, preparing to spend a day baking in it. When I finally gain my composure, I reach for her, trying to hold on to her and the only kernel of humor that I can find in this bizarre ailment that inhabits both of our frail bodies.

"Well, if nothing else, it'll be an adventure!" she says.

Rain comes out of the bathroom, modeling her purple bathing suit and matching headband. With a mother's yearning, I look at her, so wanting her life to always be filled with sun.

Bethany has gone to the gym already and Rene is clearly no cook. She quickly prepares a frozen breakfast of organic, multi-grain frozen waffles and uncured organic turkey bacon. We eat quickly, while Rene watches the time. In 30 minutes, we have eaten and slathered ourselves in sun block and steroidal lotions. Finally, we are ready to depart.

I wear a long fitted black sundress with ¾ sleeves, open-toe sandals and bare legs. Rene is neat, as always, in a grey linen T-shirt, black linen pants with sneakers to match. Both of our heads are covered with black hats; hers, a baseball cap and mine a large sunhat with a floppy brim. We take one last look at ourselves in the hall mirror and burst into laughter. Our extra dark sunglasses make us look like a parody of The Blues Brothers.

"You guys don't look like you're going to the beach," Rain says. "You look like you're going to a fune—"

"Rain! That's enough." I glare at her as she remembers the situation, slightly too late.

"I'm sorry Auntie Rene. I didn't mean to say that." She hangs her head down to avoid my scolding stare.

"It's OK, Rainy. Your mom and I do look a tad... *funeral chic*," Rene says with an affected French accent.

"People should wear whatever makes them feel comfortable—even if they're going to the beach. You have no right to judge them. Never!" My voice crackles. Rain's innocent callousness has triggered something unexpected in me. "Rain, you know that Auntie Rene and I both have to avoid the sun for health reasons. You never know why people do what they do. You can never be sure with just one look." I feel my throat locking up; my unfinished thought dangles in the air. My eyes well with tears.

Rain's face contorts with confusion.

I open the front door for her and she walks confidently into life's unreliable arms, like I once did so long ago.

Rene locks up the house and trails behind us to the car.

From the driver's seat, Rene lowers her voice, "What's the matter? What just happened in there?"

The brat in Rain mimics me, "Never judge, never judge..."

By the time my seatbelt is on, Rain is already geared up; headphones on and a cable plugged into the side of the iPad that Rene loaned her for the trip. Bright flashes of multi-colored animation jump out of the screen, sucking her in like a dragon's tongue. In an instant, she's gone.

As I struggle with my seatbelt, I say, "Nothing's the matter with me."

"Have you spoken to Jahn today? Is that what's bothering you?" Rene asks, unusually eager to talk. No Vivaldi blasts out of her speakers today.

"Not yet, but he'll call, he said he has things to do today." As I attempt to smooth out my sundress and my wrinkled thoughts, I repeat, "He'll call."

"I'm happy for you and Jahn. Perhaps you'll come visit more often."

"You must be pretty surprised by all of this... Jahn and me, I mean."

"Not really. You're both good-looking single people. Hooking up is never a surprise to me. And, I saw the wedding video. It was quite cute what Rain said. Perhaps someday the three of us will take credit for putting you two together."

I am embarrassed by my compulsion to further investigate. The blood rushes to my face at the thought of being "together" with him. "Rene, can I ask you something? What else do you know about Jahn, besides… the obvious?"

Rene turns her head to the backseat to make sure that Rain is still tuned out. "It seems that all I know, really is what you're just finding out. I don't really know much more about him—just what Bethany has told me, which hasn't been much. How do you feel about his transition?"

"Well, I don't know, yet." Quietly, I add, "Maybe, I'm kind of afraid."

"Afraid of being attracted to someone that you didn't know you could be attracted to? You sure didn't look afraid. You two couldn't keep your hands off each other," Rene jokes.

"My heart and body are not afraid. I guess my head is. I'm afraid of other people… and their damned opinions, while I'm still trying to get a hold of my own."

"Morgan, we can't stop living or loving because of 'people' or their opinions. That's what I've always loved about you—you never judged me. So, don't judge Jahn, he's just a human who's trying to *be*."

"So, why is Bethany so furious with him… and me, for that matter?"

With her baseball hat firm and low on her head, Rene's eyes stay glued to the road. The only sound is that of Rain singing a lopsided lyric from the movie that has swallowed her up.

Finally, Rene speaks. "You know, Morgan, I suspect that Bethany was once in love with him. I mean—when he was a she. Bethany has been through a lot with Jahn. It's hard for her let go of her memories. She's still adjusting to the very idea of *him*."

"Doesn't it scare you, knowing how strongly she felt about him? I mean, her?"

"I can't be jealous of a past that's not mine. The dead girl can't be my concern."

I look at Rene, surprised at her bluntness.

She says, "No disrespect, the dead girl, that's what Jahn calls her."

Rene changes lanes as the exit for Hollywood Beach comes up on the right.

"*Reneeee*," I whine, "What's this guy done to me? I have lost all common sense. But there's something about him that I... can't get enough of. It feels like love... sort of love or what could be love... He's confident, great sense of humor. He's complex and so sexy. He makes me think... differently than I ever have."

"Feels good, doesn't it?" She says. "That's how it was when I first met Bethany. Everything about her seemed so incredible. I had never met anyone like her before. She was fearless. Nothing stopped her. It was hard to breathe when she was around."

"*You* intimidated by someone? I find that hard to believe," I tease.

With a laugh she says, "Yep. That's why I had to marry her."

"Do you still feel that way about her?"

Rene's face turns serious. "I don't think that I'm meant to. Realistic is how I feel. Sometimes I see things in Bethy that I love and other times, things I absolutely hate. Like this weekend... what I see in her, *sucks*. I don't like how she's being with you and I really can't stand how she's treating Jahn." Rene's voice changes, slipping into an unfamiliar cadence. "She's cock-blocking and that shit just ain't cool."

I smile at Rene's use of slang, wondering where she ever heard such a term within the constipated circles she travels.

"Maybe Bethany senses that something has changed in you, too."

"It has. My mother, Bertha Mae Harden, is dead and I am fucking free!"

Just as we pull into Hollywood Beach, Rain's movie ends and she's back in the car with us. "Can we get something to drink? I'm dying of thirst!"

"That's a little dramatic," I say, eyeing the unopened bottle of water, next to her. I know this is the closest to the sun that I'll get all day. Eager to stretch my legs, I say, "Come on, I'll take you to get snacks."

Inside the air-conditioned concession shack, we stand behind an impossibly emaciated woman with a wheel-chaired daughter who looks to be the same age as Rain. For an instant, I am horrified, feeling a mother's pain, not able to grasp the thought of Rain disabled. I catch myself staring.

The two girls shyly acknowledge each other and Rain stands behind me, not sure of what she sees.

A hand extends, "Hi, I'm Hayden and this is my daughter, Hayley." Her leathery skin tells of an intentional life spent in the sun.

The girls giggle for a reason that only pre-teen girls can understand.

I extend my hand, "Hi, I'm Morgan," I say as her pale green eyes scan and assess my non-beachy, black ensemble. I wrestle with telling her my truth and decide there's nothing to lose with a stranger. "We're from Atlanta, so the beach is a big thing for my daughter, Rain. I'm not supposed to be in the sun for extended periods, which is slightly inconvenient for a day at the beach." I laugh to keep the conversation light.

Hayden's eyes grow with confusion, which I ignore. "Oh, I'm so sorry…" Her eyeballs fall to the sand-covered ground.

"I'm good. I just need to take care of myself in the sun, that's all."

"That's totally cool," Hayden says like a teenager trying to erase her uncool response.

Hayden is as thin as I was, when I was first diagnosed. I wonder about *her* health, as she needlessly laments mine. Back then, the doctor had described my sudden weight loss as "wasting." I assess Hayden, realizing that in L.A., visible bones are considered beautiful. Her tiny black bikini sags off of her sun-kissed frame and I shudder, remembering my own hollowness. Shame hides in so many places.

"Morgan, don't you worry about a thing. Haley is excited to have a new friend and I pledge to keep them both out of trouble, and out of the water as much as possible. Despite my daughter's… situation, Hayley adores the water. She must have been a fish in a past life."

My eyes wander back to Hayley, still curious how she landed in a wheelchair but I can't bring myself to ask. "Hayden, I'm trusting you with all that I have."

"I totally get it," she says throwing a protective glance at Hayley. "I promise to watch Rain as if she were my own. Hayley's chair has safety gear that alerts me of everything."

We both watch Rain pushing Hayley close to the counter, as if it were just another toy. Hayley's eyes sparkle at Rain's attention. The two girls load up the counter with drinks and candy bars, laughing all the while.

The sales clerk waits for payment as they nervously hover over their sugary feast.

Lost in thoughts of Hayley and Hayden, I don't realize that everyone in the line is waiting for me. "Oh! Let me get this," I say as I hand the clerk my debit card.

Hayden says, "Morgan, how generous of you. Thanks so much! I promise, they won't get too far into the water."

As we part ways, I kiss Rain, again, as if for the last time. "I'll be watching you from the car."

"I know," Rain says, rolling her eyes.

Seeing that I'm not moving, Hayden waves me away, "No worries."

I watch the three of them go towards the ocean.

The air conditioning blasts me as I open the car door.

Rene has adjusted to the chill. "Who's Rain's new friend? And, what's with the wheelchair?" she asks.

"I didn't want to be rude, so I didn't ask and the mom didn't volunteer any info. The girl's name is Hayley and her mother is Hayden."

"That's so L.A. of them to have matching mother/daughter names," Rene cackles.

"She offered to watch Rain for me."

"What did you tell her was the reason you couldn't watch her yourself?"

"I told her all that she needed to know, which was enough."

"I feel you," Rene laughs. "I always make something up. Anything to avoid explaining the details again." She opens her mouth too wide and raises her eyebrows, mimicking the look of exhaustive curiosity.

"I'm not ashamed. It's just such a downer, but we're both here, which is all that matters. Besides, everyone has something. Hayden's lucky I didn't ask her what she has, skinny as she is."

"It's called L.A.-itis. Everyone out here suffers from it."

"Rene, you crack me up."

"It feels good to hang out with you again, even if this has been a stressful time. I miss you and am happy you're here. You know what? I actually had a dream about you last night."

"You did? What was it about?" I say nervously, not knowing what to expect. I'd only ever heard men use that line when attempting a pick-up.

"Nothing really. You were just in my dream but with a different face, I think. But I knew it was you."

"How could you tell, if it wasn't my face?"

"I just could feel it was you."

"That's odd," I say. "So, how did the dream end?"

"I woke up with Bethany's arms wrapped around my naked body."

Relieved, I say, "Just as it should be!"

"It's freezing in here. I'm going to go get something from the shack. Want something?"

"No thanks."

"If I see something you'd like, I'll get it."

"No wine in there," Rene says as she opens the car door. "So, we're slummin' it! I got us both wine coolers. I hope the sugar and food coloring don't kill us on the spot. Imagine the headline: two dead of wine cooler poisoning. The headline would say, 'They had so much to live for...'" Rene's eyes dance wildly as she delivers her dark humor.

The image chills me. Death and its mention have always been my weakness, ever since I had my tussle with it as a young motherless girl, barely out of middle school.

I'm shocked at Rene's willingness to imbibe something that's bright blue. "A wine cooler, really?" I say. "You're actually going to put that into your body? I can't believe it."

"Believe it!" Rene's says smacking her lips. "The way I see it, we have no choice. Look at us, both shrouded in black at the damned beach on a hot California day. We deserve a drink or two for that matter. The only other choices were Miller Lite or Colt 45. Wine coolers are the champagne of poor choices. Only the best for you, baby," she teases me.

"Thanks," I say, hesitantly taking the chilled bottle out of her hand.

"Loosen up Morgan. It's the last day of your 'vacation.'"

"Vacation? Your mother died, remember? What's up with you, today, anyway? You're dreaming about me and there's no Mozart blasting out of your speakers. What's the deal? I'm your best friend, so just spit out whatever's on your mind."

As I invite Rene to open up, I see a dumpster outside of the shack. The image of Rene throwing Bertha's remains in a trashcan comes to mind immediately. I'm not sure that I can take another one of her secrets.

Rene takes a sip and says, "Nothing's really on my mind. I guess I kind of lied to you about my dream. I don't know if you knew, but I used to have a little crush on you, way back-in-the-day… it was very little, don't worry. It was a long time ago when we first met. I'm completely over it," she assures with her words and eyes.

I don't know how to respond. Relieved that her dream was not about death, I'm flattered and a little uncomfortable. Should I reciprocate saying I had a crush on her, too? Since I'm straight, maybe she wouldn't expect it… but she did say that often straight girls can become attracted to girls… I reach for my wine cooler. "So, what really happened in your dream, then?"

"Don't freak, Morgan. In the dream, you and I were discussing the pros and cons of us kissing."

I swallow hard.

"From the look on your face, I see you haven't realized that there is a very fine line between friends and lovers. After all, affection is affection. Now sex is a whole other thing.… I think the dream just symbolized how women over process everything. It was probably sparked by Bethany, to be honest. Don't freak out. It was just a stupid dream. It wasn't even your face. I should have kept it to myself."

"Well. whose face was it?"

"Unknown, is all I'll say," Rene winks.

I peer out the window, wishing I were splashing in the ocean with Rain instead of trying to understand how to navigate these strange new ideas that Rene has presented. Smiling, I finally say, "Well, kissing me would be awkward and ridiculous, since, I've never kissed a girl." I reach for the wine cooler, again.

Rene pauses. "Never?"

Out of respect for Jahn, I don't want to think what she's thinking, so I turn away.

"… Yeah, I guess you're right." Rene continues with a teasing smile. "Just for your information, it's no different than kissing Jahn. Only better," she says with a wink. "No beard to contend with."

"I kind of like his beard," I say loosened by the injection of booze mixed with processed sugar and food coloring. "Ya know, I've got two eyes, and as I remember, you weren't so bad yourself, back then. Don't tell Bethany I said it. She'd throw me out of the house!"

"Over my dead body," Rene says taking another gulp of her berry wine cooler. "Girl, I've got to get out of this icebox for a minute. I'm going to go down to the water and check on Rain. Wanna come? We won't be out there long."

"No, I'm fine where I am. Besides I'm the last person Rain wants to see. She's having a blast with Hayley. You go check on her and just be careful in that sun. I don't want anything swelling up on you, either."

"Being careful is highly overrated," she says as she sticks out her tongue and slams the door.

I watch Rene walk away, counting to 10. The third sip of the wine cooler feels like the cheap, sugary thrill that it is. I take a couple more sips and leave the rest in the cup holder. The swell of my tongue instantly reminds me how my body detests sugar. Closing my eyes, I recline in my seat.

There is only silence when I finger my phone, hoping to feel the vibration of a missed call. I yank the phone out of my pocket, placing it in full view, desperately seeking any indication that the phone has been called. Is it on silent? I check Settings and sadly the volume is all the way up.

There is no blue flash of a missed call. The phone lay inert in my hand like a dead insect.

Jahn said he'd call. Through the windshield, there's Rain gently pushing Hayley less than five inches into the water, both of their heads tilted back in uproarious laughter. Hayden smiles, watching her daughter enjoy the company of my precious daughter.

Rene has pulled up her pant leg, kicked off her shoes and is dipping her toes into the water. She is gesturing for Rain to do the same. Rain turns away from the water towards the car, seeking my smothering gaze. I make a thumbs-up, but she's too far away to see it. I remind myself she's big enough to stand in the water without drowning. I have to trust but trust is not easy.

This is my only chance. With one eye on Rain and the other on the phone, I push the Recent Contacts and Jahn's sly smile fills the screen and my stomach clenches. I wait for the call to connect.

It rings.

It rings.

It rings again.

Voicemail finally answers. *"You've reached me. I'll hit you back as soon as I get to it. Peace."*

But I know he's there. He said he had things to do at home... what about the stuff for Transexpression? What is he hiding? There can't be more.

The beep is expectant, waiting for me, pushing me to make a fool of myself. I stop before leaving a desperate and insecure message that I will regret.

I refuse to let him make a beggar out of me. *I promised myself... never again.*

I audibly sigh into the phone, but leave no message, hoping my silence speaks for itself.

BETHANY

In order to have something to do with my hands, I move the throw pillows from one side of the couch to the other. This is the third go-round. I hope Rene won't bring them back for dinner. I assume that they will want to be alone on their last evening. I've already washed all of Rain's clothes and packed them neatly in the Louis Vuitton that Rene gave Morgan for Christmas. I hope Rain will be surprised when she finds the silver flip-flops that I bought her with a matching T-shirt. She's such an innocent girl. I worry about her now that her mother is all twisted up with Jahn.

It's the blue pillow that just doesn't look right. Taking it out of sight makes me feel a little better.

I've also packed Morgan's clothes, leaving out an outfit for her to wear on the plane, a pair of stretch trousers, a slouchy t-shirt and black sneakers. I hope that she doesn't get all pissed off with me.

The stress headache is starting to lift as the hours tick by and Morgan and Rain will soon be on their way back to Atlanta and out of our hair. Packing their suitcase was an attempt at being civil, an olive branch.

At this very moment, I bet that Rain is putting on her sweet face and dragging them to some cheap casual dining dump that serves only fried foods with an endless dessert buffet. Rene calls those places "trash pits" but will cave in to please Rain and impress Morgan. Rene loves to spoil "her girls," as she once referred to them.

Ugh.

It's been a long tense weekend and I know that Rene will have a lot to say about it. I'll be expected to apologize, but I'm not sure why. How can Rene not empathize with my distrust for Morgan, who pretends to be her sister and stupidly parades Jahn around like they're an item? Doesn't Morgan see that she's just a garment that he's trying on for size?

When the front door unlocks, I expect to see Rene. Instead it's Morgan with her hands full of Rain's things. "She's dead asleep," Morgan says softly, "Rene's bringing her in."

Unprepared to be alone with her, I hear the tension building in my voice. Hoping to sound sincere, knowing that I don't, I ask, "Was it fun?"

"It was for Rain. She met a friend."

"Everyone needs one," I mutter. "Did Rene get you guys something to eat?"

"No, actually Rene said that you would want us to all eat together since it's our last night and all."

"Yes, of course, I would want that," I lie. "There's only one problem. I was sure that Rene would take you out for a nice dinner so I didn't cook. Luckily, there's always Plan B. Thai anyone? It can be here within the hour. You know, there's not much time before you have to head to the airport."

"Sounds good to me," she says. "And while you place the order, I'll pack. Won't take me long."

My back is to Morgan when I say, "I've already packed for you. Hope you don't mind. Your bag is already in the hall outside of the guest room with travel clothes left out."

The air stands still.

"You... Y-You've already packed *for* me?"

I can feel her stillness behind me.

"I've packed for both of you and I left a plastic bag for Rain's swimsuit on top of the luggage."

When I turn, I almost see Morgan's words struggling to pass between her gritted teeth. "Bethany, that wasn't necessary. Of course, I had planned to pack for myself."

She finally finds her manners. "I guess a thank you is in order, Bethany."

"No big deal. I was in there, stripping the beds and collecting towels to start the laundry and decided, why not? You know, I was just trying to help. One less thing for you to do," I say as I start to set the table.

With a knife in her hand, Morgan approaches me to help. She says, "It seems you're eager for us to go."

"Don't be ridiculous. I was genuinely trying to help," I say pulling the water glasses out of the cabinet. My face is red and prickly. There is a heavy silence between us, until we hear Rene stumbling through the front door, carrying Rain as if she had rescued her from a fire. All I can think is how much rescuing Rain will need. Running over to clear the pillows from the couch for Rene, she is able to drop the dead weight. My wife plants that wet familiar kiss on my lips and I am comforted that soon it'll be just us again.

Once Rain is down, I feign an embrace, hissing into Rene's ear, "Why didn't you get them anything to eat?"

"Babe, I thought you'd want to have dinner with them, it's their last night. It's just what you do with guests."

She needn't remind me. *She's so oblivious.*

"Morgan said Thai Food would be fine."

"I don't think Rain will be into it, but I think she'll eat chicken fried rice. Order that for her," Rene directs.

Feeling a bit like a servant in my own home, I obey. "Sure. Let me do that, now."

As I leave the room, I hear Morgan's lowered voice "*Can you believe* that Bethany packed our suitcases?"

I overhear Rene say, "It's a little strange but definitely something she'd do."

What does she mean by that? Have they already forgotten that I am near? I pause to hear Morgan's breathy words accelerate. "It's just weird. She even picked out what I was going to wear on the plane."

I feel the weight of new stress building up in my shoulders, when the doorbell sounds. Rain is out cold on the couch. Now for dinner, it'll just be the three of us and a wasted order of fried rice.

Polite but terse with the deliveryman, I offer him a messy wad of uncounted bills, fives and singles. In return, he gives me a wide display of stained, broken teeth. I gently close the door on him while he's still bowing, smiling and thanking.

I turn to carry the warm bags into the kitchen just as Rene is saying, "I'm surely going to miss you, Morgan. We hate to see you guys go."

My throat closes as I offer, "Surely Morgan has a life to get back to in Atlanta. We shouldn't be sorry to see her leave. We should just be grateful that she jumps whenever you need her."

"Bethany, let me do that. Thank you again for dinner and your hospitality." Morgan catches me off guard, tugging the bags out of my hands.

She has come slightly too close.

Rene brings out a bottle of wine and says, "Morgan you can put the iPad and headphones in Rain's bag. It's a little surprise for her; I know she thought she had to give them back. She'll enjoy them."

"Rene, I don't know what to say, I usually don't let her accept such expensive gifts."

"I'm her Godmother. I'm supposed to." Rene reaches for the corkscrew and opens a bottle of Stella Rosa. "Don't worry, girl, it's a light wine, it won't hurt us," she winks at Morgan.

I resent the camaraderie of Lupus.

Morgan says, "You've both done so much, I'll never be able to repay you."

We've done too much, if you ask me.

Leaving the wooden spoon dangling in the air, I ask, "More sticky rice?"

"No thanks," they both say in unison.

I dump the glob onto my plate, knowing that I will never eat it. A clump falls and lands right in front of me. I see it as a sign to speak. "Morgan, I owe you an apology."

Rene looks up from her plate with worry scrawled all over her face.

I turn to her, "Sweetie, please don't try to stop me. I have something to say."

The steam has stopped rising from their plates. They both stare at me, quizzically, putting down their forks.

"I'm sorry to say that Jahn is not quite the man that he says he is."

Morgan's eyes grow wide and afraid. "Are you apologizing for him or for yourself?"

I look softly at Rene, "Babe, Morgan needs to understand that being involved with Jahn is not as easy as he's making it look."

My body whips around to address her, directly.

Morgan braces herself.

My blood tingles. "Morgan, Jahn simply can't meet your needs. The needs of a woman, that is. He has some *limitations*. You know, I've been there since his inception."

"Bethany, you can't take credit for a man's existence. I know more about Jahn's limitations than you think."

"Pardon me if I just can't bear to see you, of all people, falling into the never-ending, narcissistic rabbit hole that is *transition*. I just really think you should do some research on it first. Think about it. It'll be almost impossible to settle down with him. Think of a life raising your little girl in the midst of his lunacy. Rain's friends will never be allowed to come to your house, ever again, when other parents hear who her mother's dating. Rain will be as much of a reject as he is. Why would you put your child through this?"

Morgan's open mouth inspires me to say more.

"Let me give you an example: are you aware of the hormone shots that Jahn will have to take for the rest of his life? You know they do have side effects." I make my hand into a fist, pulling out each finger to illustrate my points. "*One*, flattened emotions, *two*, depression, *three*, intense fatigue. *Four*, quarterly doctor's appointments to make sure his liver and heart are not failing. Oh, and *five*, did you know about the increased possibility for male pattern baldness?"

Morgan's stoic face says it all.

"I rest my case." She clearly hasn't thought of any of these things. Sitting back in her chair, Morgan's arms are folded tightly, trying to hold herself together. Her silence is an invitation for more.

"Morgan, don't you get it? Forever you'll live in his shadow, losing your own identity because of his *transition*, which is an all-consuming affair,

I might add. Your only purpose in life will be to fight for him and advocate for all the things the world is not willing to give. You'll tire of it, pretty quickly."

"How can you know how I feel?" she weakly shoots back at me.

"Let me ask you a question, Morgan. Are you at all political? Are you ready to fight for pap smears and mammograms for trans men? Gender-neutral bathrooms in public places? Are you ready to march and make cold calls begging for donations? Are you up for demanding sensitivity training for police? Don't you see that by being with Jahn, you're just taking up a *cause*, not a lover?"

Morgan pulls forward in her chair as though she has a comeback.

I wait for it.

She changes her mind and sinks back in her chair, playing with her uneaten food.

I've successfully knocked the confidence right off of her smug face.

Deliberately, I do not look in Rene's direction. "See! It's just what I thought! You've no idea what you're getting yourself into! Have you taken the time to consider that a man like Jahn is virtually unemployable in most states? Especially *Georgia*, one of the most backward states in the union! If he quits this job because of you, or loses it, because it's always possible, he may not be able to get another one. And if he does, it certainly won't be as good. Don't forget his employment was a favor to *me*. If it weren't for me, he'd be the janitor at Holly Crest instead of the coach."

Morgan's eyes close as though she'd been hit.

"The pitiful self-inflicted blight of trans life is a one-way ticket to drug addiction. It's all in the books. Read 'em and weep, Morgan. There are endless books and studies on the subject. I suggest you pick one up."

Over my voice, in the distance, I hear Morgan begging me to stop. But new words keep spilling out of my mouth. "Christ! Do you know of all the little lies that you'll have to tell to keep Jahn afloat when the world has beaten him down? Do you know that he'll come home an inch shorter every day, shrunken by the dead giveaways?"

"What dead giveaways?" Morgan shoots back.

"Like his small hands and no fucking Adam's Apple. Touting his strength and ignoring his puniness will be your life's work. Keeping him *alive* in any way you can will be your new job. He'll constantly need you to man him up."

Morgan turns away, her head droops.

Rene taps her foot on the wood floor like a percussive instrument. "Shhhh! You'll wake Rain," is all she says.

In an effort to console Morgan, my wife actually betrays *me*. In a quiet voice, she says to Morgan, "What Bethany is saying is *not* always the case..."

My eyes fly open, "Yes, it is the case! You're not helping her by coddling her."

Rene ignores me and reaches for Morgan's hand. "Some of it's true, you do need to be aware, but it's still your decision to make. I'm just sorry that you're hearing it like *this*." Rene's face glowers with disgust.

Morgan's hands are fast and frantic, twisting and pulling at her locs as if she needs to pull them out of her head for relief.

Rain turns on the sofa, making us all look in her direction.

The scratch of my chair against the hardwood floor startles her again. Heat burns my face from within. My hands shake.

Rene coaxes from across the table, "Baby, calm down. You're going out of bounds."

Using the words that are meant to catch me, the code phrase doesn't work this time. I'm a car with no brakes.

"How will you feel when you see how quickly he can shed his manhood so his attackers will let him live?"

Pushing herself up from her chair, Morgan musters the strength to stand.

I stand, too, facing her.

Morgan's face is flushed and too close to mine. Her eyes are swollen and red. Her lips tremble as she speaks, "Why can't you let Jahn have what you have? *Love*. What gives you the right to decide who deserves love and who doesn't? What has he ever done to you, besides move on with his life and remove you from your pedestal?"

She's too close to me. Close enough that I can I smell her nauseating floral perfume. I have no choice but to push it and her out of my face with my flailing hand. I don't mean for her to stumble, but she does.

Rene leaps out of her seat to catch Morgan.

Rain's foot jerks and rises in the air.

In frustration, Rene slams her hand on the table, toppling a wine glass. It hits the floor, smashing into three large pieces.

I imagine Morgan picking up a shard and slicing my throat to silence me.

Morgan stands taller than before. Her breath is sharp, hitting my face. "I choose to love him. The rest should be of no consequence to you."

Wine drips off the table, pooling like our blood on the newly polished floor. The tips of Rene's ears have turned red, and her eyes sputter out of control. Her loud voice finally tames me.

"Bethany stop it! I demand that you shut your fucking mouth! You have to stop *now!* You've said enough. It's Morgan's life. Jahn's none of your business anymore."

Rene comes towards me with a predator's gaze. Aggressively, she turns me around, grabbing my arms from behind like a police officer at a traffic stop gone wrong. Her touch hurts. I feel the blood clotting in my arm, forming a bruise underneath her fingertips.

"Shhhh… shhhh," comes from Morgan's lips, like little prayers, as she looks over at Rain.

Rene's phone's alarm sounds in the corner to remind that it's time to get ready for the airport. The sound is jolting and insistent. It blares for too long and too loudly. Her wandering eyes show that she doesn't know what to kill first.

Rain sits up, frightened by the alarm. Her eyes struggle as her body climbs out of sleep.

Rene silences the alarm and walks back over to me. In my ear, she whispers, "I'll get your pill."

Rene asks me to sit. The room spins. My blood slows as it travels through my veins, struggling to change course from the violent place that I just left.

Morgan pulls Rain from the couch, pushing her outside for some fresh air.

Fear lines Rain's voice as she asks her mother, "Where are we going?"

Morgan leaves the door ajar, pushing her outside, as quickly as she can.

Rene stands over me, pill in hand, shoving a glass of cold water in my face. "Drink," is all she says. I drink some and let the forgotten daily dose sit on my tongue, anxious to take hold.

Rene says softly, "You need to go to bed, now. I'll be back from the airport as soon as I can. Will you be OK? I'll call the doctor in the morning."

I ask her, softly, "Do you have to *go*?"

She nods her head, yes.

Rene doesn't let me walk near the broken glass and spilled wine. I feel her sweep me up in her arms and carry me over the mess. Behind me, I see a world upside down; the pair of neatly folded jeans and sweatshirt that I left on top of the suitcase for Rain are just as I left them.

Thick strands fall from my loosened bun, poking my eyes like pins. Rene pushes them away from my blinking eyes. My face feels hot and damp. The last thing I remember saying is, "You don't need Morgan as a best friend. I'm all you'll ever need."

CHAPTER

13

OCTOBER
Mid-air

*D*ear Jahn,

 I type this email with shaky hands from 40,000 feet above, gliding through the thick night, leaving things with you so painfully unresolved. I am angry that you ignored my call yesterday. Is it goodbye for now or goodbye forever?

 I'm writing because there's nothing else I can do with these suffocating feelings that you have conjured up in me. Although I want to, at this moment, I couldn't stand to hear your voice, a voice that has transformed me; helping me to believe in all things unbelievable. What a mighty gift to give and then take away by abandoning me with silence. At this point, the sound of you would only reconstruct the wall built by me, a woman scorned. The wall that I so wanted to take down for you.

 If you care to respond, please just use email. Electronics numb us, granting us the power to accept and reject with ease. Something that you have mastered.

 In your absence, Bethany revealed more details of your daunting life. She thought I deserved to know the things that you conveniently omitted. I admit, I'm angry and afraid of all that she revealed. Especially, the pain that you've already suffered and will continue forever. As bleak as it all sounds, I agree with her on only one point; that I deserved to know. Rage like hers is simply the ramblings of a world in flux.

 Bethany strongly urged me to say goodbye to you and spare myself of your "mess." But my longing for you has turned me into a wanton soul, strangely drawn to the flame that is you. Yes, I'm jealous that Bethany knows all of you. And I am also incensed that she thinks she knows me. What she doesn't know is that I am not as interested in your journey as I am in knowing that you arrive safely. I just don't care so much about your anatomy as much as I care about all the things inside of you and me that only we can see.

Jahn, you have shifted the tilt of the earth. You have shown me that I have much deeper places to dive.

With only love,

Morgan

I read it and re-read it, fearing that my maudlin yearnings will push him over the edge. Closing my eyes, holding my breath, there is a final exhale and then my finger pushes *SEND*.

In that instant that the words disappear, I want to retrieve them, pulling them back in, hoping for more perfection. Already in route, my words glide through cyberspace, unsheltered and totally exposed. He has become a stranger all over again.

I spend the rest of the flight with Rain asleep, head nestled in my lap, googling a single word: t-r-a-n-s-s-e-x-u-a-l-s.

We land as the sun tries to rise. I drag us home, promising myself that a nap is all we'll need to function. My head is filled with an overwhelming sense of loss and an unreasonable urge to check email, constantly, to see if he has responded.

He hasn't.

From my bed, all I can do is look up at the ceiling and stare at a single crack that lulls me into a half-sleep. I am muddied, struggling to escape the grief that has sucked me in. I lie alone with my laptop on the other pillow, where Jahn's head should lay.

We've overslept. My body stays still while I attempt to pull my legs over the bed. It would be good if I cared, but all I can reasonably manage to think about is getting Rain to school, signing her in, feigning parental shame and shoving the tardy slip into my purse.

As the sun comes up, I recognize the shape of the crack in the ceiling is that of a branch, bent in some places, straight in others. It's the one crack that could never be covered, no matter how many times I painted, no matter how thick the paint.

One more peek at my email is all I take before I shower. Too many hours last night were devoured by the Internet, studying, learning and listening to the how, what and why of sexual reassignment. Strangely aroused by the videos of these seductive, in-between men, I crave them and their revolutionary hearts more than I thought possible.

As the warm shower spills over me, I still feel Jahn's fingers sliding in and out of my crevices, the many places that he discovered and claimed as his own. Under the water, I struggle to hold on to whatever traces of him are left. Lathering the triangle beneath my naked belly, I watch the suds dissolve the parts of me that comprise my womanly self. For just a second, I dare to float in neutrality, imagining that I am neither woman nor man. I grasp for straws, wanting to know what it is to live in new skin, human skin, skin that allows all pieces of me, where there are no absolutes, no *should*.

Stepping out of the shower and back into my female self, I wish Jahn were here to prove what I know to be true: *there is something between us.* My stomach spasms as I recall Bethany's wrath, each word sounds off like a gong in my ear. *Reject. Unemployable... little lies that you'll have to tell...*

The sound of Rain's small blows to my bathroom door, snap me up out of my thoughts. She is yelling, "Mom! *I'm* dressed! *What* are you doing in there? We are soooo late!"

My response is unusually harsh and mean. "Who the hell do you think you're talking to like that? You're out of line, young lady!" My vocal cords feel the strain. She is not used to my anger. I have been careful to direct it only at the things that she cannot see.

It's not her fault that I've overslept.

It's not her fault that she will miss recess today.

It's not her fault that her mother has let a man take my body and turn it inside out.

～

Walking into the green door of Greenbelt Studios, my first vision is Mr. G. hovering over my desk with a disapproving look. Walking slowly, my steps are measured. "Sorry I'm so late. Long flight. Short night."

He waits for me to elaborate.

I don't.

Mr. G. touches my shoulder and I don't like it. "I really need to talk to you once you've settled in. A lot has happened while you were away. You'll need to hit the ground running."

The sound of his voice curdles my blood. "Give me a second," I hiss under my breath.

All I want is to know that Jahn was not an optical illusion. I have to know that I have not been victimized by a small passive aggressive act of cell phone trickery—me reaching out to him, and him dismissing me with a single touch. I grind my teeth as the start-up tone chimes from my laptop. I fear the silence of an empty inbox but bolded letters indicate a new message. It's him.

Mr. G. watches me from his office door.

Morgan,

It seems that someone getting hurt is the only constant when humans are together. I do not mean to hurt you but somehow, I've managed to erase some crucial parts of myself for my own protection. I apologize for my abrupt disappearance but a new snag has taken me out of the revelry of you and me. You can't understand because I've been in hiding for so long, I'm simply inept at how to be with people... how to finish what I start. There are so many more things that I'd like to tell you, but I'm wrestling with who I've become and the parts of me that I felt it was better to leave behind.

Please hug Rain and apologize for the all the things that grown-ups do. In another time and place, maybe I can make it up to you, both.

My apologies, Jahn

Mr. G. bellows down the hall, as I re-read the email. "Morgan, what the hell are you reading that's more urgent than your job?"

He stands at the doorway of his office.

I am frozen.

In response to my inertia, he rushes down the hall, now towering over me. Quickly, closing the email for his benefit, I follow behind him, walking and worrying that I have accidentally deleted Jahn's prized words.

"Morgan, what the hell is *up*?" he says as he slams his office door.

"Sorry. I'm not myself today. What's up? You said lots has happened."

"Good news! Jax will be recording his next project at Greenbelt. I'm assigning him to you. You'll be his personal account manager. It's a new thing I'm tryin' out."

"Who'll look after the production for all the other artists?"

"You leave that to me, my dear. You are going to be in charge of Jax' every comfort. Think of it as a promotion. We need to take advantage of all of his success while we can. He'll be tumbling down the charts as soon as the public comes to their senses and the next big thing happens. Music is a time-sensitive business," he says with an insider's smirk.

"Why the sour puss, Morgan?" He says, seeing my bewilderment.

"Is there anyone else you can assign Jax to? Trina? Simon? Someone who… maybe likes his music?"

"Suck it up, Morgan. We don't have to like his music. We have to *love* it. Jax pays our bills…" He sticks out his tongue like a kid. "*Besides*, Jax wants *you*."

"He does?" My stomach feels queasy at the thought of Jax wanting me while all I want is Jahn. I feel the muscles in my face regress, gathering into a little girl's pout.

Jahn,

I'll tell Rain. She'll be happy to know that you're still… somewhere.

I wish you felt safer with me.

No one else has ever moved me like you.

You've shown me how to seek the places that matter most, the underneath.

I'm still here.

Morgan

JAHN

The doctor says there's no such thing as a last session.

D r. Winston hasn't changed at all. He has the same calm demeanor, same quiet tone of voice, same black turtleneck. What's different is how he watches me while his slight hand caresses his enviable beard. "What a pleasant surprise to hear from you again," he says with a concerned look. "What brings you back? For an emergency session, no less?"

I still wonder how I could have missed the note that had not been seen until last night. I need to read it aloud:

Dear Coach Booth,

My son is having some personal issues and will not be able to participate in your PE class or any athletics for the remainder of the school year. He will be taking the online gym classes to cover the necessary credits for 10th grade PE and the High School Health Assessment.

Please let this note serve as a permanent excuse for Tina Rogers from gym class for the remainder of the school year. For your files, please note that Tina Rogers, as her transcripts indicate, would prefer to be called Teegue now. We have recently transferred from Atlanta, Georgia. His preferred pronouns are he/him/his.

Should you have any further questions, please feel free to call me at 404-269-3659.

Sincerely, His mother, Misty Rogers

"Interesting note. Jahn, when did you receive that note?"

"I'm not sure. There's no date. I just found it yesterday morning shoved in a folder of old mail from last week."

"Usually you are the consummate professional. How could you have missed this?"

"Distracted," I say under my breath.

185

"Distracted by Morgan? That's her name, right?" Dr. Winston probes.

"Yeah…" I say with some reserve.

"So, why are you here? I'm sure you get gym excuses all the time." Dr. Winston rears back in his seat.

My eyes drop. "Did you hear… preferred pronouns, he's Trans! Didn't you hear Tina, but likes to be called Teegue?"

Dr. Winston's eyebrows arch. "Oh. I guess I didn't register all of that. Is he the first trans student in the school?"

"The only one that I know of," I say with my eyes focused on the brain drawings over his desk.

"How do you feel about it?" He picks up his pad, ready to write.

"Well, it finally makes sense. That's why the new bathroom. His mother—Uh, Ms. Rogers, must have contacted the school board and threatened them. Holly Crest can't afford a reputation worse than they already have. Now I see that Coach's hands were tied."

"I repeat, how do *you* feel about this kid being there?"

My mind races, "I'm not sure… Don't know. Maybe a little exposed."

Dr. Winston shifts in his seat. "I see. It's easy to forget until something or someone like this pops up? So, tell me more about feeling 'exposed.'"

"I can't describe it. It just brings it all up again."

"Please clarify what the 'it' refers to." Dr. Winston takes his glasses off and rubs his eyes.

"You know. *It*. This feeling that never quite goes away. Constant danger and fear. Having to second-guess every pair of eyes that I meet, searching them for danger. Hiding behind designer sunglasses for fear that someone will recognize the girl behind my eyes. It's squirrelling away every red cent hoping and dreaming for something that is totally out of my reach. At the end of the day I'm just a fucking woman in a man's suit."

"Jahn, what damning words! I know you can't mean that. The experience of being trans, "it" as you call it, is not meant to go away. You're a man fighting for your life. We all are. I wish you understood that everyone is fighting for their own existence in their own way. Most give up or give in to being

186

whom the world wants them to be. We, my darling, don't give up because we can't. Being who you were meant to be is the ultimate cost of humanity. It seems that only trans folks are willing to fight for it, at all costs."

"Doc, when I read that note, all I feel is dread." I feel my pulse quicken. "Why do *you* think I feel this way? Why now?"

"Perhaps this Teegue kid makes you realize that you're not the only trans man on earth. That could feel like relief or it could be very scary. Perhaps you think, he'll embarrass you if people equate the two of you as the same. I can't say for sure why you feel this way. This is a new one for both of us."

"Maybe I'm just worried about being linked to him and outed."

"Jahn, you act like you're not eager to meet this kid. But I submit that you're actually dying to do just that. What do you think you'll see if you were to meet him and look into his eyes?"

"I have no idea."

"You'll see what's behind all of our eyes: an acute need for acceptance. Sadly, it's universal. It's just so damned hard for any of us to admit."

For the first time, I can see the pain behind Dr. Winston's bare eyes.

"Jahn, if you could be a safe place for this kid, you'd finally find some safety for yourself. I know my opinion is not warranted."

In my head, I hear only my other voice, no longer able to access the lessons that the vocal coach taught. *The testosterone will drop your voice*, the endocrinologist had promised, but it's not always true. Not when you still have your original fear that is always high-pitched.

I manage to say, "It just sucks to think that this kid will have no support. But Doc, save the analysis, it's not happening."

"It sucks, but he could have *you as support*," Dr. Winston reiterates. "But it's up to you whether you will be generous with your truth or not."

"Don't you get it? It can't be me! It's unprofessional. Not appropriate. If anyone were to find out…" I sigh. "I just can't disclose." Tears seem to come out of nowhere. I sob as I say, "What have I done to myself?"

"That's quite a normal question. We all have asked it at one point or another in transition. I just ask you to think how you'd feel to find out that there was another trans person in your midst, seeing you drowning and they chose to do nothing to save you?"

"It's a solo trip. Another trans person doesn't make it any easier. We all have to fit into ourselves, by ourselves."

Exasperated, Dr. Winston says, "Jahn, you win. It's a solo thing, if you say it is. Now, enough about that. How's your Morgan?"

I feel more tears forming and flowing down my face. I'm too weak to wipe them away. "She's gone," I say, feeling the strength coming back to my voice.

"So soon? What happened?"

"When I found that note, it fucked with me all day. All of it just came barreling back to me and I realized that I didn't have the energy to go any further with Morgan. I know I'm just not ready for anything serious."

"Well, how was the weekend that you spent together?"

"It was good. Too good."

Dr. Winston looks confused. "So, I don't understand why you're letting her go."

I say, quietly, "I took your advice. I let her see... me. All of me."

"You did? That's a huge step, Jahn. You should feel really good about that. How did she handle it? How did it feel being naked with her?"

"She was just as I thought she'd be. Open. Affectionate. Scared. I didn't like it. It was too much."

"Did she say that she was scared? Or are you talking about yourself?"

"Dammit! Don't nail me. No, she didn't actually say it. But she must have been. It's scary! Yes, it was me that was scared. OK? It's me that *is* scared. I won't do it again."

Dr. Winston leans forward. "You don't have to, Jahn. It's your choice. What else happened?"

"Bethany happened. She couldn't handle seeing me with Morgan. She made a scene. She was a total bitch all weekend."

"That's not news," Dr. Winston says with a scowl.

We both remember the tedious hours spent processing my guilt and feelings of obligation to Bethany after everything happened.

"Jahn, snap out of it! You know her condition. She's not well. All of it wasn't your fault. Some of it was hers. You can't let her illness take over your life forever. You wanted this relationship with Morgan so badly, I don't want to see you give it up because you're not able to get through the past."

"Morgan called, but I didn't pick up. Doc, it's just easier for me to get back to my own solo life. Besides, I have new things to worry about."

"Teegue, you mean? Since he won't be coming to gym class, he's just another paper transaction, right? You'll submit the letter to the school, get the proper signatures, sign off on it and that will be that. Teegue will handle it just like we all have had to. I am sure he knows what to expect."

We sit in silence. Dr. Winston pushes a button at his desk and classical music suddenly pipes out of the speakers mounted in the corners.

I feel myself releasing all that I thought was gone. I hear myself weeping and am ashamed. "Doc, just being with Morgan sends me reeling into a lazy fog of farfetched hopes."

"And, what's wrong with hope, Jahn?"

"What's wrong with hope? There's never a day that I don't feel the hours seeping out of my life. There's no time for contentment when reality is always sucking me dry. How can I plan a future when the present is always at stake?"

CHAPTER

OCTOBER
Atlanta, Georgia

L ying in bed, thinking about Jahn, the phone rings. Instinctively, I pick up, not looking at who it could be, hoping it is him.

It's my pugnacious 85-year-old, Southern-born relentless father. Our deep love for each other and his disdain for my adulthood make our relationship sweet and complicated.

"Where ya been?" he starts.

I don't know what to tell him about where I've been. *I've been places that I never meant to go.* "Funny you called, Daddy, I was just thinking about calling you."

"Ain't nothing funny about being a liar! You weren't going to call me. What happened on your trip to see Rene? And that damn boy you were so crazy about?"

"Not much happened," I say, although *everything happened.*

"You're not telling me the truth. I can hear it in your voice. Something happened to you out there... what is it?" My father's voice is finally soft but laced with concern.

He's right. I saw things that I've never seen before. I am thinking things that I've never thought I could think. I have fallen in love with a man whose body is not fully male. *How can I tell him any of that?*

Finally, I say, "Nothing happened, really. We went to the funeral. Rene took it hard. Jahn took me out to dinner. There's nothing more to talk about."

"You went out to dinner when you were supposed to be supporting Rene? I don't understand you. What's this boyfriend business, done to you? You've gone crazy."

I can't tell him anymore. It's all too complicated. He won't understand a boy born in a girl's body. He will have never heard anything like that before. He will have no understanding of the word trans. Upon hearing it, his laugh will turn to sarcasm as he'll pass it off as something that only white people do.

Lamely, I would start to explain. *Daddy, this has nothing to do with race, it has to do with knowing who you are...* But I do not venture to go there with him, it would be going too far.

"It was fine with Rene, Daddy. She was asleep when I was out with Jahn."

"You can't get me off the phone until you tell me what really happened. Whatever it is, it's *bothering* you! I hear it in your voice. You can't fool me. I've known you your whole life!"

We sit silently. He blows into his version of coffee; boiling water and Folgers coffee crystals. I stare at the crack in the ceiling. Finally, I say the words he wants to hear. "It's over with Jahn, anyway, alright? We're not right for each other," I say. "He's got some issues."

My father curses when he's getting close to the truth. "What kind of damned issues does he have?"

"It doesn't matter, anymore. Please leave it alone, Daddy."

I am a liar of the worst kind.

I can smell him from a distance. The scent of Jax' Nag Champa blended with the stink of marijuana comes through the front door in a cloud. Mr. Greenstein escorts him in, tugging him by the hand like he's a High School Principal and Jax is the student of the week. His entourage rolls behind them like a cloud of smoke. There are six of them but they feel like twelve. They half walk, half dance into the building, loose hips, bent knees, bouncing to a beat that lives only in their heads. Their wide stance carves a path, making everyone move out of their way.

Their clothes and shoes are straight out of a hip-hop magazine. $300 is the cost of one pair of sneakers like theirs. The ones that are custom made, handcrafted of suede and exotic pony skins. They're sky blue, teal and shades of purple. The crew varies in shape and size. The one thing that have in common is that they are untamed.

"Boo-ya-ka, Boo-ya-ka!" they yell with their fleshy fingers shaped like pistols pointed towards the sky. They shoot their rawness into the atmosphere, changing the air for everyone. Their darkened lips hang open; tongues wagging like dogs, their rough voices scratched from smoking too much designer weed. They repeat their favorite mantra, "*make dis money*," like a childish call to prayer.

"Waa gwan Morghaan? Me and you gwan be tight for the next few months, wukin' close togeda. It's going to be Irie, man!"

The entourage laughs on cue.

"So, let's get to work." I smile a meek, *please-respect-me* smile. Hoping that he will, knowing that he can't.

Jax looks me up and down. His extra-long eyelashes are meant to make me look. I try not to, but they bring up old rumblings and stirrings of the woman I used to be.

Black Russian, *Panama Gold* and *Colombo* are the designer strains of marijuana that Jax and his boys talk about as if they were brands of chewing gum. I recognize the names as they peek out of the thick forest of patois that jumbles their Island-heavy tongues.

Their manager has arranged it with Mr. Greenstein that Marvin, a blonde blue-eyed weed guy will deliver every morning to the studio. Shorty, the tallest of the crew, rolls the pithy joints fresh and has them ready on demand. Jax' lips tremble as he takes a long satisfying drag while I attempt to start the meeting. I find myself allergic to them.

Jax' crude face never fails to intrigue me. His "handsome" is hard to discern beneath the scars and scrapes that come with being a Nigerian born, rudebwoy raised in Jamaica. His face is dramatic, angled and shrouded by smoke, scent and attitude.

His boys shamelessly assess me as they take their seats around the conference room table. The wholeness of me disappears, melted by the gaze of hungry eyes. All that is left is my flesh. Their open mouths and bared teeth show what they want to do with me. In their presence, I move with caution, keeping my distance, shivering on the inside. I roll my chair two rolls back from the table. My presence seems to crowd them.

I attempt polite conversation. "So, guys, what's the name of the album?"

"Awhol heap of wuk gon' into dis ya know, and we a callin' it *Transition*."

I squirm awkwardly in my seat.

"So, whatya 'tink bot' tit, Morghaan?" His teeth glow white.

I shudder at the word. Suddenly protective, I don't ever want Jax and his boys to ever use the word again. I don't want them anywhere near it.

"Awhat wrong withcha ya, Morghaan? You no like it?" He says with his lips aimed at me.

"It's cool, I guess." My breath makes it hard for me to speak.

"Transition to what?" I ask, eyes down, shuffling papers and timelines around on the table.

"It means, a change from bwoys to big men. Tru dat?" His boys laugh and jeer.

One of them yells out, "We change from Yadie to Rich Yankee!"

Jax laughs and says finally, "De name means everyt'ing and nuttin' at all."

"Morghaan, just hang wit' us and you'll see. It's all good." A loud guffaw fills the room.

Jax flings his muscular arm over my shoulder.

But I'm already numb. Shaken by boys who laugh, *just because*. They laugh at everything and nothing at all…

JAHN

The Doctor says that sometimes there will be an error in judgment.

'ANITORS CLOSET* said the door that the J had fallen off, years ago. The old door and sign have now been replaced with a new institutional blue sign that reads: GENDER NEUTRAL RESTROOM.

I admire the 21 letters that grant my freedom. A sense of pride, fleetingly, sweeps over me until I look at the disturbing images above. The first two figures are familiar. These bald, faceless, "female" and "male" icons define everything the world has ever known. The third figure is the anomaly, not belonging here or anywhere. It is a mere "thing" that tries to blend the two genders together, creating something that speaks to no one. It's an image that is the product of time-sucking meetings with puzzled bureaucrats aimlessly trying to figure out whom, if anyone, this new creature represents. Sadly, this is the best they could do. If only they had taken the easy route to just say what they mean: *single user facility*, which is all that it is and all that it needs to be.

I shudder to think that soon this brand-new sign will be defaced, laughed at, tweeted and re-tweeted, tampered with, crossed out, drawn on, pulled down… *victimized*. Much like what they would do to those who use it.

I am unnerved by the automation of everything. At my slightest touch, the new door unlatches and turns on the overhead light. Fearing there's a built-in camera behind it, I wonder if the surveillance is meant to protect us or to ogle at our misplaced parts. The door locks softly behind me.

Unzipping my pants, my black khakis and boxers slide down together. Slowly I bend, folding myself into the dreaded female plié. My bared ass finds relief on the sparkling white "soft-close" toilet seat. Piss flows from me like a raging stream. I am relieved, lingering for an additional moment; pants slumped down around my ankles. Although this room was built for one-at-a-time users, it was really constructed to accommodate a single trans student who just needs privacy and a lifetime pass out of gym class.

Washing my hands, looking in the mirror, I see how the Morgan thing has broken me. She was a good woman, but it's just not the right time.

I can only hope that she won't call and persist, begging me to articulate what in me has changed so quickly. She'll wonder if it's something she's done, she'll blame herself; she'll want to compare me to the man that I was, just before I turned on her. Typical female. If she calls, I'll hang up the phone, simply unable to articulate how tenuous I have become underneath all these layers of new skin. I shouldn't still be thinking about her.

Just outside the door, is that a breath, I hear? My touch on the knob unlocks the door and the light goes off behind me. I start my exit. It's after six; the building is almost empty. With one foot outside, I step into silence and a flash of white light, slaps my face, hurling me back inside. I fall heavy against the white porcelain sink. *What just happened?* The automated door has closed, the light is on, and the lock has caught. I am safely inside and a prankster has fled. "Fuck!" I yell.

My heart beats hard inside my chest. In the mirror I see how my lips have clenched and the muscles in my face have tightened. My eyes have a whole new shape. Fear has left me unrecognizable. Regrets swirls through my body. I kick myself for giving into untimely bodily needs. Slowly, I peer out of the door. In the distance, all I see is a flash of red, running for dear life.

Coach Blande hadn't looked at me since that bathroom meeting with the staff. Trying to earn some points with him and get back into his good graces, I volunteered to work on the grant that Holly Crest is applying for. I said I'd write the section about our athletic programs. If the school gets the grant, it would mean $75,000 to the athletic department and a bonus for him. Knowing that he had once respected me, even praised me for turning the "the animals" into winners, staying late one night may get him off my back.

No one's here, I stupidly thought. It just didn't make sense for me to wait until I got home to piss, as I had done for too many years. The only people in the building were students who served their time in after school detention and the monitors who controlled them.

I needed the distraction. No longer will I have anything better to do with my nights. There will be no more dreams of Morgan or nights filled with moist words and quixotic fantasies. I miss her but I'm not ready to give her what she needs, despite her protests.

The kids all laughed at the bathroom when it was finished, questioning what we needed it for. Cruel jokes, titters and howls burst out of their careless young mouths. I heard someone say, "It's for freaks." More laughter. More misunderstanding. In those few moments, the bathroom had already been labeled, a no-go zone. No one would use it simply because there are no freaks here. So, who would dare lurk outside of this forbidden place? Who and why would anyone care that much, if we freaks don't matter?

Falling asleep, I feel a scandal wrapping itself around my body, entrapping me, holding me in contempt and forcing me to see that a change is imminent. As my eyes close, I ask myself again and again, so what if they find out? *So, fucking what?*

The next day, there are eyes following me as I walk through the cafeteria. Mine refuse to meet them. I continue getting my lunch and head for the faculty lunchroom. Stubborn, these eyes are hard to ignore. Finding my seat in the back corner of the faculty dining room, I sit armed with tasteless food and the latest issue of Sports Illustrated, which keeps me occupied.

Flipping through the pages, I look for the college basketball stats, always looking for a way to get my boys out of the 'hood and into college. Page after page, I compare and contrast the stats of boys that look just like mine. These boys have only relied on sex to confirm their manhood and sports to make them worthy. Page after page, I see them covered in ink, symbols and pictures that define their lives. Their tattoos are the flags that beg for recognition of pain endured and victories too small to see.

Rushing out of the cafeteria, a kid cuts me off right by the door. It's a kid shrouded in red, an oversized knit cap that covers his whole head. I have not seen his face before. I would have remembered the red scarf and hat, both too thick for California weather. His ears are plugged with ear buds attached to a long chord that dangles and snakes along the side of his bulky body that leads to the electronic device that keeps him alive. The kid stops and our eyes meet, locking in recognition that we are each other's reflection.

"Excuse me," I say.

He only stares more intensely.

I recognize his overdressed style, which was once my own. Baggy clothes meant to hide from being seen, pigeonholed, *misgendered.* Two earrings dangle from the left side of his pudgy sour face. I step to the left, he mirrors me, taunting and blocking me.

I feel anger rise but remember that I have been trained in de-escalation. I'm never to use my hands, despite my hormone-induced instincts.

I turn my back and leave him standing there.

Perfectly formed block letters ask an innocuous question. "WHY HAVEN'T YOU SAID ANYTHING?" is the note left on my desk.

I don't have to wonder who it's from.

I just don't have an answer.

CHAPTER

15

NOVEMBER
Atlanta, Georgia

R ene's face lights up my phone, just as I walk in the door.
"Sorry it's taken me so long to call you back," Rene says into the phone.

The sound of people being paged over a PA system is in the background.

I say, "Where are you? There's a lot of noise behind you. I've been worried; is everything OK?"

"B's in the hospital. She'll be here for a couple of weeks. That's why I haven't called."

"A couple of weeks? What happened to her?" I ask, already knowing that something is very wrong.

"She's had some kind of a breakdown. After you and Rain left, she started acting very strangely. We went to the doctor the next day and they kept her. They need to tweak her meds."

"I didn't know that Bethany was on meds. Is that why she was acting so strangely? I knew there was more to it but I didn't want to ask. What do you think it is?"

Rene sighs, "I wish I knew. Something about the weekend provoked it, but it's not your fault."

"I'd hate to think that I had anything to do with it."

"Don't. It's not you really... it has to do with fucking Jahn, but I don't know how or why, yet. Like I told you, I don't know much about their past.

I didn't really care to hear the details, until now. I think that their little teenage love affair was not as simple or innocent as she says."

"Rene, she loves you. Apparently, this is a lot for her to handle."

"I thought I was holding it together but Bethany breaking down is too much for me to take. I thought she was OK until that weekend. Seeing Jahn must have done something to her. Speaking of him, has he called?" Rene asks.

Saying it aloud hurts. "No. I think he's gone."

Rene's voice darkens. "What? I can't believe that. It makes no sense. He was so into you. The stuff from the past seems to have complicated things but he cares about you, I can tell."

"Rene, people can change in an instant and sometimes we never see it coming," I say. "He emailed me once saying that something new came up, but he didn't elaborate."

"What happened to Bethany has something to do with Jahn and I have to stop it in its tracks. Their little childhood tryst can't go on. They're both grown and it's time for them to move on."

"I'd never seen Bethany like that…"

"You were never supposed to," Rene says. "I should have told you about her… mental health issues but I really thought that it was a thing of the past. Seeing him with you seemed to cause whatever it is to come up all over again. It will take a lot to get her back on her feet."

"Why didn't you confide in me?"

"Bethany asked me not to tell anyone, even you. She doesn't want people to know. I needed to respect her wishes. Morgan, she's my wife now and I love her."

Wishing that Jahn and I had that kind of trust between us, I say. "I know you do."

"How's Rain doing? I hope all that stuff with Bethany didn't scare her too much, it was pretty intense. Luckily, she slept through all of it."

"Luckily, she did."

Rain bounds into my room, "Mom, can I ask you a question?"

"Sure, anything,—"

"Anytime!" we both say in unison.

Rain's face looks serious and scared. "Why is Auntie Bethany so mad at us?"

"Why do you say that?" I ask.

Tears start to form in her eyes as she confesses, "I'm sorry. I wanted to tell you sooner. I was only pretending to be asleep at Auntie Rene's. I heard the fight that you had about Jahn and stuff. Will we never see him again?"

"I don't think so, Rainy. Not anytime soon, at least, but it's OK."

Keeping my eyes on the TV set, I bite my top lip to manage the hot tingle in my nose, which means that tears are coming.

"Why hasn't he called?"

"Rain, it's a lot to explain. It wasn't a fight. Aunt Bethany just wasn't feeling well and she just overreacted. She's not really mad at me. You see, she used to be Jahn's girlfriend. Many, many years ago. I think she just misses him."

"But she's got Auntie Rene now, right?"

"She does, but you can still miss people you used to love," I say.

"You can? Do you still miss my Dad?"

I hate to admit it to her or to myself. "Yes, I do. Every time I look at you, I can't help but think of him. He is part of you. But my heart is all healed now, so all that's left is a little bit of missing, which is a good thing. If I didn't miss him, just a little, then I never really loved him… and I really did, back then."

Cuddling closer she says, "Why don't you call Jahn? You haven't smiled in a long time."

Getting off the bed, I walk over to the pile of clean laundry that needs to be put away. I haven't had the energy.

"Mommy, why'd you leave? We're cuddling aren't we?"

"Because, I just don't want… you to see me cry." As the last word comes out of my mouth, a warm tear falls. I sink down to the ground, letting the towel drop out of my hand.

Rain picks the towel up for me and sits beside me on the floor, hugging my neck. She hands me the towel for me to cry into. Taking it from her, I cover my whole face with it.

Rubbing my back, she says, "Mommy, it's OK for you to cry."

Sniffling, trying to pull myself together, I feel ashamed. "Rain, Mommies shouldn't cry to their kids. I'm supposed to show you how to become a strong woman someday."

"When my friends make me sad at school, I sometimes feel better, I mean stronger, when I cry. You can cry and still be strong, Mommy," she says.

I smile at her as she tries to help me make sense of a world that doesn't.

"You're right, sweetie. Thank you for reminding me." I kiss her gently on both cheeks. "Now, would you mind leaving me for a few minutes. I just need some time alone. Look at all of this laundry I still have to do!"

The love that I see in Rain's eyes melts me. I want to hug her forever. I haven't felt this deep ache since her father left us so many years ago. When he walked out, I thought I would keel over and die right there, in the living room, in front of my favorite potted plant… I never imagined that ten years later I would have lived, healed and even had the strength to attempt love again. This time will be no different. I won't let Jahn break me.

"Is there anything I can do for you, Mom? I can fold laundry, too. You taught me."

"You don't have to do that. But the one thing you can do is just give me one of those big Rainbow style hugs. That's all I need and I'll be fine."

She comes towards me with wide, outstretched arms and I know that she's the only love I need.

As she bounds out the door, I pick up my cell phone to make sure it's still working. Disappointed by the silence, my eyes perform a quick forensic review of all of the functions, trying to see if technology is to blame for the sudden death of Jahn. I pull up his name and see the smile that makes my stomach hurt. With my finger held on his name, the phone prompts me: DO YOU WANT TO DELETE THIS NUMBER? Reading the words through tears, the word YES is a blur, but I push it.

Smartphones are not smart, but brilliant. It asks me again, ARE YOU SURE YOU WANT TO DELETE THIS NUMBER? But I can't bring myself to do it.

Quickly, I push NO.

Somewhere deep inside, I feel him still out there. He's not gone. He just needs time.

Part Four

JAHN

The doctor says your story is your own. Do with it what you want.

I have no illusions. I heard how those teachers laughed at the mere mention of making room for people unlike themselves. This fucking Teegue had the nerve to ask, why haven't I said anything? Because people prefer illusion over truth, any day.

Really, who does this kid think he is? Why haven't I said anything? Because I have said enough in blood, guts and hormone shots. I have let doctors amputate, dismantle and reshape me. I've paid the price for a lifetime commitment. And I'm almost there…

Who the fuck does this kid think he is? I don't have to say anything to anyone about who I was and who I have become. It's every man for himself.

~

A sudden nausea fills me as I approach my desk. I fear that he's been here again. Cautiously, my finger flips through a pile of game schedules, permission slips and phone messages that clutter. As I look at each, I sort them mentally; garbage, respond, already done and call back. At the bottom of the pile, I see that which takes my breath. It is the picture of me, buried beneath my mess. It's the unwanted photograph that I have waited for, not knowing when and how it would surface. The image of me being caught startles me; my mouth open saying, *please don't*; my eyes squint, trying to block out the glare. I shudder at the image of my body contorting, twisting, trying to disappear.

I am jolted by the fact that I am a man. Like a homework assignment, the kid has worked on me, manipulated, photo-shopped and color corrected me. And, he added a caption. Once again, perfectly formed block letters ask another question. GUESS WHO?

Standing, I've died. Breathing hard and loud, beads of sweat form everywhere. I have never liked pictures of myself; they make me obsess over changes that never come fast enough. Seeing myself for the first time in this picture shakes me into belief; I have really landed. This is the proof. I have been caught in the act of being male.

My heart beats louder and louder. There is no denying that the image must be destroyed, but it can never… to hell with the automation of *everything!* I want to find this predator and hurt him… but I have been trained in de-escalation.

———— ⌇ ————

Teegue is brazen. Another day, another gift. Another question. "WHO'S MY FAVORITE COACH?" reads the new caption. And he's colorized the image pink.

———— ⌇ ————

Who's letting this kid into my office, so he is close enough to touch and torment me? I can no longer trust the secretaries, the other coaches or myself. Days have passed and I no longer go to my desk, it's safer this way. I have lost my appetite; food no longer stays down and everything else has come up. I long for Morgan who always said that she'd be there to listen. It was a mistake to let her go.

———— ⌇ ————

At home, searching for the lone piece of paper that will give me the out that I need, I make a mess. Where is it under the pile of old magazines, scraps, bills, papers, student evaluations, old game schedules… *Where is it?* Sweat pours from my face; droplets of my perspiration leave stains. *It's here.* I know it is. Frustrated, papers fly out of my hand. It's here. It *has to be here.* I scream out, "*Where the fuck is it?!*"

Berd moves around in his tank, showing himself, knowing that something is very wrong.

Finally… the note from Misty Rogers. "… *if you have any questions, please call,*" I read. I do have questions that only she can answer. She needs to know that her kid is threatening everything that I have ever had or ever will. He has to be stopped.

———— ⌇ ————

The dreaded meeting has been set for 6:00 p.m. on the night that the choir rehearses until 8:00 p.m. No one will be on the gym level of the school. We'll have the privacy we need.

I have cleared and cleaned off my desk. There is no more evidence of Teegue and his petty torture. He obviously knows, but I don't know how he could. Can he and others see that I'm unfinished? What could he want from me?

I see her as she approaches the door. I rise to greet her; she's tall and blonde with broad shoulders and an unwilling smile. Draped in several layers of black clothing, her pale stoic and unmade face is a perfect canvas. Only the blue of her eyes and the red of her lips show that once there was life.

Teegue appears beside her when the door is opened wider. He is surprisingly small and disproportionately stout. His blue eyes peer out from the folds of his ruddy round face. I recognize the inappropriate red hat and scarf. He wears double layers of long-sleeved shirts for self-protection.

Two bottles of water sit in front of where they will sit. I have placed a third bottle for myself for when my throat closes due to nerves. Extending a sweaty hand that shakes, I say, "Thank you for coming in." My other hand hides inside my pocket. I try to look everywhere but at Teegue. I shut the door behind them.

"We were sure hoping that the photo would get your attention. We've been dying to meet you," Ms. Rogers says with a smile.

The blood has rushed to my face. "Dying to meet me? I don't understand."

"Now that Teegue will be a student here at Holly Crest, he'll need a role model. Someone who will keep him safe."

"What do you mean, a role model? And why the hell did Teegue take a picture of me?"

"Coach, I realize that this is quite a sensitive subject for everyone involved."

The back of my neck sticks to my shirt. I ask in a low shaky voice, "What exactly do you want from me?"

Misty says calmly, "We only want what everyone wants, your truth, please." She has sat down and loosened her drapes. Her legs cross seductively. Her knowing eyes make it impossible to deny, but I try anyway.

My hands are tense, forming fists. "You've got the wrong guy. Who are you and how did you find me anyway?"

"Come clean, Mr. Booth. My sources are reliable. This is not to hurt you, Coach. It's to help my son."

Teegue finally speaks up with his head down, ears still full of distraction. "You're trans just like me."

"Coach Booth, we're really not trying to make trouble here," she says stroking her son's layered back.

"Don't you realize that I called you, thinking you were a sensible parent? I called to tell you that Teegue is harassing me and hopefully you could stop him, but you're *in on it!* What the hell?" I hear desperation on my tongue. My posture slumps. "I've been getting along just fine until now…"

"Well, of course you've been getting along just fine. Getting along only works when you're alone. But now it's the two of you," says Ms. Rogers. "You and Teegue are a community now. Teegue needs protection and you're the only one who… gets it."

"How do you think I can protect him?" I take a swig of the warm bottled water. "Every day, I have to do everything I can to protect myself."

"Your mere presence protects him. You being here makes it OK for Teegue to be here. When others know that he's like you—and you are well-respected… they will respect him. We're not asking much. Just tell the school—what you are and we'll leave you alone. Of course, by then, Teegue and you will have formed a beautiful mentor/mentee relationship. There's power in numbers, I always say."

"With all due respect, Mrs. Rogers,"

"It's *Ms.*"

"Ms. Rogers, your request is preposterous. What if I say no? What you're demanding of me is not a game or a goddamned *dare.* This is my livelihood. My gender status is no one's business. As long as I do the job I was hired to do, I owe them nothing."

Impatient, Ms. Rogers turns to her son and slaps him gently. "Tell him Teegue."

Teegue takes out one ear bud and leaves the other in. His voice is loud due to the music playing. "If you don't do it, that pretty picture of you coming out of the gender-neutral can will be all over the school. Everyone knows it's for freaks like us."

I interrupt, "Teegue what are you saying? Freaks? I thought you needed the bathroom." I turn to Ms. Rogers, "I thought you are the reason the school had to provide it."

Teegue continues ignoring my questioning.

"Then, I'll post it all over the Internet. Before you know it, you'll be an Internet star, but not a hero. Let me see…" He throws his head back with a villainous laugh, "I'll start with Facebook, then move on to Instagram and then… last stop Twitter, even though it sucks because the Prez uses it now. But tweets still have some reach… So, what do you say, do we have a deal?"

"That's blackmail," I say. My eyes dart from side to side, not knowing which of them is more vicious. "Ms. Rogers, I don't know where you got this idea but it's a bad one."

Her body softens. She tries to hold them, but tears start to stream from her eyes. "Please Coach, look at my lovely daughter, Tina. She *was* my lovely daughter… Look at what she's turned herself into. She says it's who she really is. I don't know what to do. They kill kids like her. They kill…"

I can't deny what she's saying. All I can say to her, "It doesn't always happen. Teegue will be OK."

"How do I know that? Tina, come over here and show Coach Booth your arms."

"Mom! You said my dead name," he says with sheer panic in his voice.

"I'm sorry, Noodle. Just do what I ask! He's our only hope."

"Don't call me that in public." Stubbornly, Teegue pushes up one sleeve, only to reveal another shirt's sleeve that lay beneath.

"Push that sleeve up or I'll do it for you," Ms. Roger's voice climbs up an octave.

Teegue turns away.

Taking a deep breath, Ms. Rogers, reaches for Teegue's arm and pulls at the sleeve. He shudders and releases a long, slow moan. As his mother pushes up the sleeve, she winces at the violent scars that paint his forearm and wrist.

Some of the scars are weathered and dried, while others are fresh, oozing with live red blood.

"Don't start," Teegue says.

"Now you listen to me, Coach. This is not the way it was supposed to be for me or my daughter, Tina. You see, she's not well. She says what she sees in the mirror doesn't match her mind. I've cried too many nights to lose her. But it's not for me to cry. It's for me to help her in any way that I can because I'm her mother. It's not what I wanted for her... but you know what I discovered. THIS IS NOT FOR ME TO DECIDE. We mothers cry and we pray and we talk to anyone who'll listen. No matter how long it takes, we always learn at the end of the day... love is all there is."

Ms. Rogers falls back in her chair, taking a sip of water.

We all stay silent.

Once she can speak again, she says, "You know, Coach, just when I thought I was an accepting human being, I had to come to some new understandings of everything I once believed. I have to love her in all the ways that she is. Even when she's a he, for God's sake. There's a million ways to be human."

Teegue moans, "I'm not a she."

"Sorry, Teegue, you know what I mean. Let me talk to Coach Booth!"

Wrenched by their pain, it all comes up again. The scent of this mother's love is foreign to me. I only have words that I have read in books about family ties and mothers and their kids. I recite from memory. "Acceptance and love are what Teegue needs most. He really doesn't need me, he has you... Something I never had."

"He does need *you*. Do you know what I've been through? I've searched the country to find someone like you in a school that would be safe. Those rednecks almost killed him in Georgia. Forget what you've heard about Southern hospitality. I talked to every friend and acquaintance I ever had, asking them to ask their friends. I've spent over a year searching for a place where Teegue would not be the only one. When I heard about you... we came."

"How and what did you hear? No one knows," I say, still not understanding what has landed us here.

Tears flow from her eyes. "Don't be so sure of that. Someone always knows. Either you tell the school... Or we will. I know it's a big decision. You have two weeks. Once you come out, things should start shaping up around here. Imagine... local news coverage applauding the inclusivity of Holly Crest High, you leading a new Gay/Trans/Straight Alliance.... The works! Holly Crest High will be the gold standard, instead of the dump that it is."

"Ms. Rogers, please don't get ahead of yourself. Do you really think your plan can save him? I'm just like your son, trying to survive. It's lonely. And it's hard. Now it'll just be the two of us against everyone else in the school. It takes a very long time for minds to change. It will be much easier for the school to get a new coach and to recommend that Teegue be transferred. We're disposable. Don't you know that?"

I turn to Teegue who has buds still in his ears. Gently, I touch his shoulder, straining not to shove a little harder. Trying to keep my voice calm, I try a different approach. "Why would you do this, Teegue?"

Startled by my gentleness, he says, "Because visibility is what you and I both need most. They need to accept us as we are. They can no longer feel they can chase us away with meanness. We're here and not going anywhere."

I feel myself getting angry, knowing that he's right. Youth has emboldened him.

I plead, "Teegue, the world sees us and they don't like what they see."

"That's because of people like *you*," he sneers. "Every time you don't let yourself be seen; you admit shame."

Holding my head in my hands, I say, "You *can't* do this, to me."

Ms. Rogers steps in again, "We can and we will. Just try to complain about this meeting without revealing too much. You can't."

She rises from her seat and Teegue follows behind her like a minion. As they reach the door, she turns to me one last time. "I guess you've reached a rock and a hard place, Coach Booth. See you in two weeks."

As he shuts the door behind him, Teegue whispers, "I'll bring my laptop."

CHAPTER

16

NOVEMBER
Atlanta, Georgia

s he sleeps, he sweats. His citrusy musk permeates, becoming my
new perfume. Miraculously, he is in my bed, although he dis-
regarded my original request that seems so long ago. He *called.*
I feared the fury all over again, which is why I asked him not to. I imagined
that his voice would turn me into a banshee, all fire and salt, but I was mis-
taken. The mere timbre of his voice soothed my ruffled feathers.

It was a week ago. The call was quick and desperate. It was a lightning
bolt of urgent words scattered between quick breaths and heavy pauses.
*"Something happened at school.... took a leave... I'll tell you when I see you...
only for a couple of weeks..."*

The thought of what he was asking turned my body moist, my ego
flattered, but my brain questioning... how could I be the only place that
he has to go in a crisis? Under duress, I agreed. I agreed not just for him,
but for my last shot at a second chance.

Rain likes having Jahn here because he's funny and playful and good at
math. He helps her in all the ways that I can't. He's strong, healthy, tosses
the ball around and he can play hide-and-go-seek without getting winded.
He also does magic tricks that baffle her every time. Rain can't stop laughing when Jahn's quick hand pulls pennies from behind her ear or makes her
favorite toy appear out of thin air.

"He's *good,*" she whispers behind his back.

He's almost too good. We've spent our first nights simply holding each
other. We breathe each other's breaths, speak in whispers and rely on our

hands as the sole means of contact. That's been enough. Jahn has not insti-
gated sex, neither have I, although I want to. At night's end, in the darkness, I wonder, is it me? Is it my fear that Rain will hear us making love?
Is it that we both fear the clumsiness of new intimacy? Do we shy away
because we are afraid to admit that our lust has already dried up? Is our
love not *feasible?*

This morning the sun blasts through the window, bathing the dining
room in morning light. The house feels different with a man inside. Since
he arrived, I feel my body's rhythm changing, my hips are loosened and
I move like my body knows new tricks.

Rain has changed, too. She laughs louder and falls into my hugs a little
easier. Jahn is like a rare vintage piece of furniture that goes right where it
should have been all along.

This morning, Jahn makes pancakes for Rain and prepares an elaborate
fruit bowl for me. Neither of us is used to this kind of attention. Fending
for ourselves is what we have always done.

Rain devours her pancakes like a child who has always had a Dad making breakfast for her. She eats as though she's been waiting for him all her
life. I, too, eat, voraciously, fearing that Jahn is all in my head and his lavish
treatment will soon end.

"You guys better not be late for my play tonight. I'll be looking for you
in the front row. My teacher said that I could save seats for you."

"We won't be late, we promise," Jahn says.

"Mom, you'll even have a date tonight!" she says between syrupy bites.

Jahn offers an apologetic look for me, whose loneliness has just
been exposed.

"Is it tomorrow night?" Jahn asks.

"No, it's *tonight!*" Rain yells and giggles, feeling him pull her leg.

Teasing her more, he says, "Is it at 8 p.m.?"

"No, it's at 6!" she says through peals of laughter.

Jahn leans across the table and whispers, "Don't worry, we'll be there.
You know we wouldn't miss it."

"Will you promise to do your magic tricks for my friends? I told them all about you," Rain says, her shining eyes are serious.

"Of course, I will," he says with a wink.

"How did you learn to do all those tricks, anyway?"

"I'm a magician! And you are my audience, the most important piece."

He bows in front of her. "The only way a magician can make magic is if his audience believes. That's all magic is, *belief*."

"Is that what it is, Mom?" Rain asks me with her face in a twist.

"Sort of. Believing is certainly half the battle," I linger, pouring more juice.

"If you say so," she says as she takes another bite.

As he laces up his big black boots on the side of my bed, I *almost* forget. When he changes his shirt for the third time, I *remember*.

"How does this one look?" he says stepping in front of me at the mirror holding up a sweater.

I am slightly dismayed as I watch his posture, while modelling the same shirt that he just took off, only in a different color.

"It looks good. But you already know that," I say without turning my head.

From a distance, I admire his face and the way he stands. He's delicious. His kiss at the airport, three days ago, meant something. The hard press of his lips against mine caused me to momentarily forget the tensions that persist; the strangeness of this visit, his unfinished story about what happened at school and why he stopped calling. After we clung to each other, kissing, a long, slow public kiss, he grabbed my hand and we walked through the airport like lovers who already know all the things that we don't know and wish we did.

"It feels good to be here with you," he'd said and I held his hand tighter.

When we got to my car, mugginess surrounded us, making it hard to breathe. I wanted to savor his presence for a little longer but there was too much at stake for me to be silent. I caressed his face and let my fingers lightly brush his prickly beard. I tried to sound gentle when I said, "Jahn, you owe me an explanation. Tell me what happened at school. And, why are you *here*?"

"Please, not now. Not yet. Can't we just breathe the same air for a minute? Isn't my being here enough for you?"

"It's not that simple. This is not just about us, anymore. You've asked to stay in my home with my 9-year-old *daughter*."

"Ok. Where should I start?" His temples pulse from the stress inside his head.

The sound of his voice had grown strange, stretched and weak. "You won't believe this but I'm being stalked by a student and his mother."

I ask, "Someone on your team?"

"No. It's a new kid. He's trans."

"Wow. What could he possibly want from *you*?"

"He wants me to come out."

"Why? How will that help him?" I say, quickly glancing at him and then the road.

Jahn's face is tormented at the mere mention of the situation. His face has turned hard. All of the light has gone out of his eyes. The word "*issues*" from Bethany's tirade pops back into my head. My stomach slowly turns.

As he begins to speak, my heart slows down as though it may stop at any moment. "Remember that Sunday that you called me and I didn't pick up? It was because I'd just learned about the new trans student. I had misplaced the note that was sent over a week before, but found it that day. I panicked, sensing that somehow this kid being trans would somehow lead back to me. *I just knew it.*"

"Keep going," I push.

"One night I stayed late at school when I thought no one was in the building except for the choir, practicing upstairs. I never use the bathrooms at school but I was curious about the new gender-neutral bathroom that they built to accommodate this kid. It was a stupid-ass decision. When I was coming out, someone snapped my fucking picture. The flash was so bright that I couldn't even see who it was until they were running away. All I could see was a red scarf.

"So how do you know it was the trans kid who took the picture?" I asked.

"I didn't see him but I saw the red scarf. I have no idea how this kid knows so much about me. *No one* knows about me except you, Rene and Bethany. I can't understand how he would know. He must have been watching me… but for how long?"

"Wow, that's crazy. Do you think you're in danger?"

"I'm always in danger," he says, laying his hand on my thigh.

My heart sinks remembering all of Bethany's warnings.

"He actually left a note on my desk asking why I'm not out? The note said 'why haven't you said anything?' It's totally fucked up. I don't even understand how or why this is happening."

"What did he do with the photo?"

"Nothing yet. The problem is I can't tell anyone any of this without telling all of it. This little shit was leaving me daily reminders on my desk including that picture." Jahn puts his hands to his head in frustration. "His mother said they'd blast the photo all over the school and web if I don't disclose. They gave me two weeks to decide. I'm *fucked*."

"How did you manage to get two weeks off of school? Your Coach must be livid."

"I told them I had a family emergency."

"Don't they know that you don't have a family?"

"They don't know anything about me, which is how I'd like to keep it."

"Morgan, if you're paying attention, you can see the shirts are totally different *textures*." With mild frustration Jahn pulls the fabric up to my eyes, showing me the heavier cabled fabric in a light gray knit opposed to the black cotton one or the navy rayon blend. I had forgotten how challenging it is to truly be with another, allowing and accepting all of their peculiarities.

"My bad," I say realizing that what I'm going to wear to the play is no longer a priority.

"Morgan, you always look good." He watches me ponder the contents of my closet.

Not wanting to embarrass Rain with my limp, I decide not to wear heels tonight. There will be so many parents to greet, so many introductions to make and explanations to avoid.

"OK, I figured it out," he says from the next room. "I'm not going to wear any of them. They're all too formal," Jahn says, coming back into the bedroom. His face is flushed like he has been stuggling to decide. He has decided on a black turtleneck, which suits him the best. Standing in his choice, he looks sexy and artistic. His loose jeans fit in all the right places.

"Lookin' good, babe," I say lightly, tickling his waist.

He kisses my bare lips and my agitation melts away. The excitement that he's really here makes my body quiver. But at the back of my mind, the questions remain. *Why? How long? For what?*

Tonight, the teachers' faces look puffy and pale after three months in rehearsals with children who have little to no attention span. The teachers' plastered smiles are permanently glued to their worn-out faces. Disheveled clothes are proof of the madness they've endured in order to prepare for tonight's event.

As soon as we step through the door, Jahn walks ahead of me into the Welcome Hall where student art is everywhere. I watch him as he searches high and low for Rain's work. He finally sees something that she did and stops to enjoy it. It's an abstract piece, charcoal and chalk.

I catch up to him to find that he's truly enthralled.

"She's quite an artist," he says, while he carefully holds the bouquet that we bought for her.

I am impressed that he's so interested, peering through his dark blue sunshades.

As I stand beside him, he says wistfully, "I wish all children had the opportunity to do art in school. It's so good for their souls."

"Don't they have art at Holly Crest?"

"Not anymore. Art had to go because the district said sports were more important and there wasn't enough money for both."

"What do *you* think of that?" I ask.

"It's fucked up!" he says loudly.

I look around for staring eyes.

He doesn't even stop to see if anyone noticed his outburst. "Art is the only place where kids can go to learn to draw outside the lines. It's the only class where there's never failure. Sports are just a little bit of skill and far too much risk."

His passion is showing again. His brow furrows and he shakes his head in dismay. His shoulders rise and fall. His sigh is of loud resignation.

From behind we hear, "Hello, Morgan. And who's this?" It's a squeaky voice belonging to the mother of one of Rain's classmates but I'm not sure which one. Her husband stands beside her while she shamelessly admires Jahn, her eyes hungry with interest.

She stares until I clear my throat and answer. "This is my... friend, Jahn," which is an incomplete and awkward way of explaining who he is to me but I am not ready yet to say what I hope for.

His hand extends to shake hers. "Yes, but it's spelled J-a-h-n."

She holds Jahn's hand for a second too long. "I'm Keely, nice to meet you. You new in town?"

"Hi Keely, interesting name. I'm from L.A. and am just visiting Morgan and Rain."

"Bless your heart for saying that. Keely is a family name. Well, y'all have a nice visit," she says in her deepest Southern belle accent. "By the way, y'all make a real cute couple." And she drags her husband away like a piece of old luggage.

"Friendly folks," Jahn says as he remembers to retrieve the bouquet from the table where he left it.

We find our reserved seats at the front of the darkening auditorium.

"They're friendly enough but they're *Southerners*, famous for their hospitality and total insincerity," I whisper.

"I don't find them insincere at all. In fact, I knew exactly what they were thinking," Jahn says as we find chairs with our names written in Rain's large scrawl.

"What were they thinking?"

"That you need a man," he whispers back.

"You, my dear, are not my first. I've had plenty," I flirt.

"Clearly, none like I," he says, kissing my lips while the curtain rises.

We hold hands throughout the whole play. His hands are warm and smooth and wrap neatly around mine. Rain's performance in her first *Gilbert and Sullivan* play is amazing. She doesn't forget any of her lines and her singing is perfectly on pitch. Our shared giddiness translates into intimate touches and subtle squeezes every time she's on stage.

At the end, Rain comes out for her curtain call. Jahn surprises me as he stands holding the bouquet in the air walking towards the stage, yelling, "Bellissima! Bellissima!"

Rain is surprised to hear his voice and not mine. As she goes to reach down to take the bouquet, her face tenses with embarrassment. I blow her a kiss from my seat and suddenly her worry melts. She bows and then curtsies, which is humorous in her male suit.

A crowd of proud parents flows into the cafeteria where we reunite with our children. Rain is all smiles as her teachers and friends shower her with kind words and sloppy hugs. Jahn and I stand on the sidelines, proud but unintended parental units.

Wrapping his arm around my waist, he whispers, "Don't you find it's interesting that Rain was cast in a male role? There are plenty of boys in the school."

"Of all people, you're questioning gender bending? Shame on you!" I say, discreetly. "I'm sure it's just because she's the bossiest one in the class."

"Yes, she did play that part quite well," he agrees.

Rain runs up to us with two friends behind her. She hugs my waist. "Mom! Jahn! Did you guys like it?"

"We loved it," says Jahn. "Good job, Judge!"

"Jahn, can you do some magic for my friends, Skylar and Astor? Can you do the trick with the penny?"

"Pretty plee-aase!" they say in unison.

"Rain says you do good tricks. We want to see `em!" says Astor.

Jahn smiles a toothy, strictly-for-children smile. "Hello, you two! Ready for some magic?"

I wander away, leaving Jahn to his own devices, while Rain and her friends cheer him on with wide eyes and gaping mouths. Astor's mom catches my eye across the room and I go to her. Walking through the room I observe couples of all types. Confusion washes over me. Suddenly, I feel alone and lonely. At these times, I wish for my other half. I wonder if it's true that they're all looking at me with pity. Are they thinking, as Jahn says, that I *need* a man?

"Who's your friend?" Astor's mom, Shonda, says to me when I finally reach her on the other side.

"His name is Jahn, J-a-h-n, that is. He's from Los Angeles."

"He's cute. New boyfriend?"

"Not sure yet," I say, wishing I hadn't come all the way across the room to be interrogated.

"Obviously, he's into you. He flew to see you. Girl, just enjoy the ride."

"I will," I say slightly embarrassed, knowing that romance didn't get him here.

"Morgan, don't you get lonely? It's hard doing everything alone."

My armpits start to sweat. "Is it incredibly hot in here? I think I need to get going."

Shonda is one of the few parents that knows the secret of my health. "Are you not feeling well, today? No, I'm comfortable. Hey, I just got an idea. Why doesn't Rain sleep over tomorrow night so you can have some alone time with Jahn?" Her eyes brim with mischief.

"That would be a treat. Both of them will like that. I'll give you a call in the morning for details."

I see them coming towards me as I stumble through the crowd to meet them halfway. Jahn steers Rain with both of his hands on her shoulders, as if they were on a party train line on a cruise ship.

"Where'd you go, Mom?" Rain says as she gets closer. "Jahn did another epic trick that you haven't even seen yet."

"Perhaps he'll show me another time. Let's get going, now," I say with sweat now dripping from my brow.

"More, let me drive," Jahn says as we hit the cool night air.

"You don't need to, Babe. I've been driving for years." *I didn't mean it that way*, but my nerves are pricked because he even felt the need to offer.

Jahn's eyes close with the sting of my words.

I squeeze his hand, so he knows that I didn't mean anything by it. I am acutely aware that his being here is causing a strange discomfort. Although I know that soon I'll get comfortable with it, I resent him, in advance, for the hard truth that he won't be here forever.

As soon as we get in the car, Jahn asks Rain about the play again. "Sweetheart, was it hard to play a man?"

"Not really. Men are just people," says Rain, giggling.

"What about the voice? Did you have to change your voice to make it *lower*?" Jahn emphasizes the word by dropping his voice two octaves.

"Sort of, but not really," she explains, "My teacher said, just be natural. The audience will see that I am not really a man but my acting is what will make me the Judge, not my voice."

"I see." He ponders that for a moment. "Well, what about the role of the bride in the play, the one suing for breach of marriage. You didn't want that part?"

"That's a small part. I wanted an important part," Rain says, sleepily.

He says, "Is that why they gave the Judge role to you?"

"Jahn, they didn't *give it* to me. I earned it. Isn't that right, Mom? It's because I have a good singing voice and I could remember all of my lines."

"Those are all fine reasons," he says. "You deserved the part."

"Thanks for coming, Jahn. Going to sleep now," she says as she slinks beneath the seatbelt to get comfortable.

"Sure thing, Princess. I really enjoyed your performance."

"Yours, too," Rain covers her face with her jacket as she falls into a cozy fetal position in the backseat.

I whisper, "She does that with her jacket to mean, 'do not disturb.'"

"I feel her on that. I do the same thing when I'm tired of talking," he says.

As we pull into the driveway, he says, "Let me carry her in."

"Usually, I make her wake up and walk herself in. She's a little too big to be carried, I think."

"But I'm here and can carry her. Give the little thespian a break. She has had a big night." He whisks her heavy body out of the backseat, effortlessly.

"I'll put her pajamas on, later. You can just lay her down," I whisper as I stand at the door, watching Jahn's effort to co-parent.

I go back to the kitchen to prepare tea.

Jahn comes back into the kitchen without his turtleneck. He's changed into a crisp white short-sleeved T-shirt and black pajama bottoms that slightly drag along the floor. His feet are small, pale and bare. He comes up behind me and plants a sweet kiss on my cheek. His whiskers tickle. "You seem tense," he says, massaging my neck.

I moan at his touch.

The boiling water and tea bags go into each of our cups which both bear the letter M.

He teases, "One of these cups needs a J on it. Don't you think?"

I ignore him, not wanting either of us to dream too big. "Let's go into the living room. It's more comfortable in there."

"Anywhere you are is comfortable for me." He pinches my ass.

I kiss him gently on his cheek. "Jahn, you're really good with Rain. She adores you."

"I actually *like* kids. You never hear teachers say *that*, do you?"

"What do you like about them?"

"With kids, I'm not so wrapped up in my own bullshit. Watching them try to sort out the world with their pure, innocent eyes helps me to see things more clearly for myself. Take Rain, she's a blank slate. She just sees what's in front of her, magic and all. She doesn't need a backstory to trust. In her eyes, what she sees is enough."

I ask, "Do you ever regret not having kids?"

"Sort of. But mostly when I'm with you." He pauses, lost in thought. "But everyone is not meant for parenting. Like my parents, for example."

"It's never too late, you know."

I kick off my shoes and rearrange myself on the couch.

"Touché." He caresses my arm and adds, "But you should have heard the trans kid's mother. Her name is Ms. Rogers. She has such a fierce love for her son. It made me really get the depth of being responsible for another life. She told me all that she's been through to find a safe place for her son, Teegue. It's like she's obsessed with finding a place where he wouldn't be the only one. Somehow, she found me at Holly Crest. They actually packed up everything they had and moved across country. Being a parent is intense."

"Being *alive* is intense," I reply.

We soak in the warmth of being together. What I think, I say aloud,

"Would you ever quit your job and move somewhere else? Say, Atlanta?"

"Is that an invitation?" he asks. "Shit, I may have to after this situation at school unfolds."

"What if you can't find a—" I leave it there, not wanting Bethany's rant to stick.

"—*job*," he finishes my sentence. "I've already been thinking about it. I could work for myself here in Atlanta. Or I could probably get another position at a high school. My real dream is to open my own gym, someday."

"Interesting. You really don't want to come out, do you?"

His anger starts to flare, "Why the hell should I?"

We wade in the silence.

I close my eyes, imagining this house with Jahn in it. I see every change, re-touch, re-paint, re-stain and re-creation of every surface there is. I think of all the money I spent, saving to make things the way I wanted them. Jahn's presence excites me but troubles me when I think that he'd want to make his changes too; adding his taste to *my* things. He'd bring his turtle, despite the fact that I don't like the smell of animals. He'd bring all of his stuff into our lives and nothing would ever be the same. I'm not sure I am ready to give up all that I created. My neighbors would see him as a hero; the man who pulled me out of my singlemotherdom… He'd be the rescuer, stealing me from myself.

Another part of me craves him. I yearn to embrace newness. He'd bring something unpredictable into my banal existence. He would be the brawn. Isn't that what they say every woman should want? Finally, I would be a part of the natural order of things, no longer standing on the sidelines of Noah's Ark. Only he and I would know the truth of his below. He would help quiet my restlessness.

Jahn's sudden touch takes me out of my wanderings. "There's something else I need to tell you."

Eager for the next piece of him I say, "Please, do."

"I know you want to know about me and Bethany... you need to know."

Suddenly, I don't want to know. I rush to say, "You don't have to tell me. It's none of my business."

He looks confused.

"But you know I'll listen," I submit.

"When Bethany and I were in our late 20s, we tried to date again... I'm sorry if this is hard for you to hear."

Nervously I say, "Go on."

"She really fell hard for me the second time around. I hadn't transitioned yet, but I was seriously considering it. She wanted to settle down and take our relationship to the next level. We fought a lot. We'd have these terrible fights... yelling and screaming, slamming doors, throwing things... It was *bad*. She'd walk out, then I'd walk out and then we'd get back together. I never told her what I really wanted. I was still too scared to admit it to myself.

"The last time we broke up, she said that she felt confused, no longer sure if being with a woman was what she really wanted. She said she wanted to experiment with dating men."

"Really?" My heart speeds up. "How did you feel about *that*?"

Jahn says, "I wanted her to do whatever she felt was best for her. I did care about her and I wanted her to be happy."

"So?"

"She started seeing a guy. She got pregnant."

"*Whaaat?*" I gasp.

"The thing with the guy didn't last long. He didn't like that she had been with women in the past. He broke up with her without knowing about the pregnancy."

"Why didn't she tell him?"

With his eyes down, he says, "She didn't want him, I guess. She missed me and wanted to have the baby and settle down with me."

My heart races to keep pace with the story. "So, what did you say when she told you of the pregnancy?"

"I didn't say much. It wasn't the right time to tell her of my plan to transition. I supported her the best I could. I was still confused and scared of transition. Bethany knew something was up with me. She was angry that I wasn't excited about the kid, but she never left my side."

"What did you do?"

"I moved in and as soon as I did, I knew it was a mistake. I didn't know what else to do… The idea of settling down with her sounded… feasible, possible, almost desirable at the time. It was foolish thinking. Hell, she deserves to hate me."

Looking at him, I can see how this part of his life still stains him. "Go on," I say abruptly pulling out of his embrace.

"I see you're getting mad, Morgan. It's just the past. Everyone has one."

Eager to finish his story, he says, "… Anyway, she carried the child for 12 weeks."

My heart sinks in anticipation. "And?"

"She miscarried."

Conflicted with sorrow and jealousy, I lean over to kiss him, gently. "So sorry to hear that."

He says, "Maybe it was a blessing of some sort. We weren't ready to have a kid, together or alone. Neither of us was sure enough about what we needed from life. I tried to force myself to want her dream, knowing deep inside that transition had already gripped me."

"How did Bethany handle the miscarriage?"

"As you can see, she never got over it. She resented me because she knew that I never wanted the child in the first place. When I finally told her that I was going to transition, she blamed the miscarriage on me, saying that I willed it with my thoughts. She's always hated my transition, but held on to me, still."

"Goddammit, Jahn! Poor Bethany," I hear myself saying.

He defends, "She told herself that transition would not change me… that I'd be the same person that she always loved just in different clothes. She needed that to be good enough."

"That was stupid of her! You couldn't have stayed the same… you're a *man*, now."

Bitterly he says, "People only see what they want to see. Seeing clearly requires too much truth. The crazy part is that although I should not have asked her, but I did… to help me through my transition. She agreed and kept her word. It's me who didn't. I changed. As I should have."

Tears fall from my eyes.

Jahn says, "Don't get me wrong. I did love her when I didn't know what love was. When we met again, I admit, I forced it. I was so lonely. But when I was being real with myself, I knew I couldn't see Bethany in my forever. She no longer fit. She knew too much, which would have held me back from being who I want to be. Now, I only wish her happiness and for her to know that I'll never forget what she did for me."

With nothing to say to this, I pick up the cups and the platter and take them back into the kitchen. Jealousy and anger strangle me. How could I ever fit into his mess of dreams deferred? He has told me more than I need to know. He has confessed his ragged humanity.

Following me into the kitchen, he yells, "More, you can't do that! I was just being honest. You needed to know…"

And I did. I hear myself shriek. "But it's far too complicated. I didn't expect your history with her to be so deep, so painful and so *justified*."

He gently pulls me to him. "Tell me what you're feeling at this moment."

"Angry. I feel like a fool! I feel sad for you both. I'm pissed off at how life laughs at us, cheering us on, pushing us to make the big mistakes, leaving us to spend the rest of our lives making bigger repairs. Poor Bethany," I say again, meaning it like never before.

His hands flail as he says, "It just takes time to figure out who we are and which life we want. Each of us serves as a just a tool to help us carve ourselves out of the ball of clay that is life. Bethany helped me see that I almost rushed into a life that I didn't want. I was sort of saved by something bigger than me—something that had its hand in what happened…

to all of us… including the baby. I have to believe that or I would hate myself for living."

Jahn looks at my tear-stained face. My lips are pursed tightly with nothing else to offer.

Somberly, he says. "The end."

His eyes are teary as he walks me back to the couch. We are both numb. He sits first and lets me lay my head in his lap. We stay right there, like that, for the rest of the night as he bleeds with more memories and stories of a past that is no longer his. I listen, slowly grasping for compassion.

He is a refugee, seeking asylum.

JAHN

The doctor says there's so much more to one's life than their gender.

I open my eyes and she is asleep in my lap. We fell asleep just like that. My mouth is dry and I feel the flaking salt stains on my cheeks from a night filled with tears and truth. Untangling myself, I slide her onto her side while I slip out from beneath her. She'd be embarrassed by me seeing her unadorned: mouth wide open and a purr of a snore slipping out of her open lips.

Laying her down on her side, I pull her bent legs down and slip off her socks. With a cushion under her head and a throw covering her body, I kiss the top of her head. Creeping down the hallway to her bedroom, I peek in on Rain, who's still in her clothes. A blanket of peace surrounds me. This house soothes, like nothing at home could ever.

Climbing into Morgan's bed that has been ours for a week, the smell of our blended bodies lives in every fiber of the sheets. The scent wraps itself around me as I sit in its crumpled midst. It has felt so good to be here, folded into her heat, tasting her love. Finally, I know I am in my rightful skin. I wish I could stay here forever; *attached*, a family man, seamlessly slipping into the mainstream, enjoying the luxury *of "no-one-knows."*

CHAPTER

17

NOVEMBER
Atlanta, Georgia

I am startled to find myself alone and, on my couch, kitchen lights still blaring and total silence all around. The space is unfamiliar, despite how familiar it is. Jahn is not on the couch, Rain is in her room and I'm feeling like an outsider in this patchwork family that we have temporarily become. I lay here, not knowing whether to go forward in love or resistance.

It's still early, a little after 7am. The story of him and Bethany has penetrated my bones, frightening every part of me. Walking towards my bedroom where he sleeps, I stop outside the door to peek in. Loving him is a different kind of work, but I can't do without it.

Am I as afraid as he is, that people will detect that he's trans? Am I too 'heterosexual,' not fluid enough? Is that why I've tried to keep us at home, building our nest, avoiding strange public looks where we'd have to dodge the questions for which there are no answers? Is it them, me or him with the problem? Am I afraid that I can't protect him like Bethany accused?

When will the day come that questions of his sex will no longer exist? When will our gender curiosity no longer sit at the top of our heads like recurring migraines? When will transition no longer be something to speculate on, gossip about and something we'd kill to know... When will it no longer *matter?*

Gently, I knock at my own door. His dark round eyes open and invite me in.

"I missed you," he says as he rolls over to where I stand beside the bed. "I left you on the couch because you needed the sleep."

I say, "The Bethany story was difficult for me."

He sits up in bed. My heart aches as his perfectly sculpted chest calls to me. The scars are the constant reminder of all that he's done just to be sitting with me, shirt off, settled into manly skin.

"Come here," he summons me.

I say nothing, I just remove my pants and pull my shirt over my head. I no longer fear his gaze, trusting that he sees only what matters. He squeezes me gently and we lay on our backs, holding hands.

"I just want to be near you." His soft lips nuzzle into my neck when I arrive next to him.

We both find solace in the cracks and imperfections of the ceiling. Looking up, we are free to think our own thoughts. As he lay beside me, I sense him inching closer. He's like a magnet. The closer he comes; the less will I have to remain an individual. My body pulses helplessly, genetically programmed as a human to meld with another.

"What's on your mind, Babe?" I end the silence.

"Jenna is on my mind." He exhales with his eyes still closed. His body deflates. His words are like cold water, making me jump.

"Who's Jenna? Another old girlfriend?" My words land with a sour note. I immediately regret the jealousy that spills out of my darkest parts. I remember Rene's words; *how can you be jealous of a past that you weren't a part of?*

"Morgan! Jenna is the dead girl. The name she was given at birth," he says, slowly turning over on his side to watch me.

Tears bubble up and my eyelids blink. I don't know what to do with this burden of trust. I shiver. The more he tells, the deeper I fall.

I say nothing, letting it sink in. *Jenna.* A name that I didn't expect. Soft and pretty. It's a name that I may have chosen myself upon first sight of a beautiful baby girl. It is a name that I perhaps would have come to me when I peered into his large onyx eyes and exquisite lips that have not undergone transition. Hearing the name that was never meant to be heard brings me close. Maybe, too close. I grip his hand, tightly, but he releases mine to caress the outline of my shaking body. The sun has already begun its ascent, light slips through the blinds.

His hand starts at my shoulder blade, down my arm until it reaches my fingertips. He plays with each finger, lifting up and laying down. Next, he touches the side of my thigh, enjoying the length and girth. Then he moves to my behind, caressing it with careful motions. His hand is warm as it glides over the curvature of my body, sparking the nerve cells to dance. His touch relaxes me.

I take a long meditative breath, audibly exhaling. "Thank you for telling me," I whisper.

"You asked," he says.

"Do you regret it?"

"No. It was a small request that will bring us closer. It's scary and comforting to have you so close to me. I just don't want to feel the pain all over again. Now, we both carry in us the places to which we can never return."

The air is now pregnant with the noise of lungs breathing, hearts beating. Dozing off, my hand brushes over his skin. When I open them again, his troubled stare greets me, once again. In these short moments of rest, a new worry has aged him.

At the end of the bed is a metal box, secured with a shiny metal latch.

I eye it with curiosity. "What's in there?"

His eyes are afraid to say. "I need you to do something for me," he says humbly.

"What?" I sit up to brace myself.

"It's Saturday."

"So?"

"It's shot day. I want you to help give me my shot."

"Shot day? You don't need me for that," I say.

"I don't like to admit it, but I can't stand needles. After all these years. The fear never goes away," he admits.

"How have you done it for all these years, then?"

"Only because my life depends on it. But that doesn't make it any easier."

"I can't do it," I say.

"Would you at least try?"

I think about all the things that Jahn said he wouldn't do, couldn't say and refused to talk about, but has for me. "If, I were to do it, where do I shoot? Thighs, butt, abdomen?"

"We do it in different locations so that one spot doesn't get too tender. Will you do it? Pretty please?" he says with the same persuasive eyes that Rain and her friends gave to him.

I can't say no to him. "Just tell me what to do," my voice fades.

"You know this won't go away, don't you? I have to do it every two weeks for the rest of my life, without fail."

"I know. I know. I just never thought I'd have to be involved."

"You don't have to be, but it would be nice," he says with a kid's grin.

"OK. Let's do it," I say, shakily.

"Give me your hand," he says and I obey. "Let me show you."

I follow him into my tiny ensuite bathroom made for one. He carries the silver box. It hits the toilet seat with a solid thud. Once open, he spreads out the elements of the ritual on the top of the toilet seat. His hands work fast and efficiently. Surgical gloves, alcohol pads, a single Band-Aid and a little brown bottle that reads "1.0 cc's TESTOSTERONE."

"What's the Band Aid for?"

"Sometimes there's blood," he says casually.

My stomach turns.

"Too bad you don't have a biohazard box for the used needle," he jokes.

I can no longer speak. I'm too fearful, reminded of the quarterly blood draws and doctor's appointments that have defined my life. I dread the medical nature of it all. The life and death of it… the trauma, blood and pain. My hands shake and my stomach churns. Jahn pulls his pants down and shows me the last place that he injected himself. Still reticent, he contorts his body to shield me from seeing his front.

"Don't do it there," he says as he exposes his honey-colored backside, which is smooth, except for the places that he has recently shot.

My eyes wander across the plains of his bared backside. His hands have memorized the landscape.

"It was the left cheek last time. Let's go for the right cheek this time," he instructs.

I survey the area again, still not understanding how I will feel doing this with him for the rest of our lives.

"How about *here*," he says, as he twists backward, like a gymnast, reaching around to indicate a safe inch of skin. He points to it with an extended thumb.

I see the remote area, a spot I would have missed.

"Rub it first with the alcohol pad," Jahn's voice is instructional and clear.

Every two weeks for the rest of our lives?

I rub the spot a couple more times to buy time. He hands me the little bottle of T and I rub it in my hand to warm it with my body's heat. It's what I used to do for my father when helping him with his insulin shots.

The oily elixir feels heavy in the little bottle.

Jahn takes the warmed bottle from my hand and injects the syringe into it. With the pull of the plunger, we watch the T being sucked slowly from the bottle into the barrel of the syringe.

"Ready?" he whispers, his eyes close. "Don't forget to pinch the area before you shoot."

I say nothing, too nervous to respond. I am in position behind him. The complexity of the ritual illustrates the need for companionship on this tumultuous journey on which he has embarked. Taking a deep breath, surveying the area again, I pinch and then place the needle directly above the spot that I plan to inject.

"Any moment now, Babe," he says.

"Don't rush me. It's my first time," I snap back.

"It's not mine!" he says, laughing to ease our nerves.

"OK. OK. I'm ready now," I say, taking a breath.

"Do it now," he says, eyes closed, bracing for the initial stick.

As the needle heads toward the skin, we hear, "Mommy, I'm up!" Rain's voice is loud enough to wake the neighbors.

I sigh, putting the needle down.

"Just a minute Rain! I'm doing something. I'll be done in a second."

"Don't be too long!" she yells.

We both groan at the sound of her.

"OK. I'm ready," I whisper as I prepare to jab the needle into the area that we agreed on. I pinch the skin again and on a silent count of three, there's a small sigh of relief from Jahn as I slowly inject the manly potion.

I pull the needle out and look down to see if there's blood. As he said, there is a tiny speck but not enough for the Band Aid.

"You did it, Babe! Thank you," he says as he pulls his pants back up and tightens them with the drawstring.

I lean over to kiss his lips and he accepts me with an aroused tongue. The kiss lingers and I lose myself in its clutches.

"That was great," he says licking his lips and patting my backside. "It means a lot to me."

It does mean a lot, but I'm not sure what.

Jahn has put the silver box back under the bed. We have smoothed our clothes, wiped our faces, brushed our teeth and are ready for Rain to enter.

"What time is my sleepover?" she bursts through the now unlocked door, jumping on the carelessly made up bed.

"What were you two doing in here for so long?"

We ignore the question.

"I don't know what time; I'll have to call Astor's mom. I'll let you know soon."

"More, I don't know about you, but Rain and I are ready to eat. I'll start while you get the sleepover sorted out."

To Rain, he says, "I'm starving, aren't you?"

"Yes! Pancakes, please!" she cheers as though she's in a commercial.

"Settle down, the both of you. I'll call Astor's mom."

Rain and Jahn rush out the door in a bubble of giggles.

I close the door behind them, needing a moment to think about a future of injecting him to keep him male. Like a thief, I go back into the bathroom to seek out the little brown bottle that he's discarded. I hold it in my hands, peeking through the brown murky glass, afraid and reverent.

"Hello?" Shonda answers the phone.

"What time should I bring Rain over?" I say, abruptly.

"*Hello?*" Shonda chastises. "What's wrong, girl? You sound uptight? Man trouble?" she says with a laugh.

"Maybe a little. Sorry to be rude. What time will be good for Rain to come over?"

"Girl, anytime is the right time, Rain is always welcome here, you know that," Shonda says with her perfected 'go-on-girl' affect. "I'll take the girls to lunch and a matinee. How's that sound to you?"

"It sounds like Rain will love being with you and Astor, as always."

"So now that you and your honey are freed up for the rest of the day and night, what do you have in store for him? He's a hottie, don't let him get away. So, what's your plan? A stroll through Piedmont Park? A romantic dinner? Girl, let me in on it!"

I hadn't known that I should have been planning things to do with Jahn to keep him. His presence is enough. "Those are all good suggestions," I say. "Which restaurants do you recommend?"

I let Shonda talk so I don't have to.

"*Chez Amour* is my favorite. Then there's *The Sizzle* in Midtown. *Tommy's* is also good, a little pricey though… And don't forget to put on a little something more colorful than your usual. Girl, get out of all that black stuff you wear! Men love red. It revs up their engines!" Shonda laughs, loudly.

The more she speaks, the less equipped I feel to have a man in my life. It seems, I've lost the woman parts of myself that I can't seem to recover.

Bitterly, I say, "How about I just leave him here doing yard work while I shop for red clothes. How does that sound?"

She doesn't get the irony.

"Yeah, Girl, men love that kind of stuff. Makes them feel like men! Or you can just leave him alone with the remote all night and he won't even get up to eat," Shonda chuckles.

None of it is amusing to me. It's as if she's transmitting an unintelligible code of behavior that I never learned.

"Look out for Rain. I'll call you when we're on the way. Thanks!"

"Ciao, Bella!" says Shonda as she hangs up the phone. "Remember to enjoy yourself tonight! Let yourself go go go!"

I put the phone back into the cradle and hear Jahn and Rain making silly sounds and pancakes. Rain is making a mess and I know that Jahn is dutifully cleaning up every drop that she spills. The two of them are already a family. I never realized that Rain needed someone else around. She comes alive around him; he gives her a Daddy experience, real time. I regret teasing her with something so rapturous that may never be. I scold myself with the golden rule of single parenting: *never introduce your kids until you know, for sure.*

Falling back onto the bed, the tingle of tears stings me. He's here now. And as much as I care about him, *something* still doesn't feel right. When I listen to Shonda rambling on about what I should do to be a woman,

I feel less and less like one. "Making romance" feels like too much of an effort. Being with someone you love should be as natural as breathing. My body's disrepair has left me a sexual recluse, accustomed to being invisible. He's the only man who has shown that he sees me and wants me, just as I am. The thrill of being wanted has taken over me. Feeling as much as I do, already, the hurt has already begun.

———— ～ ————

I need more time to prepare. Jahn has convinced me to let him drive Rain to Astor's. He's been dying to drive somewhere. He says he wants to conquer the brutal Atlanta traffic about which I constantly complain.

We have decided that we will spend our free night at home making dinner together so we can drink all we want without worrying about the drive home. A simple pasta dish with capers, cream and salmon will be easy to make with sautéed vegetables. The bottle of South African wine that I have been saving for a special occasion will complete the meal.

When Jahn finally returns from dropping Rain off, he has taken a detour. In his hands are a bottle of champagne and a dozen red roses. A single kiss turns into many. Before I know it, he has led me back to the bedroom, both of us panting and sweating, our clothes strewn down the hall, making a path to the bed, where we happily land. His hunger for me is contagious. I can't deny what he's causing in me. If only we could stay here forever without all the other earthly concerns that lurk and destroy.

Without a penis, we fill the rest of the evening making innocent love. Together, we discover the pleasure of each other's bodies. As we meld, we continue to study and learn new uses for fingers and tongues. We fall asleep in between countless rounds of affection. There are giggles, gasps and hollers that shake the walls, but there's one thing that I can't help but notice…

He keeps his underwear on. He's adamant about me not touching him below. Whenever I reach, he moves my hand, kissing away my objections. His reticence dims my fire. He's a voracious lover, but he doesn't receive my touch well, which is worrisome.

In between kisses and caresses, I listen and learn about the beginning of his transition and the unseen world that is his. I feel ashamed at my negligence, never before grasping the weight of this never-ending journey. I listen with rapt attention.

Jahn glistens as he tells of the early days, when he finally saw the world through a man's eyes. There were days when he actually forgot his conundrum ever was. He tells me of being visible and feeling whole, claiming the privileges of being served first in stores and the other subtle preferential treatment that men enjoy. "Now I understand how it feels to not be cat-called on the street by disgusting men," he says with an ironic wink.

Already spent by our impromptu tryst, I'm no longer in the mood to cook and chop and clean the kitchen. What we're doing feels right. As the hours tick by, the deeper we cocoon, the harder it is to leave.

"Shall I go get the wine?" he whispers.

"Sure, I'd like that. The wine glasses are above the dishwasher," I yell after him.

When he returns with two chilled glasses of champagne, I suggest giving him a massage and he accepts. He sets his glass down, kisses me gently and then turns onto his stomach. His underwear remains.

His skin is warm. In between sips of champagne, I massage his broad back. I feel his muscles succumb to my touch. Naked, I feel self-conscious as I rub the cotton of his boxers, with no clue where my own underwear has landed in the melee.

I asked, "Have you heard of *The Book of Questions?*"

"No, I haven't. What's it about?"

"It's a list of 300 questions that are great conversation starters. I thought it'd be fun if we'd give it a try."

"Sure. Ask me a question," he says.

I choose my favorite, Question 153. I read, "What do you regret most in your life?' "

Jahn thinks about it long and hard.

"Luckily, I don't think I have many regrets."

"Not one? I find that hard to believe. We all have regrets."

"Maybe I regret how things turned out with Bethany. I wasn't honest with her, but I couldn't be until I was honest with myself. I also would have regretted not coming back to you. Now, it's my turn. Here's a question that's not in the book. What are you most grateful for?"

Without hesitation, I say, "Rain."

"What has she taught you?"

"She keeps me humble and every day she teaches me to keep my mind open and never to close my heart. She's the reason that you and I are here. She's the reason I want to try this with you."

"Should we try or should we just do it?" Jahn asks, his face now serious.

"Jahn, I wish it were that simple. There are so many pieces of me that you still don't know. I have some painful things from my past, too. There have been plenty of mistakes made; some that I still can't talk about. I just don't want to make another mistake with you. I don't want you to be the tool that helps me find myself."

"I don't believe that's what I am to you. You have found yourself already. You've been through too many things to not be found. You lost your mother as a kid, you've been hurt in love, gotten sick, raised a kid on your own and you're still here. I trust your love. It feels right on me... it feels true, like a bold step. Morgan, your love is a little messy and even unsure at times... but you're here, shaking and sharing your fears with me. That's all I could ever ask."

"What if I make mistakes? What if I don't want to do your shots anymore? What if I can't fight for you in a bar brawl? What if I insist that you are naked in bed? Will you hate me for that? Accuse me of not understanding what it means to be trans? Will you no longer think I'm right for you and disappear again?"

He responds, "What if... I don't want to play ball with Rain every single day after school. What if sometimes I tire of all of her questions? Does that mean that I no longer love you or her? Morgan, we're going to change. Just being together is a major change. But I want to be there to see the good, the bad and the worst of you. What else do you want me to know?"

I take his hands in mine. "You have to know about my rage... that my husband cheated on me, made a fool of me, left our child... I can't tell you what being here with you means to me… how good it feels. I hate wanting you so much. I was hoping that if you came back, I'd convince you that I'm worthwhile. But now that you're here, I'm not so sure, I am."

"Morgan, if it'll make you feel better, I'll say that I want to try, too. But I know we both want more from each other and ourselves."

"Jahn, no matter what happens between us, promise me that you know that you are a lovable man. You are worthwhile and all that I've ever dreamed of. But the world is ugly, careless and resistant to love without labels. I want nothing more than to prove the world wrong, but I'm just not sure I have the strength to fight that hard. I've been fighting my whole life."

With tears in his eyes, he says, "I know. It's OK. Let me be the strong one now."

JAHN

The doctor says dysphoria can be cured with surgery...

I t's true that I lived many years pissing in the dark. My whole life, I've been afraid of myself and my nature. Dysphoria doesn't mean that I'm insane, it just means that I am painfully aware of the truth; knowing what belongs there and isn't. Despite what my flesh says. I thought I had shed it for good once the T started, the beard grew and sex dominated my every thought, but the dread remains, tugging at every part of me, keeping me mortified at my own flesh, using boxer shorts as blinders, keeping me from seeing myself.

Morgan needs to know these things, the things that trans men go through. She has to know that although I have bared my soul, it's my body that still requires counsel.

I still have one last question. Why is it so easy for her to accept my female genitalia? How can she show such desire? Doesn't that fuck with the rules? Or, are the rules all fucked up?

CHAPTER

18

"Wanna put Rain to bed with me?" I ask Jahn when we finish cleaning up the kitchen.

"Sure," he says drying his hands.

Her lava lamp is on, shining its precarious dimness just enough to keep her from fearing the dark. Rain is sitting in bed, drawing a picture, which she quickly shoves under her pillow when she sees us.

She asks, "Jahn, you're going to do prayers with us tonight?"

"Yes, I thought I'd give it a try. If that's cool with you?"

"Of course, it is. Welcome," she says like a hostess.

On our knees, we form a uniform line across her bed frame.

"Let us pray," Rain starts. "Jahn, you go first since you're our guest."

Jahn smiles as if praying is not something that he has ever done. He closes his eyes. We all do and then there is silence.

Rain prods him. "Jahn, you're supposed to pray now. Say something to God. Remember?"

"Yes, of course. Let me try this again. Dear God, thank you for Morgan and Rain. They are showing me what a true family looks like."

I wink at him but his eyes are tightly shut.

"Mom, your turn," Rain directs.

"Dear God, we ask that you continue to point us in the right direction. Amen."

Rain concludes, "Dear God, thank you for Jahn. He makes Mommy happier. Thank you for Mommy because she makes Jahn happier. And thank you for me because then Jahn gets to have a kid in his life. Amen."

"That was a cool prayer, Rain. I appreciate it," Jahn says stroking her head.

"Don't let the bugs bite the bed!" she says to us.

"We won't!" I respond.

We both kiss her forehead and step over her clutter to enjoy the precious hours that we have left.

"What was that thing she just said?" Jahn asks me when we get into the hallway.

"It's her version of 'don't let the bed bugs bite.' She's been saying it for years and I never corrected her. It's kind of cute and unique. Thanks so much for making dinner. It was really good."

"It's the least I can do. Told ya, I've got a l'il sumthin' sumthin' in the kitchen," he boasts.

"Rain ate a lot and she's a very picky eater, you know."

Settling in on the couch, I say, "We only have one more week left."

Jahn throws the pillows on the floor and I get the blanket from the closet for us to snuggle under.

"I have a little surprise for you," he says with a glimmer of naughtiness in his eyes.

"Funny, I have a surprise for you, too. Mine is probably not nearly as exciting as yours."

"Ladies first," he says nodding at me.

"I talked to my boss, Mr. G. and he said that you can come to work with me tomorrow. Fridays are usually short days. We have an artist recording tomorrow so that may be cool for you to see. You up for it?"

"Definitely. Babe, that's a wicked surprise! I'd really love that."

"Since you're so into music, it's time for me to officially burst your bubble with the horrors of the music industry! And when I come to visit you, you can introduce me to your smelly team of ball players."

"I hope that I still have a team. Or even a job for that matter," he says no longer smiling.

"You will. That thing at school will work itself out. And if it doesn't, that may be a good sign. There's nothing wrong with new beginnings. I have a good feeling about it, either way it turns out. So, what's your surprise for me?"

"It's a bedtime surprise," Jahn says holding my hand.

"That sounds exciting. Shall we skip the couch and start the surprise?"

He kisses me on the lips and says, "Would you mind starting the dishwasher while I get the room ready?"

"No problem. Only if there will be more of your delicious kisses," I say, waving him off to the bedroom.

Before I start the dishwasher, peeking in, I see that he has packed the dishwasher, perfectly. Plates in the corners, glasses and mugs up top. He has hand washed all of the pots and they are neatly arranged on the drying mat. Pushing the start button, I anticipate the surprise. Excitement grows in my belly, knowing that it would be almost impossible for this to get any better.

The room is pitch black except for the candlelight of the pillar candles that Jahn has placed in all four corners of the room. He greets me at the door, linking his arm with mine and leading me to my tiny ensuite bathroom. I quickly change out of my work clothes and leave them on the hook on the back of the door. I brush my teeth and put on the red satin bathrobe, which has never been worn but hangs on the back of the door like a wish. Shonda would approve.

He kisses me as soon as I walk out. While I was changing, he must have run to the kitchen. Full wine glasses sit on each nightstand. He unties my loose robe and it falls to the floor. Naked, I step out of the heap of satin and lay across the bed on my stomach. He begins slowly massaging my back, relieving all the stress of a week filled with Jax and Mr. G. Once my muscles have melted in his hands he reaches for his wine. After one sip, he gets off the bed and from underneath he pulls out a leather pouch with a velvet drawstring.

"Close your eyes," he says and I do.

"Now, turn over," he whispers. "I'm going to put your hand inside this bag. You can pick out whichever one you like."

From the open bag, the putrid stench of rubber fills my nostrils. My heart is beating irregularly and I notice that his face is flushed with arousal. Shutting my eyes, my fingers tentatively tinker around inside the bag. They recognize what they are feeling: rubber phallus' large and small, thick and thin. My heart sinks. Hovering over me, waiting for me to make my selection, Jahn breathes heavily.

Aghast, I look away.

"What's the matter, babe?"

"Why? Why this?" I say sitting up, grabbing the sheet to cover myself.

He moves closer, his breath warm, his tongue wet. "They're for us. So that I can make love to you... The real way."

"No! No! You must have misunderstood me." I pull the sheet tighter, feeling dirty and exposed.

His voice tightens, "Morgan, *you* have misunderstood! It's the only way the boxers will ever come off. It's the only way that I can be with you the way you want me to be."

"What are you talking about? I never wanted more from you. Weren't you being with me before?" My voice turns to a shout. "Have you been faking it all along just to build up to *this*?" I push him away as he tries to come closer.

He resists, pulling me harder towards him.

"Excuse me, please," I say as I shove him aside. I don't want him to see how I tremble. Hiding my tear-stained face, clumsily I crawl off the bed. My foot pushes the leather sack off the edge and what falls out are metal rings, buckles, straps and a thick, curved hideous rubber penis. Disgusted by the lifeless playthings, I kick them all under the bed.

Slamming the bathroom door behind me, I sit on the toilet seat with my head in my hands, waiting for this appalling moment to pass. How could he have misunderstood? He should know that I only desire truth. I don't like to fantasize. I only want the real him, the one that can't stand the sight of himself but trusts me enough to tell me.

Those frivolous rubber toys only bring up bad memories of marriage. Promised to revive a dying marriage, objects like these only amplified how much our feelings for each other had dried up. Angrily, we threw them to the back of a closet, knowing that our marriage was over.

Jahn waits just outside the door, breathing heavily. I switch the light off, reeling with confusion. Why did he feel the need to do this? I never indicated that anything was missing.

Knocking urgently on the door, with no response, he opens it slowly and speaks through a tiny crack. "Morgan, I apologize. I already put them away. It's alright, you can come out now. I should have asked you… I shouldn't have sprung them on you like this."

Acute sadness washes over me. Opening the door, he stands shrouded in shame. "Jahn, I want you, nothing more, nothing less."

He lifts his head.

As I touch his arms, his hands, his fingers, I say, "This is you. I don't want anything else. We don't need anything extra. All of the parts we need for this love are right here."

Sitting on the side of the bed, his left knee moves slowly up and down with a nervous tic.

"Morgan, the 'all' that you speak of has never been enough for me, so how can I ever be sure that it'll be enough for you, forever? Your loving me feels like a cruel joke sometimes. Today you love and accept me, when the reality is, one day, you may not."

"So, you think that love only dies with trans people? Sadly, none of us are special. It happens to everyone. Waning love is a universal glitch, but it's up to each of us to commit to our commitment, choosing each other every time."

"Morgan, these toys let me exist. They are the only way that I can love *me* enough to love you."

"I just don't understand."

"You must," he says. Tears well up in his eyes as he turns his back to me.

My words are no comfort.

I crouch down and sit at his feet. "I don't care about the damned surgery. I don't need it to love you. But if you need it to love yourself, I need it."

He backs away from me. His eyes shift from sadness to rage. "What is it that you want? Do you even know? Have you ever thought that you may be like Rene and Bethany? Maybe a real man is not what you're looking for! Maybe I am just the safest way for you to get what you really want; a hybrid, a woman that simply looks and acts like a man."

The four candles in the corner of the room flicker and dim.

His words are not new. I've wondered myself. "Is that supposed to be an insult, Jahn? If it is, it's *not*. It wouldn't be a problem if I was like them, but I'm not. Do you need to hurt me to protect your own insecurities? Are you saying that being a lesbian is such a terrible thing—an insult even? I just want what I want."

His voice is deep and thunderous. "What the hell can we do in a world where being a man means having a penis? There's no way around it. It's impossible to exist on the fringes when the world has already drawn all the lines for us. They tell us how we should live... Who we should love... How our bodies should look and who's lovable and who's not."

He continues, "I *try*, Morgan. I *try* every day to feel good about this body I've been given. I finally know that my life is neither a mistake nor mental illness. I even tried to settle with the wholeness of myself until I saw *you*, a woman who deserves everything beautiful that life has to offer, including *sex!* Am I wrong to question your love for me? Am I crazy to think that you can't be any different than the world that created you? It wouldn't be your fault."

"Jahn, every single time an individual does the opposite of what's expected, they create another possibility. People like us always find each other, if we stay open. This is a far deeper problem than if I am a lesbian or not. It's about if we are living or dead." Tears pour out of my eyes. My body is spent, unearthing all these truths that I didn't know I held. Finally, I concede, "Maybe we're just not the same. We don't believe the same things."

Jahn grabs my hands, "You're wrong about that! We can *push back*. We can do what's right for us, despite what we've been told. I just don't want to exist like everyone else who's prescribed to a life they never wanted."

I come up to my knees and kiss him on the cheek. He pulls my mouth to his lips and we fall into a wet embrace. We stay there, clinging to each other as if we are each other's last gasp.

Driving to work with Jahn in the car, it dawns on me that Jax could be a problem. He seems harmless most of the time, almost likeable, but I don't trust what I see in his strange green eyes. I don't mention the complications of Jax to Jahn, in case I'm being paranoid and there's nothing to worry about. I hope the weed that Jax smokes this morning will mellow him out, not like the days when it makes him act crazy. *It's always a crapshoot.*

The giant G above the building summons us from the parking lot. As he uses his strength to hold the heavy glass door for me, Jahn has turned giddy while I take another deep breath, hoping for the best. Dazzled by being inside the music industry that TV has portrayed so well, I hope he's not disappointed. Black and white pictures of familiar and famous artists hang from the rafters in the lobby. It's only 10:00 in the morning, but the sound of thumping bass greets us as we step through the door.

"This is off the chain," he says to me. "Thank you so much, More!"

Greenbelt buzzes with a new normalcy as we all adjust to the new structure, all of us having the same job, too much to do, for one demanding artist at a time.

"Here's my desk," I say to Jahn, showing him my pile of Jax' requests and the phone log with all his calls registered. The high stack of Jax stuff covers my favorite picture of Rain and me with my father, Roy. The small handwritten notes on the log document every single one of Jax' demands.

"It's my responsibility to make sure that Jax' experience at Greenbelt Studios is like no other," I say to Jahn, mimicking Mr. G.

Jahn glances at my desk and tries hard not to be nosy, but I recognize his hunger to know. I leave him to find a chair so he can sit with me while I work.

As I approach him, Jahn takes the chair out of my hands, "This is too heavy for you. A room to smoke? What's a room to smoke?" He asks, having read one of the requests on my desk.

"Jax' manager called requesting that we find a designated room for him and his boys to smoke. I guess *someone*," I nudge him, hoping he gets it that the "someone" is me, "complained about the smell of the weed. They said they're allergic or something."

"Wow. That's crazy! So, did you find a room for them?"

"Yep. There's a small conference room in the back of the building that Mr. G says we can use. We have ordered signs for the door and a special Century Air filtration system so that the smell is sucked into a carbon filter."

"Yo! The music industry is crazy!" says Jahn, eager and exuberant, neatly forgetting the issues of last night.

"So, what time will he get here?"

"He's supposed to come around 11," I say, already dreading Jax' arrival.

"What will he be doing today in his session?"

"It's not just him," I say nervously. "It's him and his boys. His tour manager and entourage."

"Entourage? Really? I thought entourages were just on MTV."

"You know that a big famous rapper can't travel without protection. I'm sure that lots of people would like to kill Jax, including me if he doesn't act right today."

"Do you want a bottle of water?" I say forgetting that he usually doesn't drink in public because he'll have to go.

"Sure. Thanks," he says without hesitation.

Mr. G. likes to keep the refrigerator stocked with water, soft drinks, beer and small bottles of wine for guests, as Mr. G. calls everyone who enters Greenbelt.

When I return to my desk, I see Jax and his boys arriving.

"He's here," I say to Jahn as we watch Jax and his boys pile out of two black shiny SUV's.

"Dope!" Jahn says sounding like a teenager.

"To answer your question, we're supposed to be recording a couple of tracks today but it always changes so I never know what we're doing, exactly. Remember, I'm at his beck and call. No matter what, I'll order them lunch at 12:30 and as soon as it's delivered, we'll have a couple of hours to ourselves. And I've got the perfect place for us to have lunch."

As they burst through the door, their energy is high. "Bo" "Bo!" The boys yell to each other with air guns and egos in the air.

"Waa gwaan Morg-ahn," Jax says as he circles my desk. "A whodis?" he says looking down at Jahn.

"This is Jahn… my boyfriend," I stutter.

"A wey ya say, Gal?" he says, laughing a filthy laugh.

Jahn extends his hand to shake Jax's, but the rapper leaves him hanging. My stomach drops. I say, "He's visiting from L.A. He's a real fan of your music."

Jahn clarifies, "Yeah, actually it's my students who love your music."

"So, you a teacha?"

"Yeah. PE and I'm a basketball coach." Jahn postures to show his strength.

Jax turns away to talk to his boys gathered around him. "Fellas, Morgahn have a man. *Blood clot!*"

"Dat little nigga there?" Shorty says, pointing at Jahn.

My knees shake. "Enough, gentlemen! Now, let's get to work! What track will we start with?"

Jax' voice is raspy and slower than usual, "Let's start with *Killing Me*," he says eyeballing Jahn. "Gal, what gwaan wid' the clearance from Roberta Flack's people? Da Fugees dem get the clearance, man in '95. We shouldn't have no problem den, man. Me sure say dat bitch need the money!" His crew laughs a risky laugh.

I offer my stock answer, "Still waiting. Jax, remember, The Fugees didn't have the reputation that you have. You're famous for a song called, *Blood Bath*."

"Blood clot!" says Jax.

"I'll get the track set up in the booth. Vocals today, right?" Walking down the hall, some of them follow behind while Jax lingers to get close to Jahn.

"Yaah, dessa we a go start. Dis goin' to be a long night, Jonny Boy," Jax says to Jahn as he passes him. His leather backpack clips Jahn's shoulder with a sound. "Which part can we smoke?"

Jahn's body reacts to the hit to his shoulder but he stops when he hears my shaky voice.

"Jax, it's the C Conference Room across from the booth. It's almost ready but you guys can still use it. Please just keep the doors closed tightly until the air system is put in next week."

As the rest of them follow Jax down the hall, laughing and joking, Jahn says to me, as I get close, "I'm not afraid of those assholes, More, they're dicks. Why the hell did you say I'm a fan? I'm definitely not. I hate that shit, to be honest."

"I just thought it may soften him up a little," I whisper.

Jahn says, "The only people they soften up for are women they want to fuck." Jahn takes sudden offense. "Soften them up for me? *Please*. Don't get yourself twisted up in trying to understanding men's egos." He stops and says, "Jax wants to get with you, I take it?"

"Jax wants to sleep with anyone that he hasn't already. It's not about me, believe me. Sorry for saying that you're a fan."

"You didn't tell me about him because you knew I'd be pissed, right?"

"Jahn, listen to me. I almost quit this job when Mr. G. gave me the assignment to babysit these fools, but Rain needs a roof over her head. That's the only reason I'm still here."

"It's getting hot in here. I'll take another bottle of water, please," he says as he watches the staff moving in and out of their cubicles, cell phones melded with their ears.

"Sure, the closet is right there. You'll see the bottles stacked behind the door. Help yourself."

"Thanks." He walks away, shaking his head.

Heading for the booth to make sure the engineer has pulled up the right tracks, I leave Jahn at my desk.

When I get back, he is seated with a second bottle of water and a bag of gourmet chips.

I whisper, "I know that Roberta Flack will never give them clearance, but I'll let them work on it, anyway. Some of Jax' lackeys will be able to come up with a copycat beat, which will save Jax a ton of money. Until he gets sued, of course," I laugh.

"We reddy," Jax says as he comes back down the hall smelling like a grow house. "Me gwan keep you up all night gal. Get reddy?" he flirts.

The boys laugh, heartily.

I back away from Jax.

"I don't think so," Jahn stands in between us.

I turn around to stop him from saying anything else.

"Whodis puny nigga talkin' to, anyway?" Shorty says standing behind Jax, glaring at Jahn.

"Stop it, Shorty! You need to chill. It's not necessary. The booth is ready. The engineer is expecting you in there, now. Go," I say with the most authoritative voice I can muster.

Jax' body relaxes, momentarily. "You're lucky me like you. Me no wan no problems wit' ya. Mor-ghan's tuff bad. So, no mess' wit' her."

As he walks past me, he whispers, "You need a real man who does *wuk*."

Although he didn't hear it, just the idea of Jax coming so close, whispering in my ear, turns Jahn rabid.

"Fuck you, nigga," Jahn yells down the hall.

I look at him and he's all puffed up like a peacock. His eyes are beady and his jaw protrudes. His muscles are like carved rocks behind his shirt. With one look from Jax, Shorty is in action, preparing to pounce.

I don't know what to do.

Jahn is posturing like he's ready for Shorty and perhaps he could fight him if it were just him, but Jax rolls deep and has four other guys all programmed to fight, all of them wild-eyed and high.

Suddenly Mr. G. appears, walking towards us.

"Is everything OK here, Jax? Morgan is doing a great job with you guys isn't she? She certainly works hard." Mr. G says as he pats my back to calm me down. My body sinks under his touch.

"Yah, Mon, she's a-lright. Let's go in here and break one off," Jax says and he and the boys glide down the hall and into the recording suite.

When they are out of sight, I can't look at Jahn. I don't want to insult him with my concern.

"That guy is a *dick!* Excuse my language. I never use *the N* word but my students use it all the time. It seems to level the playing field."

"Let me try to get us out of here early. They don't need me once I have ordered lunch. I can shoot another email about the clearance from Roberta Flack and perhaps we can go after that. I can catch up on other emails over the weekend at home."

"Fuck them. We're not going to let those guys ruin our day. I'll be right back. Where's the bathroom?"

It's a question that I answer a dozen times a day. It's automatic when I mindlessly respond, "It's all the way down the hall, make the first left at the end. It's right across from the booth."

As Jahn starts following my directions, a call from Jax' public relations firm comes in. I have to take it, but my instinct says I should have escorted him to the bathroom. *He'll be OK*, I tell myself.

The assistant to Jax' publicist is asking me ridiculous questions about a track. He keeps me on the phone for a long time, asking redundant questions, making me look up phone numbers, putting me on hold. He asks me to send an emergency email to a producer and to cc him on it. Eight minutes have passed and I'm still on the phone, on hold again.

As I hold, I look at my messy desk. I see that I have several emails that need to be answered and the flashing light on the phone indicates there will be more calls that need to be returned.

Time slows when I hear glass crashing from a distance. I freeze as I realize that Jahn has been gone for too long. I drop the phone and run down the hall. As I get closer, all I can see is Jax' boys circling a melee. They are standing and jeering at Jax and Jahn as they fight. I hear punches being thrown and the thunk of flesh hitting flesh.

I run faster, calling for help. "Help! They're hurting him!"

A couple of interns follow me down the hall but stop when they see that Jax' crew is involved.

"*GalDat*, muthafucka," I hear them saying to each other, the only word I can extract out of their lush accents.

This unknown word keeps coming. I break through a wall of muscular backs and musty dreadlocks to push my way into the circle. I see that they are not hurting Jahn, at all, instead Jahn has Jax in a headlock. The entourage is surrounding them but nobody makes a move when they see me and the interns, who've stopped short of the circle. It has been rumored that Jax' crew carries guns.

Like a robot, I run fearlessly into the circle. My body has no feeling left. I am cold inside, no longer human, just watching the scene and wanting to protect Jahn, at all costs.

"Stop!" I yell. Fear burns my throat. Under their breaths, I hear that strange word again.

"*Girldat*, man."

"*Girldat*, indeed."

"No way."

"Yeah, playa, *Girldat*."

When Jahn sees me, he blurts out, "He tried to jump me in the men's room."

"Let him go!" Mr. G. is behind me and speaking to Jax.

But it is Jahn who removes his arm from around Jax' neck. Jahn's face is swollen with adrenaline and stress.

Shorty walks into the circle to pull out a flustered Jax who cusses, incoherently. Discreetly, Shorty passes Jax a joint to calm him.

Mr. G. points the crew down the hall, back to the recording suite and disperses the crowd with one look. "Jax! In my office, now!" Jax and Shorty walk slowly towards Mr. G's office. Mr. G stays to make sure Jahn is OK.

"Mr. G., this is my boyfriend, Jahn Booth," I say, trembling.

"Mr. Booth, are *you* OK?" Mr. G. says as he notices the blood on his cheek and his swelling eye.

"Yes, Mr. Greenstein, I'm fine. That guy is a little out of hand. You should keep him in check," Jahn says with a righteous tone.

"*What happened* here? I'll take care of that Jax but Jahn, you're not fine, you're bleeding! Call an ambulance. Don't worry, Greenbelt will take care of all of your expenses. Morgan, did you see anything?"

"Nothing, I was on the phone with his publicist."

"Get Jahn to the hospital, now. These rappers are *animals*! This is shitty for my business!"

"Morgan, keep me in the loop. Good luck, Jahn. Now both of you get the hell out of here! I'll deal with Jax!"

———————

While Jahn is getting his brow stitched up, I text Shonda.

Can you please take Rain home with you tonight?
Will call you later. At the ER with Jahn.

Then, I text Rene.

Jahn has been in a fight. At the hospital now. Call later.

Walking out of triage with Jahn, my heart hurts. His left eye is black and swollen and his right brow is all stitched up where the bottle hit him. Blood seeps out of the bandages.

"That asshole hit me with a beer bottle! We ran into each other in the men's room. He kept saying this thing, '*GalDat*.'" Jahn shakes his head as if to shake off the contentious word.

I embrace him with all of my might.

Pain pulls him away from my touch.

"Sorry! What do you think the word means? I heard them say it, too." Locking arms, I lead him out of the hospital.

"The muthafucka was waiting for me. He saw me going into a stall instead of the urinal, he jumped me and hit me with the bottle."

"How could he *know*?" I whisper.

"Why else would he hit me with a glass bottle for no reason. I fought him off me, but then he called for his boys. It is obvious that the bitch can't fight. Then another one of them jumped on me. It all happened so fast. Next thing I knew we were falling out into the hallway, throwing punches. His boys didn't do much when he saw who they were working with," he says proudly. "That's when you came down the hall. If there had been more time, I would have kicked all of their rapping asses," Jahn says.

I shudder, blaming myself. "Babe, I'm so sorry. I never thought that they'd act like that in an office full of people."

We walk to the car and he weakly squeezes my arm.

As I fall into the driver's seat, my eyes fill. I drive slowly out of the parking lot but by the time I turn onto the main road, I can't see a thing through my tears. I pull over into an empty lot. As I put the car into park, all of the fear, anger and embarrassment of the spectacle takes hold of me, making me shake.

Letting me weep, Jahn massages my neck with a swollen hand.

"Don't worry, More, this is not your fault. Is Rain taken care of for the evening? Did she get picked up?"

"Yes. Shonda has her," I say as I fall back into my seat and close my eyes.

"Let me drive." He has already unbuckled himself and is headed to the driver's side.

As Jahn pulls out he winces at the soreness of his hand on the steering wheel. Soberly, he says, "Morgan, are you ready for this kind of stuff? It doesn't always happen, but shit like this does happen. It's fucked up! What if Rain had been with us?" he says, eyes on the road, tears falling from his eyes, too.

I say, "Let's go home. What's most important is that you're OK."

"And that I can handle myself," he adds.

Jahn knows the way home. We drive, held by a hard silence. When we get there, I head straight to the shower without another word. Jahn grabs a beer from the fridge and collapses on the couch.

I let the hot water beat down on my back, punishing me.

Rene's face lights up my phone. Before I can say anything, she speaks.

"Morgan, I got your text. What the hell *happened*? How is he?" Rene's voice is full of concern.

"He's OK. I'm the one who's a wreck. It's all my fault," I say feeling my throat closing.

"Don't be ridiculous. It could have happened anywhere. This transphobic stuff happens all the time. It's completely random."

"Rene, they were chanting *Galdat*. What does it mean?"

"It means that they have detected something. Islanders seems to have a weird, almost bionic gaydar. I think the phrase is patois for 'That's a girl.'"

"I should have known. Why are straight men so threatened?"

"Beats me. You think he'll want to press charges? I have a colleague in Atlanta that I can call. Just give me the word."

"He's just a little bruised up. He needed stitches, but he seems to be OK, just a little sore. We'll call you back if he wants to go any further."

"Morgan, are you going to be OK? You sound terrible," she says.

"I'm OK. Still dealing with the shock of violence. I've gotta just breathe through it. But you know, Rene, I'm really proud of Jahn. He held his own. He's a strong man."

"Exactly," Rene says. "Now all he needs is a strong woman."

BETHANY

I see Jahn's face on my phone on the hospital nightstand. I hesitate but answer, not knowing what I'll say. I was told to avoid things that upset me. The last time I laid in this hospital she was here with me. Nearly a decade has passed since I was rushed here for bleeding. Rushed here because the child I carried and the dreams I had would never come to fruition. I wonder if he can still remember the things that happened to her?

When he hears the call connect, without me saying anything, he speaks, "I heard you're in the hospital. Just wanted to make sure you're OK."

"I appreciate that, Jahn. I'm surprised to hear from you. I feel better. Nothin' like stronger meds to solve a girl's problems."

He laughs lightly. We both wait for each other to say more. He remains silent.

I whisper into the phone, "I just don't know what happened..." The last thing I remember is being carried out of the living room, seeing everything upside down. The flashes of angry women running through my head happen less and less. Still struggling to put these images together in sequence, causes my fists to tighten.

Sounding like he cares, he says, "Maybe you just need rest."

"I heard you were in the hospital, too. Rene told me you got into a fight in Atlanta. That's where you are, right?"

He doesn't respond.

"Are you OK?"

"I can still see out of my eye, so the fight wasn't so bad. I just ran into some assholes, but I showed them who's who," he brags.

"How is she?" I ask.

"Morgan?"

"I just want you to know that I don't hate her," I say. Leaning against the bed rails, I can't say anymore.

"Are you still there?" Jahn sounds impatient.

"Yeah, I'm here. There are things that I need to say to you."

"Nah, Bethany, you don't owe me a thing. It happened and it's over now."

"It's not over."

"Why not? We have to move on," he says.

"I can't accept… Jahn. I still remember *her*… she was so vivid. I can still see her face in yours. I can't help it. I still can't understand how could a person choose to change themselves like this?"

"I didn't choose it. He already was. I just had to realize him. I hope that someday you'll be able to understand that—"

"—you're happy," I complete his thought. "I know you are. I can see it."

More silence and then he asks, "Bethy, don't you want me to be happy?"

I blurt out, "Not without me. How can you love a woman that's not me? We could have had a fulfilling life together." Jenna's image is stuck to my brain.

"Bethy, I regret… so much of it. But mostly that I should have told you that this is the life that I really wanted before things went so… crazy. I know now that there's never a good time for truth that breaks people's hearts. I hate myself for hurting you. I really do. Morgan says I have to forgive myself."

"She does? Does Morgan know how you turned my whole world upside down? I was afraid for you. I still am. I just don't know how we can put our friendship back together. We're broken."

"Things change. Life goes forward," he says.

"Where does that leave me? I'm still stuck in mourning. Do you even care? I know that you lost someone that you needed to lose, but I lost someone that I *needed*."

Jahn asks, "Why didn't you ever say these things before?"

"You didn't need to know how desperately I loved… the girl that you murdered."

Jahn's voice builds, "What do you want me to say, that I'm sorry I saved myself? That the girl you loved so much was actually killing me?"

"You don't have to say anything. It was me who had something to say and I've said it."

The stark hospital walls stare back at me.

He says, "Bethany, transition is a selfish act, just like life. What screws us all up is that we're told to pretend that we should care about others more than we care about ourselves. But nobody can do that, really. So, we all become liars just by being truthful with ourselves."

As he speaks, memories of Jenna flood my brain. Blood rushes to my cheeks. The phone shakes in my hand. I still hear traces of her when he says my name. It makes me weak. I ask one last question of him, "What about Jenna? What if she wanted to live? Did she ever have a say?"

"*Yes!* For God's sake, she told me that she wanted to be Jahn."

CHAPTER

19

NOVEMBER
Atlanta, Georgia

J ahn was different this morning, lingering in bed despite the sun being at full blast and my aromatic efforts to arouse him with fresh coffee beans brewing. Most of the day he's been sullen and weary, burrowing under the sheets, putting pillows over his head.

There's something on his mind. The fight with Jax got to him more than he's willing to admit. I don't know what to say about it. I just hold him when he lets me. I don't know how to soothe his fear. Fears is a given in his skin.

It was too late to talk when he finally crawled into bed. He spent hours staring at the TV, only wanting to be sucked in to TV shows that he doesn't know or even like. He hasn't used the word, but I can read the fear all over his face. It is in his silence, as he lay next to me, quiet as a corpse. Unable to spoon, he is rigid, flattened by all that has happened. He's getting close to being outed, his livelihood has been threatened and he has been assaulted. He can't even seek justice because he would have to tell too much. And then, there was our sexual train wreck...

Finally, Rain was able to get him out of bed with her giggles and hugs. We made him waffles to cheer him up but he didn't eat much. Just outside of my kitchen window, I watch them play. I am warmed by how Rain sparkles every time he chases her around the yard or catches one of her crooked throws. He is the playmate that she's never had. Jahn is the fun one, ripping, running and tumbling to the ground with her. He possesses none of the physical burdens that I carry; swollen knees and perpetual fatigue.

I do love him. But I'm not sure that I will be able to be whom he needs me to be. There are so many unseen hurdles, ahead. Everyday it's something else. What if Rain had been with us? How would we have explained the rabid look in Jax' eyes? How could we explain the reality that some people live in constant fear for their lives? How can I explain to anyone how much I love him but still fear the complications?

My mind rambles while I season a naked chicken; caressing it with layers of aromatic spices and lemon zest. Elbow-deep in minced garlic and thyme, I am unnerved and excited by the possibility of Jahn suddenly dropping into our lives. The strident ring of the phone snaps me out of my fretting. I see Rene's face on the phone. My hands are too messy to pick up. I do need to talk to her. I need to tell her what Jahn suggested and grapple with the fact that it may be true. I need her to remind me who I am, because I no longer know.

I hear Jahn and Rain coming through the side door, just as I slide the chicken into the oven.

"We're thirsty," Rain announces.

"What's there to drink?" Jahn asks.

"You guys know what we have to drink. You were at the store with me. Have at it," I say anxious to get on the phone with Rene.

Rain goes to the refrigerator and pours two glasses of lemonade.

"Don't drink too much, you'll spoil your dinners," I warn, sounding like my own mother.

"Meet you outside," he says to Rain, as he heads back to the side door. "Now, we're going to do laps around the block. It'll be good for us, girl," Jahn says to her with a coach's tone.

"OK, Jahn. Just let me catch my breath! Hey, what happened to your eye?" Rain says, just noticing the stitches under the glare of the overhead light.

"Nothin' just a stupid accident…" He turns his face away from her to avoid her raging curiosity.

Rain interrogates, "Doesn't look like an accident to me. Are those stitches?"

Caught off guard, he says, "Yes, your mom stitched me up with her very own sewing basket. Now let's get back to our workout." His voice fades as Rain looks to me for the truth, knowing that I have no such basket. I turn my back on the conversation, pretending not to see her questioning eyes.

"Have fun you two, I've got to call Rene back. I'm sure she's calling to check on *you*, babe," I say as I kiss his stubbly cheek and head to the bedroom.

"Tell her I'm fine," Jahn yells as I hurry away from his impending run-in with Rain. "Just fine!"

———— ～ ————

"Hey," Rene answers the phone on the first ring. "How's he doing? Does he want to press charges? If so, my colleague in Atlanta is ready to pull the trigger."

"I don't think so. I think he just wants to move on," I speak for him, knowing that the scuffle with Jax is the least of his worries. "I need to talk to you about something else…"

She jokes, "Uh-oh, let me sit down. I hear that you're-gonna-need-a-drink tone."

"I shouldn't be telling you this but Jahn's involved in something weird at school. There's a new trans student who's forcing him to come out to the school. The kid's mother is behind it all. He snapped a picture of Jahn coming out of the new gender-neutral bathroom and is threatening to post the picture online."

"What do you mean forcing him?"

"I don't really get it either, but they are threatening to out him on the Internet or something."

"What do they think that Jahn coming out to the school will do for him?"

"I don't know. The mother sounds a little crazy. They gave him two weeks or else they'll blast the picture of him all over the Internet. At least, that's my understanding of it."

"That's blackmail," Rene says, flatly.

"Yes, it is, but he can't tell anyone or he'll be outing himself. Do you think he'll lose his job?"

Always the realist, Rene says, "Not legally, but if the school wants to get rid of him, they'll find a way. He could press charges; it sounds like a simple harassment case to me."

"No matter which way he goes, he'll be outed. Is there any legal way to stop this kid and his mother?" I wonder aloud.

"There is, but Jahn would have to get Holly Crest involved to take the kid's mother to court. We'd end up right back at the same place... he'd have to come out."

I say, "The big question is how this woman and her kid even know about Jahn being trans. He's so secretive about his transition. He says only the three of us know, anyway."

"That's a very good question but it's not the most important one now. They already know and he has admitted it to them. The question is now, what's he going to do? I'd ask Bethany if she has any clues, but she's still in the hospital and heavily sedated. I'm sure she hasn't told anyone about Jahn in years. She's trying too hard to forget. This is strange, though," Rene says, slightly exasperated.

"Jahn feels that this job is the only way he'll ever be able to afford the surgery. That's why this is such a terrible thing to happen to him," I say. "He's so close to getting the money. Only a few more years left to save."

Rene says, "You know jobs come and go. You never know, someday he may get a better job somewhere else."

"Remember what Bethany said... *he'll never get another job.*"

"Don't listen to what she says. She's a basket case when it comes to him. I'm still trying to investigate what happened between the two of them."

I take a deep breath before I say, "He told me. But I can't tell you."

"What do you mean? You *have* to tell me."

"Rene, he told me in confidence. He trusted me with it. Bethany will have to tell you someday when she's ready."

She says nothing. Because I know Rene so well, I know from her silence that she's angry.

Trying another way in, she says, "Can you at least give me a hint? I am your very best friend, remember that?"

"I do remember. And you will always be. But's it just not my place to tell you. Just like you didn't tell me about Bethany's mental health issue, because she asked you not to. Let me keep his confidence. It means a lot to me that he trusts me. I'm sorry, Rene."

Rene is reluctant to let it go. We breathe on the phone as she processes it. Slowly, she comes around. "I do understand. I can only hope that some-day Bethany will be able to tell me."

"She will. But that brings me to the other thing. Jahn said something that really tripped me out. Brace yourself. He wondered if I'm a lesbian. 'Like you and Bethany,' and I quote.

"No shit? He said that? Why would he say that to *you*? You're the straightest woman I've ever known."

"He was angry. Frustrated when I rejected his... damned sex toys. He thought I'd like them. He thought I *wanted* them, even though I never gave him that impression. I wish he wouldn't even get the surgery, to be honest. I know he feels he needs it to please me, but as his lover, I don't think he does. Not all trans men get bottom surgery. I read that online. Did you know that?"

"Everyone knows that but you, Girl! This thing with you two is really getting juicy," Rene says as she takes a long sip of her drink.

"Rene, those *things* made me feel so *gross*. When I laid eyes on them, it brought back so many memories of... You know..."

"I do know. Sounds like Jahn's seduction scene didn't go over very well."

"It was amazing, Rene. He actually turned *mean*. He had never shown that side of himself before. He actually suggested that maybe what I really want is a *woman*."

"Wow. How do you feel about that accusation?"

"I don't know how I feel about anything, anymore. I adore Jahn, but it gets more complicated by the day. I never thought that I could be so attracted to a man... like him."

"Are you attracted to women, too?" Rene asks.

"No. I'm attracted to *him*. He's not a woman."

"So, the lesbian thing is off the table. Sounds to me like you're both just scared. You've fallen for each other."

"I'm scared to give up so much of myself. Both of us have had to do so much to get to this place. He's a lot to handle."

"And, so are you." Rene teases.

"How will I ever remain *me*, with Jahn in my life?"

"You won't. You'll still be you, but a different version. Loving someone changes everything. He, too, will become a new person with you. He'll be a *Dad*, think of the significant changes that will mean for him."

"Rene, I'm afraid of him hurting me."

"So, your plan is to hurt him, first?"

"No! But I promised myself... I'd never let another man hurt me again."

"Morgan, you think hurting others is reserved for men? Check again, hurting others is like a basic human trait. It's what we do to protect ourselves. And, we all do it, constantly."

"Maybe I don't know anything, anymore. Jahn has emptied my brain. I can't even think straight."

"You just sound afraid of vigilant love, which is what he needs. You both do. You both have had to change, adapt and fight for your lives. Now the two of you can fight for each other's lives."

RENE

It was a random and simple question. "Does anyone know of an LGBT high school teacher?" It was a little over a year ago when my colleague, Attorney, Patricia Clinkscales, was asking that question around the office. In the throes of planning my wedding and my part in it, it must have slipped my mind. It was a long time ago, not to mention all the things that have happened since, like the sudden death of my mother and Bethany having a nervous breakdown.

Yes, it's all coming back to me now...

That same night, driving home from work, Jahn Booth's name came to mind. I never asked why Patricia needed a name, but because *she* asked, there was no question it was for a good reason. It just never dawned on me that I was breaching any kind of confidence. I didn't even think to ask Bethany if it would be OK to mention his name. So, the very next day, I went straight to Patricia's office and said, "Good news! I do know someone in the LGBT community that teaches at a high school."

"Great," she said and invited me into her corner office and shut the door. She offered me a cup of coffee and we small talked for a bit. Then she thanked me profusely and confessed that the name she needed was not really for a professional purpose. It was personal. Actually, it was for a friend of a friend who had a friend with a trans son who was in crisis. This mother didn't know where to turn, so she started asking everyone she knew, which is how the question got all the way to Pat.

According to her, the kid had been bullied, threatened and almost beaten to death at a football game. The kid had even started slashing his wrists with razor blades. The friend of a friend's friend was *desperate*.

Once I heard all of that, I knew that sharing Jahn's name was not only the right thing but the *only* thing to do. Somewhere a mom was in crisis and perhaps by sharing Jahn's name, it would help in some way.

"His name is Jahn Booth," I told Pat. "He's trans and he coaches at Holly Crest High School. He's an old friend of ours." The words tumbled out of my mouth with such ease. It actually felt good to be able to say that a trans man had found a solid job with a large school district and had even received accolades for shaping up a basketball team that was once considered hopeless. The world *is* changing, I thought.

It never crossed my mind that by just saying his name, I'd wreak havoc. After hearing the fallout from Morgan, this is one of the rare times that I am truly at a loss for words. I was just thinking of that poor kid. It was an honest mistake. And I hate myself for not thinking more clearly, not hesitating, just freely giving away something that was clearly not mine to give. There is no fix for what I've done, but what's done is done. I've got to keep my mouth shut and hope that it all works out in the end. No one can ever know.

I've lived long enough to know that most of the time, things that seem like it's the end of the world, always seem to work out, somehow. Of course, I'm not religious, but I do believe that there exists some force that moves things around when they need to be moved. Maybe this kid's life will get better at Holly Crest High School, just because he won't be the only one.

I hear that Jahn will be back in L.A. in a day or two, where he'll be forced to tell the truth to a boss, to a school and to a world that doesn't want to hear it, can't understand it, wishes it would just go away. When and if he tells, he'll lose many things like his job and his reputation.

He won't appreciate it at first, but most of all he'll lose the burden of his shame. He will undoubtedly be taunted and teased and driven to the brink, but hopefully he knows that hell doesn't last forever. I would know. Just when it will seem that all hope has been lost, new possibilities will come out of the shadows. I hope he's ready.

Chapter

20

NOVEMBER
Atlanta, Georgia

Hoping to not be reminded of the Jax incident, my body is wracked with fear, walking into Greenbelt. Head down, trudging to my desk, I hope not to be seen.

I recognize his scribble. "*Come to my office*" is the note that Mr. G. has left on my desk. Not knowing what to expect, I put my things away and head towards his office. Taking a slow walk down the busy corridor, I look at every face and hear every voice, differently, wondering how I'll say good-bye to all of them.

Without standing up, Mr. G.'s secretary nods at me and waves me in. I knock softly on the glass door.

"Come in," Mr. G says from behind the door.

I tread lightly. "Hi, got your note."

"Sit down, Morgan." He looks up and says, "That Jax really pissed me off! How dare he bring that thug stuff into a respectable place of business? How's your Jahn doing, by the way? Is he going to be OK?"

"He's doing fine, thanks," I say avoiding eye contact.

"Will he press charges? I'd understand if he did," he comes around the desk to get closer.

My palms sweat. "No, he didn't. Really, he's OK. I think he just wants to move on."

"How are *you* holding up, dear?" His tone softens as he sees my hands shake.

"I'm OK," I whisper. "I'm sorry, Mr. G., I don't want to be rude, but I can't stand this small talk. Are you firing me? I'd understand..."

"Morgan, are you kidding me? What happened here was not your fault. I called you in to tell you that Jax will no longer be recording here. I banned him and all of his hooligans. I called you in to tell you that I have a new artist for you. Her name is Silver."

"Oh," I say. Knowing Silver's music and loving it, a smile spreads across my face. "What about the money? I know what a huge loss this is for Greenbelt."

Mr. G. says, "Honey, you're not kidding! But it's the only outcome I can live with. Jax was a menace to one of my favorite staffers and... her boyfriend."

Since Jax is not coming in this morning, there's time to call my father. I've avoided him for too long, not knowing what to say, unschooled at disguising my sorrow. I have shied away from his nurturing father's voice, knowing how it always shrinks me. So many things have happened, so much has changed inside of me, so quickly. I don't want my voice to show how raw and naked I feel. But as he always says, *I'm all he's got.*

As the phone rings, I pray my silent prayer that my father will pick up, that he's still sitting in his old brown chair, near the bed, not fallen and not dead on the floor; an image that he has prepared me for since birth.

"Daddy?" I whisper, trying to be discreet as Greenbelt buzzes around me.

The rant begins. "Where in the hell have you been? I thought you and that boyfriend were over. Last time we spoke, that's what you said. That's the only time I don't hear from you, when you've found yourself a boyfriend."

"We weren't over when I thought we were, but now we really are." I realize that I am speaking in riddles. "Jahn came for a surprise visit, but he leaves Friday. Probably for good."

"Good, get him the hell out of your house! You better be careful having strange men around your daughter."

My father digs deeper, "Did he treat Rain all right? I know he slept in the guest room, so I won't even ask about that."

"Of course," I say, still feeling Jahn's agile hands all over me.

He probes further. "What happened to y'all? I guess I should say, 'I'm sorry,' only if you are. Why's it over?"

I try to explain the inexplicable. "It was just bad timing. We're both going through some changes in our lives."

"Baby Girl, take your time. There's no rush when it comes to these things. You just have to wait for the stars to align. They always do, if you just wait on 'em. Look at how the world is constantly changing. To keep up, you have to forget what was. I may be old, but learning to change is the only way we old folks will survive this earth. What kind of issues has the boy got, anyway? Something with his health, you mentioned before?"

"I think he's worked that out. He seems to be on the road to recovery."

"That's good… but what about your health? How *you* doin'? Don't let this thing get you down. Don't flare up and start swelling again. You know you can't take too much stress. If he's not right for you, the right one is on his way."

"I've gotta get back to work now, Daddy. Thanks for the good words. So glad you're always here for me."

"God willing, I'll always be."

When the call ends, I love him all over again. He's always right and always wise. Maybe there will come a day that I'll be able to tell him all the things that live inside of me; my deepest desires, my hopes and all the ways that I want to change. Someday, I'll tell him all sorts of things that I never thought I could, like what it means to love a beautiful trans man named Jahn.

Since Jahn has been here, I find myself short of breath. Tomorrow at the airport will be awkward, trying to wrap up these two weeks with perfunctory hugs and kisses. There will be so much that will choke us. So much that we'll want to say, need to say and will decide not to. There aren't enough words for all that lies between us. How will I ever gather enough courage to even attempt to love someone else? How will I not shatter into a million pieces?

The only way I can express what I feel is to write him a letter that will be *handwritten*, neither typed nor spell-checked. He can do whatever he wants with it. I will have done all that I could.

Dearest Jahn…

———————～———————

The night before he leaves, it's his birthday, November 11th. Rain calls him to the table that she has set for his last dinner.

"Jahn—you can come out now for your last dinner." Her voice is soft, full of emotion.

"I'll be there in a second, Rain," he calls from the back of the house.

I feel my heart racing.

As he enters the dining room, he sees the drawing that Rain put on his placemat to surprise him. It's an elaborate drawing of the ball that they have thrown every evening after school since he's arrived. "Happy birthday, Jahn. Remember me. Love, Rain," is how she signed it in her familiar hand. Jahn said that her handwriting means that she will be great someday.

Sitting down at the head of the table, he says, "Rain, thank you so much! You know, I can never, ever forget you." Intensely, he studies the lines and the shadings of her drawing.

"What can I get you to drink?" she asks him with a waiter's proficiency.

In that English accent that he pulls out from time to time, "Water please, with lemon," he says, smiling.

His tongue hugs the roof of his mouth when he says his L's. I will miss that.

Standing in the doorway to the kitchen, I watch her skip away from the table and right past me as if I was no longer there. "Coming right up!" she says as she fetches a glass of water with a slice of lemon floating in it. Trailing behind her, I carry a wine glass filled with his favorite red.

Rain has prepared wine-marinated cheeseburgers with sweet potato fries and salad. It's a meal that Jahn taught her to make during the visit and they called it, "The best burger ever!" He beams when he sees the familiar dish coming out of the kitchen on the fancy serving platter that Rain asked me if she could use.

I bring out the other two plates and we sit in uncomfortable silence.

My heart is weak, already fretting about tomorrow and the next day and how we will go on without him. Jahn looks at the burger but only takes a small bite. Rain watches him from the side. The table is noisy with the sound of grief. The burgers are flavorful but I can only nibble and Rain picks. Jahn takes small, ineffective bites. We have all lost our appetites.

This pain feels just like the night that Rain's father left all those years ago. It was another 'last dinner,' but Rain was too young to know that last meant final. Her father had picked her up, tickled her belly and deceived her with his kisses, pretending they would always be. But there would be no more Daddy kisses at the dining room table for her. She was a baby then; now that's she's older, maybe she feels the same lump in her chest that I do.

"Jahn. What happened to your eye?" Rain asks twirling a single fry between two fingers.

"Silly freak accident but your mom stitched me right up." Changing the subject, he says smiling, "So, Rain, who will you throw to after school when I'm gone?"

With her head down, she says, "Mom doesn't stitch. Tell the truth about your eye." Surprising tears fall from her eyes. "You make my Mom happy. I wish you'd never leave! When are you coming back? Mom and I want to know." Rain pouts and looks at me. Consumed by my own despair, I don't scold her. She sulks for both of us.

"That's a good question, Rain. I hope it'll be soon but there's a lot of things that I have to do before I come back."

"Like what? Pack your clothes and buy another plane ticket?"

"That's enough now," I say, feeling the same indignation.

"It's alright, Babe," he says to me. "Rain, those are a few of the things I have to do but I also have to make sure that I'm not leaving anything or anyone behind."

My stomach drops, thinking of him having a someone else to leave behind.

"Like, I'll have to pack up my stuff, sell some stuff, throw stuff away and bring Berd," Jahn continues.

"Who's Berd?"

"He's my turtle. Didn't your mom tell you about him?"

"A turtle… that's super cool," says Rain.

Jahn says, "I think he may like you better than he liked your Mom. He wouldn't come out of his shell with her. I bet he'll prefer you. He's never met a cool kid like you."

Rain warms up, "I can't wait to meet him. So, what else do you have to do before you come back?"

"Just things…"

"Oh," she says, another French fry sticks out of her mouth.

I save her from a conversation that she won't be able to finish. "It's getting late, Rain."

Jahn gets up to get another glass of wine. I send her to get pajamas on. In their brief absence, I try to take a bite, but my empty stomach is too full of sadness.

When Rain comes back, she's in her pajamas. "Thanks for all the fun times in the backyard, Jahn. And thanks for doing magic tricks for my friends." She hugs him tightly, laying her head on his shoulder. Her eyes are puffy and red. Her hand presses hard into his skin, leaving an imprint of herself.

"Rain, let me tuck you in now," I say, not wanting Jahn to see me falling apart.

"OK. But can we do prayers since its Jahn's last night?" Rain asks.

"Sure, let's just do them here at the table. You go first," I say.

"Let us pray," Rain begins. "Please close your eyes and hold hands."

We all do but I'm torn between wanting to hold his hand and afraid that I won't be able to let go. He grabs my hand with a confidence that says it won't be the last time. I want to believe him.

"'Dear God. Thank you for so much fun with Jahn. He's so cool and so nice to me and my Mom. Please get his plane back safe, so he can come back again soon. Amen. Jahn, your turn. You remember how to do it, right?"

"For sure. God—," he peers at me. "—I mean, *Dear* God. Thank you for these two amazing ladies, Rain and Morgan. Tell them that we will see each other again, soon. Amen. More?" he turns to me, relieved to have gotten through it.

"God, thank you for giving us strength. Amen." Feeling the tears, I pull them in with a sniff. "Be right back. Come on, Rain."

Walking down the hall, I hear Jahn clearing the table.

Looking up at me, Rain says, "Mommy, are you crying?"

"Maybe just a little. I saw you shedding a few, too."

"Will Jahn really come back? I like it when it's three of us."

"That's what he says. All we can do is breathe and wait."

"Thanks, Shonda, for taking Rain to school this morning," I say as she pulls up.

"So, how did the visit go?" Shonda whispers.

"It went well. I wish it weren't over," I whisper back.

From behind me, he says, "It's not over."

He's unshaven and more handsome than ever. Weighted down with his leather duffle bag, knapsack, cell phone, book, his headphones and a bottle of water he looks like a man going off to war. I pop the trunk with the key fob and he throws it all in.

Shonda eyes him and strokes her blonde weave. "It's been so nice to meet you, Jahn. Hope to see you again soon," she says, extending her hand.

"You, too," he says, holding her hand in his. "Astor is adorable."

Jahn always knows what to say and do.

"Thank you, how nice of you to say that," Shonda's smile widens.

Rain gives Jahn a careless hug and climbs into the back of Shonda's car without looking at his face.

Leaning into Shonda's back window, I remind her, "You'll go home with Astor today, too. I'll pick you up around 7 or 8. Have a great day. Get your homework done!"

As I turn, I bump into Jahn, who stands right behind me like the shadow he has become. When the window goes back up, Jahn stands in front of it making funny faces and waving frantically at Rain.

Rain holds her gaze, only staring straight ahead.

Slowly, Shonda pulls off, hoping that Rain will finally acknowledge his waves and funny faces. But inevitably, the slow crawl of the car gains momentum and in seconds the car is in the distance and then out of sight.

Jahn's face is defeated, as he says, "Rain didn't wave goodbye to me."

"She *couldn't*, that's all," I say as I pass him to go lock up the house.

"This is hard for all of us," he says shaking his head. "I thought we were…"

"Don't worry. You'll be back. If for no other reason, to introduce her to Berd. That's what you told her. I know you're aware of how damaging it is to lie to children."

Throwing my purse, a little too hard, onto the backseat, my compact, tube of lipstick and lip gloss all fall out, rolling off the seat onto the floor and under the passenger seat.

Just as I start the car, he says, "More, I forgot something inside. Will you pop the trunk and give me the key to the front door, again? I know how to put the alarm back on."

"Hurry up, I don't want you to miss your plane," I say wishing that we had gotten the day and time wrong.

Quickly, he grabs something out of his duffle bag that he doesn't want me to see.

"I'll be quick," he assures me.

In two minutes, he's back. "Here's the key."

He looks at the house one more time. "Let's roll."

~

Driving out of the driveway, I attempt to make conversation, despite my drained heart. "So, what did you decide?"

Annoyed he replies, "There's many things that need to be decided. Which one are you referring to?"

"Let's start with Teegue and his mother. Will you come out at school or not?"

Out of the corner of my eye, I feel his body rigidly sitting beside me like a toy soldier. His head no longer turns. "Don't know yet," he says.

"Did you think any more about the surgery? I told you, I'd support you if you decide to go through with it."

"Dammit Morgan! I can't say right this minute, on my way to the airport, on my way to losing my job and being publicly humiliated. I just can't say a goddamned thing right now! ... Because I don't know what *to* say. What *should* I say?" Tears stream down his face.

"I'm sorry, Jahn. I didn't mean to—"

"—pressure me? Well that's exactly you're doing, Morgan. I don't want to hide, anymore. I'm a forty-five-year-old man, for Gods sakes, still wearing boxer shorts to bed with my woman!"

I can't respond, seeing how upset he is.

"Where does that leave you, right? I know that's what you're thinking. I can't answer that right now. I know you and Rain are waiting for a date, time and flight number but I don't have any of those things and it will take me a while to get them."

Consoling him, I say, "I know. I know,"

"I know you don't trust easily but all I can do is hope that you will trust me."

As we pull into the airport, Jahn finally speaks. "I don't like long good-byes. You can drop me off at curbside. No need for you to wait and be late for work. Silver comes in today, doesn't she?" His voice is rushed.

I pull out of the lane, impressed by how he remembers my every word. We inch towards the drop off area. "Mr. G. knows that I am taking you to the airport this morning." I say, hoping he will want me to linger.

"Well, you've taken me. Now, get back to work, my Beauty," he says. He leans over and kisses my open mouth with his.

I hand him an envelope. "It's a letter. Read it on the plane."

"Mmmm. Roses. It smells like you. Thanks. I'll check it out. Pop the trunk," he says, peering out of the window at the long line. His voice goes from weak to strong. "What can I say? Thank you will never be enough. I left you guys something on your pillow."

"You know I don't like surprises. What is it?" I ask, my voice breaking.

"Learn to be surprised," he says.

There are too many words and thoughts and feelings to fit into a final moment. All I say is, "Thank you."

He gets out of the car and I want to also. I'm too flustered, no longer remembering how to turn the car off with its keyless ignition. I need to hug him one last time, to feel his body close to mine. As he pulls the duffle out of the back, I bite the inside of my lip to hold in all that I feel but can't name.

One last time, I take a mental picture. My eyes take in all that my brain can hold: how the morning sunlight catches his warm brown complexion, those deep-set eyes, the jutting jaw line, the dark wiry hairs that explode on his chin.

He looks at me with equal intensity; eyeing all of me, tugging one of my unruly locs and putting it back in place.

"Babe, I've got to go! I'll text you when I land." He has dropped my hand and it falls to my side.

He picks up his bag and slips into the long line at the curbside check-in. All around me I feel the push and pull of the human experience. Hugging, crying, laughing, eating and struggling to go or come back. *We carry so many heavy things.*

I stand by the car and glance at the top of Jahn's head one more time. I watch him in the line, looking straight ahead, not texting and talking like everyone else. *He's a man with things on his mind.* I watch as the porter takes the duffle and checks it in. He must have called Jahn, "Sir."

I see Jahn slide multiple dollar bills across the counter in gratitude.

I watch him don his headphones; hike his knapsack onto his back and take the last swig of water before he goes through Security. I see him head for the revolving door then pause to let an older woman go before him. *Always the gentleman.* Not once does he turn to look for me.

Standing at the door to my car, he suddenly feels like a dream. My mind grapples, was he *just* here a moment ago? Was his hand in mine? Has it been days, hours or just moments ago? Did he even happen?

Numb, I drive forward, not thinking where I'm headed, only feeling the car move. Traffic is blurred by the tears that fill my eyes.

Thoughts of him only barge into my head when the sun has set and I am heading home after a distracted day at work. Frazzled, I rush into the darkened house, past the kitchen, past the untouched guest room, down the hallway to see what Jahn has left for us. As the light switches on, I see it. The same leather drawstring bag with something round inside. I go to it with caution; a flash of the past stops me, briefly. My hand shakes as I pull out Jahn's handwritten note:

More, please give this ball to Rain. Tell her I said,
"Remember to throw straight and I'll work on my prayers.
I left you my chain.

Wear it until I return.

I sit on the side of the bed, the same spot from where I had furiously kicked the same bag only a few days before. The feeling of us as a family washes over me, again. Looking up at the ceiling, more tears flow.

Lying down, eyes closed, I imagine Jahn settled into his window seat. His seatbelt tightly clasped around his waist as the plane prepared to take him back to his unshared life. I am hopeful that he didn't hear the loud sound of engines whirring and the thunks of wheels retracting into the body of the plane. I pray that he was deaf to the clanks and the bells in the cabin and the flight attendant's drone. I hope the only sound he heard was the pitch and the rhythm of my voice as he read:

Dearest Jahn,

I am constantly shaken by how hard and how beautiful it is to be alive... to have experiences with another person that shake you to the core. You are the reason that I want to live a very long time. Even longer, if it can be with you.

I know what lies ahead for you is terrifying. I so wish I could be there to support you, hold you up and keep you strong. Just remember if they lose you, it's their loss.

Jahn, I want you to know that you'll never be too far from me, because I will see you in every person that I meet. I will shamelessly compare everyone to you, searching their eyes for your kindness, gentleness and courage.

My love for you is as whole and complete as you are. Thank you for letting me in and shaking up every piece of me with the magic of your love.

More

He never texted me when he landed. But I know he did.

FEBRUARY
Atlanta, Georgia

THREE MONTHS LATER

F or three months, babies cried, dogs barked and the phone no longer
rang. Since he left, I've had trouble sleeping, startled by the slightest
sounds that all remind me of the riotous season of Jahn.

"Have you still not heard from him?" Rene asked every single week.

"He just needs time," was always the answer.

Today, a letter arrives.

My Dearest Morgan,

*This is probably the first letter I've ever written. I wanted to wait until
I was sure. Thank you for giving me time.*

*As soon as I returned to school on that Monday in November, there was
news. Teegue Rogers passed away. I don't know whom to blame. Was it my fault
for leaving? Is it the world's fault for not understanding us? Or is it just the way
that life works, sometimes? People die.*

I won't give the world the benefit of saying that Teegue's exit was "mental illness." That's too easy. He was too smart, capable and clever to not understand his actions. Perhaps Teegue was saner than the rest of us, able to discern when enough pain is too much. He chose when and how to find his ultimate peace. I know this sounds like a dangerous supposition, but it gives me comfort, leaving Teegue with his dignity intact. I want to trust that he knew what he wanted. He found his power in the weakest moment.

I've met with Ms. Rogers a few times to offer my condolences and support. She's alone now. Teegue was all she had. I just hope that she knows that our meeting was not in vain. As you once said, children teach us. Teegue taught me that every time I keep my existence a secret, I'm admitting shame. I'll never forget the sneer on his face when he said it.

Ms. Rogers and I met with Coach Blande. I told him everything and she tried to explain being trans, from a mother's perspective. Morgan, I wish you could have seen the look of shock, rage and disgust on Coach's face. He rambled, accusing me of duplicity and non-disclosure, neither of which are crimes. Maybe only crimes of morality.

Once Blande calmed down, I told him of my eventual plans to relocate to Atlanta. But for now, my job will stay secure, despite him. Rene has offered to represent me, pro bono. I didn't ask her to do it. Strangely, she volunteered. Like Teegue said, "We are here to stay."

Ms. Rogers apologized for the whole blackmail debacle. She said she never intended to let Teegue do what he threatened to do. They just needed my attention. To make amends, she has donated $175,000 to the school to create the Teegue Rogers LGBTQ Center for Acceptance. Channel 7 News is doing a story on it and I've agreed to be interviewed. The Center won't be completed for another year or two, but I don't plan to be here. My hope is to be with you.

Jahn

Epilogue

There are no accidents, no coincidences or chance meetings; there are only small tremors in the earth that remind us that we are alive. Only when the seismic shifts seem to deceive us, we question the solid ground on which we stand. When we dig deeper into the cracks below, we see that the only thing that holds us together, keeps us standing, keeps us fighting are the vicissitudes.

ACKNOWLEDGMENTS

A ll of my love and gratitude to Nordia Lee for her unwavering support for this "strange" story that I had to tell. Thank you for listening to my excitement every time I saw deeper into the truth of what it means to be human as I created these characters who live in all of us. Thank you to Sasha Carter who read and read and read and read, each page, each chapter, each word with such love and commitment. Thank you to Carol Lee Lorenzo and Atlanta's inimitable *Fiction Intensives*, the group of writers who gave me the gift of their listening and who honored these characters with their love and understanding as they slowly came to be. Much love to Susannah Wilson who did not live to see this book published but whose wise and pristine commentary exalted every word.

I can't forget to mention Vivian Scott Chew, whose loving critique, sparked the need for creating a man like Jahn. Thank you for your perpetual truth. Thank you to my family, the Cincinnati crew, for your endless pride and expectation. You mean so much to me.

Writing deserves a place that is not always our own. Endless thanks and appreciation to the amazing Joy Borra, Nordia Lee and Jen Sincero for lending me their beautiful sanctuaries where me and my characters found our voices.

Special thanks to the amazing author, speaker and consultant, Zander Keig, LCSW for his unwavering interest in this story and his willingness to brainstorm with me to bring it to a solid end. A million thanks for your kindness and patience. Thank you to esteemed author; Mitch Kellaway and all of your precious truth, vulnerability and wisdom. Also, thank you to Alex Santiago, Trina Strickland and TF for sharing your truths with me. Thank you to Ernie Mosior and A.S. Turner & Sons for showing me the way death is done. Professor Annaliese Singh and Katie Leikam, LCSW for meeting with me and taking tentative interest in this book before it came to life. I also want to thank Jim Farmer, Director of the OUT on FILM Festival in Atlanta, Georgia whose provocative film choices made this story mandatory. Big thanks to Vanessa Blake for your editing excellence.

Thank you will never be enough for Trystan Cotten for his admiration, support and belief. Endless gratitude to the staff of Transgress Press for seeing what I see and needing others to see it, too.

Thank you to D. Lammie Hanson, artist extraordinaire, who is always painting what I am thinking. Thank you for your generosity, allowing me to use your masterpiece, "Coming Into My Being," which makes Vicissitudes complete.

Many thanks to Xavier Guerra for his excellent touch with the art.

And, to my dearest Jim DeBarros, who designed the cover of this book with patience and your trademark elegance and style. Thank you for squeezing this in when there was absolutely no place for it to fit.

ABOUT KIM GREEN

Kim Green was the ghostwriter for "Life Is Not A Fairytale," (Simon and Schuster) the autobiography of 2004 American Idol winner, Fantasia Barrino. The book was listed on both the New York Times and Wall Street Journal's Bestseller Lists and was made into an original TV Movie, directed by Debbie Allen. Her self-published novel, "hallucination" received an honorable mention from Writer's Digest Magazine. "Vicissitudes," her debut novel explores the intricacies and complications of being human.

Kim owns and operates *Words, LLC*, a creative words studio *and Blank Page Consulting* where she coaches writers and their lives. She currently lives in Atlanta, Georgia with her spouse, her son and her perfect dog, Mixx.

Scan the QR code below to access Kim's thoughts on the book cover.

ALSO PUBLISHED BY TRANSGRESS PRESS

Tomorrow, or Forever
And Other Stories
Jack Kaulfus

Trans Homo…Gasp!
Gay FTM and Cis Men on Sex and Love
Edited by Avi Ben-Zeev and Pete Bailey

Lou Sullivan
Daring To Be A Man Among Men
Brice D. Smith

Life Beyond My Body
Transgender Journey to Manhood in China
(Lambda Literary Award)
Lei Ming

Queer Rock Love: A Family Memoir
Paige Schilt

Love Always
Partners of Trans People on Intimacy, Challenge, and Resilience
Edited by Jordon Johnson and Becky Garrison

Now What?
A Handbook for Families with Transgender Children
Rex Butt

Giving It Raw: Nearly 30 Years with AIDS
Francisco Ibañez-Carrasco

Trunky (Transgender Junky)
A Memoir of Institutionalization and Southern Hospitality
(Lambda Literary Finalist)
Sam Petersoon

New Girl Blues...or Pinks
Mary Degroat Ross

Letters for My Sisters: Transitional Wisdom in Retrospect
Edited by Andrea James and Deanne Thornton

Swimming Upstream: A Novel
Jacob Anderson-Minshall

Words of Fire!
Women Loving Women in Latin America
Antonia Amprino

The Wanderings of Chela Coatlicue
On Tour with Los Huerfanos
Ananda Esteva

Manning Up: Transsexual Men on
Finding Brotherhood, Family and Themselves
Edited by Zander Keig and Mitch Kellaway

Below the Belt: Genital Talk by Men of Trans Experience
Edited by Trystan Theosophus Cotten

Hung Jury: Testimonies of Genital Surgery by Transsexual Men
Edited by Trystan Theosophus Cotten

Made in the USA
Columbia, SC
21 June 2021